Mr. Samuel's Penny

11/15/14

Kate,

you have a lonely Aunt
who obviously loves you
very much.

Best Always.

[signature]

Mr. Samuel's Penny

Treva Hall Melvin

The Poisoned Pencil

An imprint of Poisoned Pen Press

Copyright © 2014 by Treva Hall Melvin

First Edition 2014

10 9 8 7 6 5 4 3 2 1

Library of Congress Catalog Card Number: 2014938597

ISBN: 9781929345045   Trade Paperback
       9781929345052   E-book

The Poisoned Pencil
An imprint of Poisoned Pen Press
6962 E. First Ave., Ste. 103
Scottsdale, AZ 85251
www.thepoisonedpencil.com
info@thepoisonedpencil.com

Printed in the United States of America

To my loving parents Vance and "Bernie,"
who supported me in all my endeavors and told me to
dream big! This book would never have happened if it
weren't for my father, who encouraged me to write for
many years because my stories made him laugh, and to my
mother, my best friend, who always held my hand.

Acknowledgments

Thank you, God, for giving the greatest gift of my life: the love of my children, Olivia and Eli, and my husband, Tim, for having to put up with my late-night writing.

To my Aunt Alice, Great Aunt Ode, Aunt Algurnia, and Uncle Felton, whose love help me create these characters, and to "Tootie" and Terry, two of the very best cousins I could ever imagine to have in my life. I love you all so much.

There are many friends who have supported me along this road for the past five years in becoming a writer, but I must give special thanks to my friend and personal editor Anne Dubuisson Anderson. She taught me how to write, to actually craft my thoughts into meaningful stories. I could not have done this without her, and I never will.

Prologue

It is peculiarly bright this evening. Will not be dark for another hour or so. The headlights of the '68 station wagon are on, but their worth cannot be seen until the fog seeps between the slats of wood. The sweet smell of honeysuckle floats through the air on a blanket of steam rising up from the river as the car makes its way across the threshold.

The old bridge aches aloud, for its back has carried many a passenger the last hundred years to and from Ahoskie, North Carolina. Known as "The Only One," Ahoskie has existed as a settlers' town and with the Indian name since 1719, but without the Indians' permission to do either.

For a moment there is a sense of unsteadiness.

Got to get across.

Just one more time.

Sometimes easy.

Most times hard.

Then sometimes someone never crosses back.

One

For several hours, I'd done nothing but unpack and eat. I was ready for something to happen.

But I wasn't ready for anything like this.

I was standing at the front door that 12th of June evening, waiting for Aunt Alice to come home from the grocery store, when I heard the piercing sound of horns and sirens unleashing their fury, synchronized to the flashing red and white lights leading the way south, away from town. The pimples that ran down my spine were tender from the screeching noise. At least five vehicles rushed down the narrow road, leaving great clouds of dirt as though dragged by invisible ropes . Heading for a place where something god-awful was happening.

I could see Auntie's car trotting at a nervous pace behind them, then veering off to the left, down our street. I focused on her torso behind the wheel, then her head, then her eyes, steadfast with purpose.

"Hi Auntie, what's going on down there?" I asked, with my hand shielding my eyes from the fading sun as she opened her car door to get out.

"I don't know really, Lizbeth, 'cept Uncle Frank was called

to come in a hurry with his wrench truck to help down by the bridge."

As the jarring sounds washed out through the tall bushy head of the forest, Aunt Alice stared out toward the road. With her chin tucked in, she spoke.

"Lizbeth, I'm going down there to see what's going on. It's going to be dark out soon. You can stay here if you want to, or go over to Mrs. Cooper's if you get scared." She placed her hand on my shoulder to reassure me that all would be okay.

"Scared? I'm not scared; I just want to go with you! See what's happening down there!" I exclaimed, shaking her other hand in a tantrum, dividing her fingers between my two hands.

"You couldn't fit in there anyway Lizbeth, I have a car full of groceries, girl. And besides, by the time I finish putting them away, I may as well stay home." She had me there, but I wasn't about to give up. My eyes darted around the yard looking for a way out of the problem.

And there it was.

"You're right, Auntie. I can't fit in your car, but I can ride my bike!" A prideful smile burned in the flesh of my cheeks.

"But Lizbeth…"

"I got a light on my bike, Auntie. Besides, I bet I get there before you do!" That was all that needed to be said.

I arrived at the bridge before Auntie, thanks to my cousins showing me a narrow path just that morning. I rode right on up to the bridge and oh-so-quietly kicked my kickstand down. There wasn't one holler, mostly because the police and other officials were concentrating on the sadness below. Good thing I had enough sense to leave my bike where it stood and walk the rest of the way so as not to call attention to myself. As my excitement grew, I tried to hold my breath, feeling my heart thumping through my chest, hoping that my good fortune in not being shooed away would hold out until I got a closer look.

By now the sun was so low the river looked like black ink angrily slapping the shore for letting Uncle Frank's crane drop into its waters, with men bobbing up and down like red and whites. Flashlights dotting and dashing about like lightning bugs searching for their supper. A few orders jabbed out amongst the men here and there. Other than that, there was silence.

A startling shout came from a man with a white hat, and a tremendous *swoosh* broke through the dark water. When the crane pulled the car up, with a solemn grinding motion, something burst free from one of the car's open windows. Shocked me so bad I nearly fell over into the deep, so shaken from the sight.

A man's hand had set itself free from the car.

At first glance, the hand seemed to be riding the surface of the water, waving happily without care. But then the ashen skin with its grotesque wormy veins made it clear it was not waving. Something glistened in rhythm with the ripples of water flowing over his fingers—a gold band. But before I could focus, the shoulder and the head of the man slipped through the window like an eel. I could have held on a little longer but for the man's face turning upward; his eyes bulging out of their sockets like strained ping-pong balls. I threw up right then and there on the bridge, and luckily not on my brand new checkered shirt.

"Hey, hey you there girl! Get off the bridge before you drown your fool yourself! We don't have time to be searching for no more bodies tonight. G'on now!" The man with the white hat again. I wanted to say sorry, but my wobbling legs took the best of me. Luckily I spotted Auntie on the shore, so I got my bike and stumbled to her side. Auntie held me close to her breast for a little while, still keeping her watch over the damage in the Ahoskie River.

I gathered myself and sat on the hood of her car, still hot from the engine, with a sweater between it and my legs. Auntie stood like stone beside me. Even the soft jowls of her face looked hard above her densely clasped hands.

I caught Uncle Frank's eye across the river, and he waved to me in return. Not the free and *happy to see you* kind of wave, more like the *I am here and so are you* kind.

The rumble of a car moving fast toward us made me turn behind myself to see who was in such a hurry to see death. The Spring City emergency squad had already arrived, though late if you ask me, and there was nothing left to do except get that poor soul out of there. As the car's lights peeked through the woods, I could see a turquoise Ford Country Sedan with a woman behind the wheel. A black woman. She steered wildly, like a cartoon character scripted for disaster, nearly hitting us as she drove up beside us. Punishing the brakes to screeching tears. Barely before the car had stopped, she ran out toward the bridge.

She had on a light blue dress that ruffled at the collar and short-sleeved cuffs. Her black hair, which was once held in a knot, was fast becoming a ponytail with every step she took. And she was beautiful. Only when she reached the water's edge did I hear her crying. No, not crying. She made a sound like an animal being torn apart from its limbs. She did not get far, thank God.

"My babyyy!" She hollered. Fighting to break free of the man in the white hat who had taken both her firm arms.

"Noooo, not my baby! Emma! No God, no!"

I looked over to Auntie's grim face.

She could have been mistaken for a totem pole. I was afraid to speak; to interrupt the stranger's pain seemed rude, but Auntie must have read my mind.

"Emma is...was their baby." Aunt Alice swallowed hard when she said 'baby.' "The man you saw down there, her husband, Joseph Samuel." I've known my Aunt Alice all of my life. She obviously had some kind of affection for these folks for her to well up like this. "Joseph and Violet Samuel...and their daughter Emma."

Lost in misery, we hardly noticed that Uncle Frank had crossed the bridge to meet us. He gave Auntie a long hug, then ushered me in to join them.

"What happened?" She whispered.

"I don't know, hon'. Sheriff Bigly said the skid marks show Joseph drove that car clear off the bridge." He stroked her back, gently rubbing the information in, soothing her like oil on a baby's bottom. She let his powerful strokes sway her back and forth without resistance.

Out of the corner of my eye, I saw a man dashing to the grieving Miss Violet. A man named Benjamin Samuel, I gathered, from the loud and thankful greeting made by Sheriff Bigly. Must be someone close in the family, I thought. He barely grazed her arm, when she suddenly turned to see who it was.

"My baby's dead!" she cried to him.

His long fingers got a hold of her petite arms. As he pulled her closer in, she fought with the strength of twenty slaves to be free from his grasp. But he wouldn't let go. She kicked her feet wildly to get free of him, but she failed. I could see her chest heaving hard, until her body became limp in his arms.

That moment was hard with silence.

After what seemed like forever, Auntie finally broke her trance, got into the car and turned the engine on. I nearly fell off the hood from the suddenness of her intentions. Thank goodness her headlights were already on. I grabbed the handle and swung myself into the seat. As soon as my seatbelt *clicked* she was heading out. She braked with a jerk, and then yanked the gear hard into forward. As she pulled around to get back on the road, a dust cloud gathered around the wheels. Crackling bits of dirt and gravel pricked the skin of my arm dangling out the window.

"You okay, Auntie?" I asked. I wanted to touch her hand, but both were clinched with a mind to stay on the steering wheel; ten and two o'clock. So I went for the flapping short sleeve of her shirt instead.

She nodded at me with a fleeting smile.

Try as I may, I couldn't get that man's bulging eyes out of my mind. Auntie must have sensed my distance on the ride back. Trying to erase those images, she told me a story; a Miss Melanie Neely had walked around town for most of the day with the back of her skirt tucked into her voluminous panties until Auntie shouted out at her at a red light. We laughed. I smiled at her twinkling eyes, knowing that whatever was behind them would soon find its way out.

In the darkness, we let the crickets' chirps lull us a while, until she told me about Joseph Samuel. How he didn't want to insult his father or his siblings, but still refused to work in the family business before, during, and after his time in the army. Not until the bank threatened to take the lumber yard did he finally succumb to their wishes.

Uncle Frank was sorry to see him go. He always said that Samuel was the best man he'd ever had working for him in his shop, smartest one, too, but always whistling a tune for the devil.

Daring him to come.

He'd met his wife, Violet Nightingale, at the Annual Candied Yam Festival. The first for him since he'd come home from the service. Every eligible woman wanted him, smacking their lips like he'd jumped straight out of the syrupy sweet can himself. Not love at first sight for Violet, but the world and beyond for him. She was grateful for a man who would provide for her without question, so she married him, and begot a wondrous child. Wondrous, for after a year and a half of four miscarriages, this child took its first breath from Violet's womb. Life's sweet kiss had planted a seed named Emma. Nothing bound to this Earth would ever matter more than she.

We arrived at home with the story told to its finish, then carried the groceries inside and started to prepare dinner.

Beep-beep!

Leave it to Uncle Frank to finally arrive at home, after helping out with the towing of Mr. Samuel's car and retrieving my bike, just when the rolls came hot out of the oven.

"Hey, hey there family!" He shouted as he slammed the truck door, trying to be his jolly self.

"Hey to you too, Uncle Frank!" Lena and I shouted back at the front door.

We watched him drag himself to the back door, heavy in sadness. He left his boots next to the brick steps along with his spongy socks, and then hosed his feet down on the grass. Auntie opened the screen door and passed him a towel to dry them off. He grunted and groaned a little, as he was a big man sitting on the low stoop, trying to reach his toes. I managed to leave the poor man alone trying to do his business, but Lena couldn't.

"Come on, Uncle Frank, dinner's waiting for you!" my baby sister, Helena, exclaimed, trying to light a smile on his face. "Here, you'll need these." She scurried over to his favorite chair and retrieved his thick navy-blue velvet slippers that exposed his toes.

After he slipped them on, he stood up and hugged us. Lena giggled since he was hugging the top of her head, leaving a sprout of her braid sticking up through his thick arms. Auntie held his huge hand and led him to his seat in the kitchen.

We all sat around the table waiting; all eyes riveted at him.

"Let's say the blessing," he said low. We all held hands; my sister and I squeezed particularly hard into Uncle Frank's to let him know that we were proud of him.

"Amen!" we all said together. Uncle Frank took a deep sigh spewing his hot breath mingled with the smell of a wet cigar. Things started feeling back to normal again. I could tell because my belly relaxed so I could eat.

"It's your favorite, stuffed pork chops and gravy!" I poked at his belly, and pried a giggle from him.

"Well thank you, ladies. Now pass that plate right on over here, please!"

Once he piled the homemade mashed potatoes and green beans on his plate, he became the lovable Uncle Frank again.

"Tell us Uncle Frank. Tell us what you saw!" Lena asked.

He looked to our aunt for her permission. She nodded that it would be fine.

"Well..." he said after taking a gulp of grape Kool-Aid, "once I was able to get the chains underneath the carriage, the hooks got that car up. Hmh, watchin' that winch haul it up in that darkness just like it was a casket seeping through the black waters of death." He took another gulp of Kool-Aid to keep him going. I wanted to drink too, but I dared not take a sip and miss hearing something from the swallow.

"The bodies hadn't been in the water too long. It was cool too, so the skin was wrinkled and kinda' pimply, same as when you get goose bumps but bigger. Nothing remarkable at first 'cept a few scratches and a missing finger to Mr. Samuel's right hand." Uncle Frank held on to his own finger, then snatched it quickly, to demonstrate how it must have happened.

I fought to smother a gasp, remembering again the sight of Mr. Samuel's face. I saw Lena clasp her little fingers to her chest, then slowly slide them underneath the table.

"Anyway, he, Mr. Samuel, was found floating facedown, sucked to the roof of his car with his eyes wide open. Sheriff Bigly thinks that he had to have watched his baby drown, still strapped in the backseat with one of the two seat buckles undone, the other jammed. He could no more set her free from that one mischievous buckle than fly home on the grace of God's breath. Can't imagine how it felt, the water fightin' to bust into his lungs. Jesus!"

"That's enough now, Frank." Aunt Alice spanked his enormous hand.

"Okay, okay, Alice…funny thing though…."

"Franklin!" Auntie scolded this time.

"Just let me finish, woman. This ain't so bad for the kids to hear. Like I said, funny thing though, when we took him out of the water his right hand was knotted up tight in a fist missing a finger, holding on to a coin—a worthless penny. Heck, maybe he had a spasm or something, it just seemed kind of an odd thing a dyin' man would do. How 'bout that Lizbeth?

You being the expert about pennies and all." I smiled at his compliment, although I was far from an expert.

There we sat eating our meal, dying to hear more without Auntie getting in the way. But Uncle Frank was smart. He timed it just right to tell us something sad but kind of thoughtful.

"As for Emma, she was wearing a sweet lilac dress with ruffles on the bottom, with a white homemade sweater. A pattern knitted with little puffs like popcorn scattered about in rhythm. Just sittin' there sleepin' like an angel. Shame is, that was the first time Joseph had picked her up from the babysitter or else she'd be alive now," he said.

"Shame for Violet, to lose them so soon," said Auntie, forking up some string beans.

That stripped us speechless. I had to remind myself to breathe after that.

"Stranger still, the tire marks show that Mr. Samuel was breaking hard to the right, but there wasn't a thing there to make him to go off that bridge, as far as Sheriff Bigly could tell. In fact, a boy along the Spring City bank saw the car plummet right into the river. Can't imagine what would make Joseph run off that bridge like that."

"Or who," I added.

"What do you mean, who?" Uncle Frank demanded.

"Makes more sense than a cow or a deer running him off the road." I swear Uncle Frank looked at me like I had two heads and twice the horns sprouting out of them. "Come on, Uncle Frank, he'd a' hit a darn animal before…you know… with his baby girl in the car."

The table went quiet.

"What?" I said softly.

They knew, we all knew.

We all stared down at our plates, twirling into the crystal ball of mashed potatoes and gravy for an answer.

Nothing.

Tasted good, though.

Rrrrnnnng, Rrrrnnnng

Auntie answered the phone while the rest of us washed down a piece of 7-Up cake with a glass of frosty milk. I tried to eavesdrop, but her deep voice was in a whisper until....

"Shush now, sweetie, I'll take care of it."

Auntie hung up the phone and headed out of our sight down the hallway. Moments later she came back across the room with a light sweater on. In one swoop she picked up the car keys, her purse, then she was gone. Uncle Frank started to holler after her, but he nearly choked on his words thinking it might be best not to.

We were asleep by the time she came home.

Two

My name is Elizabeth Parrot Landers. I was fourteen years old that summer, in the year of 1972. The time when Mr. Samuel and his baby daughter, Emma, drowned in their car after it went off the Danbury Bridge into the river below.

Although my parents told me that we'd spent a few weeks in Ahoskie when I was four or so, I don't remember. So this would be the first, official time my nine-year-old sister and I spent the summer here. I was to spend many a summer in Ahoskie afterwards, but not one held me captive for the rest of my life like that one.

Born in the borough of Queens, New York City, and having lived there all of my life, I was officially a city girl, despite my parents. After living on a farm in North Carolina, with a variety of cows, a cackle of hens, and three to four horses, tobacco, and cotton, my parents couldn't fly fast enough on a pig's rear end to get to the big lights of New York City. The closest I'd ever been to cotton was my underwear, until my Dad tricked a cotton plant into believing that it could grow in our backyard.

By the time fall came around, amazingly enough, a white fluffy ball of cotton blossomed. Only thing, it seemed as though the cotton had sucked the life out of the stem that had given birth to it. It was dry, hard, and brown. It was as if it had given its very existence for the white cotton, without ne'er an apology.

Nothing new really, if you understood how life worked. The poor brown stem working hard, toiling in the dirt day and night, forever sacrificing so the white cotton ball could become all that it could be. Happy to drench the best rays of the morning sun or worthy enough to be plucked into the finest robe.

And a seed would drop from the dry stem, back to the soil, to labor all over again.

Both of my parents had six siblings to kick each others' butts every day until the sun went down; from running through green fields of fat tobacco leaves, to dreaming about yellow cornbread in the morning. Making your own soap out of pig fat and lye had to have become a drag at some point. In New York City, soap comes from the grocery store, all pretty in a package, smelling nice like lilacs tucked in a cotton pillowcase. Can't beat that with a stick.

———

It was coming on to the last two weeks of school when my parents shared a great idea with us, my sister and I—living down south with our aunts, uncles, cousins, second cousins, and third for the summer. So many cousins, hell, my grandmother told me that I would hardly be able to "talk to" a boy in town, due to the fact that he would most likely be related to me! Anyway, down south we came for the summer, planning to be passed up and down the road like wandering Jews behind Moses, but more akin to the plant.

We started out at my Aunt Alice and Uncle Frank's, and I was already working it out how to stay there more so than not.

Franklin was his baptismal name, since he was born the same day as Franklin Delano Roosevelt, our thirty-second president of the United States. I just couldn't imagine who popped up with that piece of information. It's thought that my Great Aunt Ode was behind this, since she was there when he was born. She was the only one of the family who had graduated from high school at the time. It was said that she was some kind of woman. I couldn't wait to meet this woman.

My Aunt Al, Alice Morgan, she was the principal of the local high school at the time of the Samuels' deaths. She had schooled just about everyone in town at one time or another, even taught math to Mr. Samuel and Miss Violet. She cared for all her students as if they were birds of her own nest. She didn't have any children of her own. The Lord had decided that she had too many children in school to look over.

Auntie was a cool customer, to say the least. Even her skin was cool, as dark as black coal lit up after dark. Slow. Deliberate in every way, with the greatest intensity. She never had to shout or tell me to do something twice. It wasn't that I was afraid of her; she never raised a hand to me or my sister. I just knew she meant what she meant, and that was that. Her jet-black curly hair made you want to reach out and wrap the glistening threads around your finger. As soft-spoken as she was, her hands were equally as hard, the palms had stiff tough skin. The creases that were once supple had aged to brown, and would not bend without the aid of Vaseline. Tough as rawhide, when it came to digging up the earth. But to hold my face, where a smile was always there behind them, they were as soft as a dove's feather.

I loved this woman from the moment I met her. I always will.

My parents gave my aunt enough money to buy me a used bike for the summer. A purple Stingray with white and purple streamers sprouting from the handlebars, saddled with a purple banana seat sprinkled with silver to complete my ride! What a piece of magnificence. To lock my heels into the groove of life. God, and the sun burning hot on my face, matched by the cool wind against it. I'd shut my eyes and smile with the unabashed feeling of the pure joys of life as I stood tall on that bike. That moment and every other moment to follow, new and fresh. Then almost at the end of the road, surely just before my poor demise...I'd open my eyes!

Not too many things in life have ever affected me that way.

I couldn't have kept that bike in New York for more than a month, especially if I'd left it out on the porch, like I did at Auntie's every night. All my bikes had been stolen from our garage in New York at one time or another, after hours of my dad cussing and bleeding as he put them together. Sometimes, some fool would have the nerve to ride it down our street the very day after it had made its escape from our garage, just as happy as a clam. Right in my face.

Daring you to do anything about it.

Sometimes I'd tell my dad that I saw it rolling down the street under someone else's behind. Most times I didn't. Because I knew he'd about kill that boy.

All those years of sweating in a tobacco field. All the time he'd spent sleeping in a tent in Germany in two feet of the whitest snow on Earth.

Every night he drove our station wagon as a cab for every hooker and hoe, as Lena and I slept in the very back, so our mom could work overtime at the hospital. During the day he was a chemist, his real job, working his way up the white chain.

Every painful moment he walked on this Earth, shielding us from the awfulness of simply being. Stripes on his back from the daily whipping of being a Negro man in America.

My dad would surely be in jail for some part of his life for giving a well-deserved beat down that the *boys'* Daddy should have given him long ago—if he were around, that is.

Thus, I was keeping Dad.

The only other thing I loved as much as my family was my coin collection. I collected pennies. Nothing amazing, but any penny that caught my eye as being special, I collected it. I knew enough that a "wheat cent" was valuable and not too hard to find. But a Lincoln wheat penny, that's the one I held out for. The one that looked odd, like it didn't belong. President Lincoln's nose with a tiny pinhole on the tip of it or a ripple through the back of his head. I'd read books about these pennies, but I'd never seen one live or held one in my hand.

Three

The morning after the deaths of Mr. Samuel and his daughter Emma Samuel, I awoke, startled with the freshness of a sunny yellow guest bedroom that was mine—alone—for as long as I lived with Aunt Al and Uncle Frank. My baby sister had the pale blue room across the hall, which was fine by me. We shared a room with bunk beds back home, since Pop-Pop, our dad's father, was now living in my bedroom. We each had our own dresser, but we shared a fairly large closet. My nicer shirts and dresses hung in that closet. That was the one that I had to guard in order not to see my "best" walking out the door for school each morning on Lena's back. At the very least, here at Auntie's house, Lena would have to work harder at sneaking into my closet to steal some of my outfits.

I'd slept so soundly last night that there was not one dream that I could remember. I jumped from between the apple crisp sheets in my brand new pajamas. Pink silky-like polyester set with shorts for the bottoms. I didn't want to take any chances that they wouldn't have air conditioning, and I'd sweat clean through the sheets to the slats of the bed in the heat of the night.

And God, privacy. A big heaping word for a teen who shares a bathroom with her grandfather and a pain-in-the-butt little sister back home. I relished the thought of using my very own bathroom every morning. But before doing so, I had something on my mind.

I stepped in front of the dresser mirror, slipped my pajama top off to the side and unbuttoned the first two buttons. I stared into my eyes first—proof that I was confident with what I was about to do. I carefully watched that arm, my arm rise before my body to my chest.

I uncovered my right breast, my nipple already hard from the act of being. The wisp of air created by the shift of my top. I was amazed by the supple roundness of it as I cupped my palm around the bottom. I bit my bottom lip, fearful of the sensation I was awakening between my thighs.

"Lizbeth!" My aunt hollered from the kitchen. I almost dropped to the floor.

"Yes!" My hand fled from my chest.

"You up yet?"

Sure I'm up. I'm talking to you, aren't I? "Yes, ma'am!" I said as I scurried about my room like a squirrel trying to hide a nut in January.

"And Lizbeth…"

"Yes, ma'am," I whimpered as I slumped down at the foot of my bed, half shaken then stirred.

"When I ask, 'Are you up?' it's a courtesy down here. We're no dummies, despite the fact that we're still here after the Confederates lost the Civil War. You may be talking, but maybe you're still not *up* yet!"

How does she do that? "Yes, ma'am."

———

I should have known something was afoot when Aunt Alice whipped up a huge breakfast on a Wednesday. Just as she gave the kitchen table its last swipe, she stopped to make an announcement, accentuated by both hands on her hips.

"Lizbeth, since you're the oldest, we've got a lot of work to do this morning. We've got to get to an understanding that chores need to be done around here."

My sister smirked at me, which caused a drop of milk from her spoon to run down her chin as she ate her Fruit Loops.

Fine, I thought. She *is* my mother's big sister.

"Lena, you're going down to Mrs. Cooper's house to keep company with Margaret while we're gone, okay? Mrs. Cooper has some chores around her house to take care of. She needs Margaret to stay out of the way, since Bob can't be depended on."

My jaw dropped like a jackhammer leaving my mouth opened so wide that a fly could have choked me before I ever had the chance to protest. Lena saw the look on my face, and out flew the milk and colorful life rafts in a stream through her nose. Aunt Al fussed over the mess she'd made, but chuckled at Lena having to pluck a trapped Fruit Loop free from a nostril.

"But Auntie…" I stomped my foot under the table, which caused her to give me the eyebrow.

"Never mind what Lena is doing," she said softly, stretching her neck to make sure I understood my place. "Just pay attention to what you're going to be doing."

"And that is?" I questioned in my most obedient voice.

"To the *laundry mat*."

Lena about lost it again.

———

Just as Aunt Al and I were loading up the car with tons of laundry, a brown car was speeding down our road. The sheriff's car. As it steamed its way closer, I could see him through the dust ball. The man with the white hat.

"Sheriff Bigly." Auntie frowned some at his presence, but kept a smile.

He was frowning hard like cement, slipped with a cut for lips. Something troubling must have been on his mind. "Good morning, Miss Al, Miss." He tipped his hat with one hand and shut the car door with the other.

Sheriff Bigly was thin, but not in good shape, to say the least. He wore his belt strapped low beneath his belly. Anyone could have mistaken him for being a few months pregnant, if he wasn't a man. His lips were thick, dark like his skin until you got to the inner part, which was very pink, as though the skin had been burned off with a torch.

"Morning to you, Sheriff. What brings you here? I'd figure you had much more important things to do than drop by for a howdy here. Or maybe you smelled the trail of a three-layer coconut cake settin' in the window yesterday?"

"Well…" he said as he wrung his hands.

"Bigly, what's going on with you?" My aunt sounded truly concerned for him.

"Can we go inside, Miss Alice? I don't want to talk about this in front of…can we just go inside please?" He leaned his head toward Auntie, taking a glance at me, to make himself clear on the matter.

"It's okay, Auntie." I said.

She curled her lips up, feeling bad about excusing herself. "Come on in, Sheriff." She looked back at me again, saying *sorry* with her eyes.

I stayed fixed to the car door with my arms across my chest until I was sure they couldn't see me anymore. Then like a shot, I bolted like a sprinter out of the blocks, which I was since I won the one hundred-meter dash All County Championship last year. I was the only girl on the team that could do twenty push-ups in less than thirty seconds, too.

To the back of the house I flew.

Then I quickly crept down into the root cellar making sure to close the latch softly behind me. The steps creaked underneath my tippy-toeing, making my face wrench with every step with the thought of being found out. It was a bit musty and smelly, like old wet socks that were left in the dirty clothes hamper for too long. It wasn't as dark as one would expect with all the cracks of light coming through little holes in the hatch. I guess Aunt Al and Uncle Frank rarely stayed down here for more than a minute or so. I, on the other hand, had already spent a good half-hour here pouting when Uncle Frank wouldn't punish Lena for wearing my brand new blouse. Instantly I realized that I could see and hear folks in the living room through the pleats in the air vent.

Sheriff Bigly had no ability to whisper. No more than if his life depended on it.

"No Alice, thanks, but I can't sit. Not now with what I have to tell you." The man was sweating himself to death, dabbing his shiny forehead only for the sweat to bubble up on his face again.

"How about some water?" My aunt was already heading to the kitchen, which startled me for second thinking she had spotted me.

"No Alice, just hear me out!" He took a deep breath, now ready to account for his fears. "The medical examiner from Spring City came by early this morning. We had taken pictures of the body and all last night, so we left everything as it was; shoes, shirt, wallet, even his wedding ring. Didn't think anything of lockin' things up and what not. Just left it all nice and neat for the examiner on the gurney. "

"So what's the problem?" Auntie took a step toward the couch. She was going to have a seat whether he wanted to or not.

"Well when we, my deputy and I, rolled out the body of Joseph Samuel, we'd sat the manila envelope with his belongings on top of him. We…I… didn't think we had any problems until the coroner started going through the list of evidence we made, checking it against what was in the envelope. When he asked me 'Where's the penny?' I told him that it was in a plastic baggie, marked clearly 'Mr. Samuel's Penny.' To keep it separated from Mr. Samuel's other things. The only other item in the envelope was another baggie with Mr. Samuel's ring in it, and he found that just fine, but he said that there was no such penny in the envelope anywhere! I ran back into the storage room, tracing my step looking for the damn thing. I didn't find anything! I just don't know, Alice. It's gone!"

My heart leaped up into my chest at those words.

"You saw me put it away, Alice…didn't ya?" His body leaned slightly toward her for an answer. "When you were there to identify the body?"

She gathered herself before answering. "Well, yes, I think so, there in the bag." Her eyes began to fix on him oddly now. "Do you think that I took it?"

"No, no Alice, of course not," he stammered. "Thing is we've had quite a few folks come through here just doing their job. You see I made a list here, Alice, a short one but I remember these folks being there. Of course you're on it, the family, and the regular nosy folks. Then I have Deputy Sherriff Duncan, Mrs. Clover, my secretary, who by the way wouldn't steal a dollar bill if it were sittin' on her nose. Mr. Moore, with the weekly delivery. Lastly we have Bob Jr. He's the office technician, which is a fancy word for janitor."

"You mean Sara's son?"

"Yep that's the one. But he's no smarter than a bushel of peanuts, Alice. I'd ask him, only thing is, he didn't show up for work today. I mean…sure it's possible someone could have come through without me noticing."

The sheriff went back to dabbing his forehead again. My aunt sat back and studied the situation before speaking. I tried to breathe through my nose, thinking that through my mouth would give me away.

"There's somethin' else, Alice…" He sat down, this time in a chair too small for his frame. It was probably best that he wasn't comfortable for what he had to say. "We found a bullet lodged in one of the wooden trusses of the bridge. A fresh gash. That's where the skid marks begin. Someone other than the Samuel family was out there on that bridge that evenin'."

"What's that you wringing to pieces in your hands?" my aunt asked.

"Oh, oh yeah, these are photographs of the penny that was in Mr. Samuels' hand when he drowned to death."

Ouch! I bumped my forehead against the wall when I heard about the penny.

"What was that?" said Sheriff Bigly.

"Nothing but your imagination, Sheriff." She smiled a little, then the smile dropped when she looked my way.

How does she do that? I said to myself.

It was getting hot in there. Through the too-tall grass, to the front of the house, I flew, just making it back to the car before them.

"What were you doing, gal?" Auntie asked me. "You seem out of breath for some reason or another."

My forehead was as sweaty as the sheriff's. I swiped my brow, catching a drop of sweat just before it hit my eye. "Oh,

Auntie, I was just chasing that cat off from the chicken coop. Wouldn't want to catch him with a chick in his mouth, would we?" I asked, as innocent as I could stand myself.

Auntie gave me an up and down once-over. "If you are not too busy chasing cats, could you please take a look at these pictures?"

"Oh no, Alice, I couldn't have no youngin' look at something like this. It's official police, I mean sheriff's business!"

"You need help in identifying what you're looking for don't you?

"Yep, But eraaa…," said the Sheriff.

"Then Lizbeth can help you." Aunt Al drew the folder slowly from his hand.

"Fine, that's fine. She's just a kid. What could she hurt?"

Auntie took the bent photos out of the folder and placed them in my hands. Both sides of the penny had been photographed.

"Well gal, have you found anything?" harrumphed the sheriff.

"It's a Lincoln wheat penny which was struck in Philadelphia. Folks lined up a block long for two of these pennies. This was struck with the initials V.D.B., the man who designed it. Right away it became a source of controversy. On August 5, 1909, three days after the coin had been dispersed, the initials were changed to just "B" for Victor David Brenner. This penny is worth something. Not a whole lot, but more than one cent. That's for sure."

"Well, tell us how much gal? Is it worth…you know… dying for?"

I looked up at Auntie for the answer.

"Anything is worth dying for if someone wants it bad enough. Its value is in the secret it contains." Auntie held my shoulder as she thought about it.

"One more thing, Auntie. There's a pinhole in Lincoln's ear, which would make this penny super special. Why, to have this in your collection would be unheard of."

Auntie took the photos from me and handed them back to the sheriff. "Thank you, Lizbeth. There you go, Sheriff. Maybe that'll help you in your investigation."

My excitement suddenly evaporated like a wisp into cold dread at this reminder of who had owned the coin. Why would Mr. Samuel hold on to a valuable penny while he and his daughter drowned to death?

"Now don't you worry about a thing, Lizbeth, this is the sheriff's business, here on out."

How did she do that? "But if I should find it, you'd want me to give it to the sheriff, right?"

"If you find it."

I didn't know many people in Ahoskie. I hadn't even met all my relatives yet. As I watched Sheriff Bigly drive away, I knew I'd have to change that if I wanted to find the answer to that one…big…fat…question.

Four

The Town Laundry Mat was smack dab in the middle of Ahoskie on the main street, Main Street. Lord, I soon grew to hate that Mat. There was nothing to do but wish you were somewhere else. Even the threat of going to the local grocery store was starting to sound like fun to me. So killing time became a profession for me. I looked through the window of Young's Real Estate, next door, at all the homes for sale in town. I ate two bags of chips from the vending machine, with an orange pop on the side.

Then I had the bright idea to toss rocks from the gravel pit parking lot. I started out tossing them into the street, but when I hit the side of a Piggly Wiggly truck, I thought better of it. So I began to throw them straight up into the bright blue sky.

No cars around, except for Aunt Al's Dodge Dart, which was at least three car spaces away. Everyone else had walked to the Mat or was most likely dropped off.

Straight up, then straight down. I side-armed the next two about ten feet into the air.

Straight up, straight down…kind of.

When that went well enough, I gave a little more sling to my shot. The rock took off like a rocket. As I watched it begin to descend, in awe of my wondrous skill, something started to go wrong. Way wrong.

The arc was too wide, traveled too far to the right. To the right where the naked Dart was parked.

"Uh oh," I said to myself.

For a flash, I thought I might try to lift the car from the rear and move it to safety. You know, kind of like those stories you hear where a desperate mother lifts a car off the ground, saving her child pinned beneath it. Unfortunately, I felt no wild surge of adrenaline pulsing through me. What I did feel was my body sway to the left, trying to convince the rock to mimic my motion away from the car. But it wasn't working. All I could do was watch…and cringe…and wait.

It's a little rock, how much damage could it do?

I watched in amazement as I witnessed *what* it could do.

Crack!

I crept up to the car with my teeth grit for the worst. Good thing.

If I had tried to hit the backside of a barn ten feet away, I couldn't have done it. But a wild, innocent toss managed to find its way dead center in the front windshield.

My movements were calculated, trying to act cool (shaking in my sneakers), as if I was shuffling around the car for another good rock. I glanced over my shoulder to the hard plastic window in the Mat's door, praying no one had been standing there to witness my crime. My heart was pounding in my swollen throat as I opened the passenger door to slide my butt across the front seat. It was burning hot, hot enough to blister my skin to a sheet of thin bubbles, but that didn't stop me. I pressed my hands underneath to the seat, as my thighs peppered up and down to escape the burn between my fingers.

"Ughhh," was my reaction as I viewed my handiwork from the inside. No way was she missing that, unless she was Helen Keller in disguise.

A diamond-shaped crack about a pinky finger long screamed out at me no matter how I squinted my eyes or turned my head. My gut churned with the fear of seeing my aunt's disappointed face once she saw the damage.

I gathered my courage, thinking that I might tell her beforehand. As my wobbly legs made their way toward the Mat with the rest of my body dragging behind them, I heard the crackle of parking lot gravel kicking up with a fuss.

A green car, moving a little too fast, blazed into the parking lot. I watched in hopes of a rock hitting the windshield to cover my tracks.

No such luck. There was nothing left to do but confess.

A small woman with a big bottom flew out of the car, with a half-full plastic basket of whites resting on top of her bloated belly. I had only seen her once before, but I knew her name: Mrs. Melanie Neely, aka "Miss McMeanie." That's what the kids around the park called her, my cousins Tommy and Terry, and some grown folks too, I'd heard. She was a schoolteacher, used sarcasm as her weapon of choice to punish her students. A woman equally small and petty in height and compassion, as I would find out on my own soon enough.

One story that went around about her at our dinner table had to do with Mr. Wilson and his son George. Mr. Wilson owned the only gas station in town. A strikingly handsome Negro with green-hazel eyes set in caramel skin stretched tall and lean. McMeanie liked him when they were in high school, but Mr. Wilson loved him some Miss Jean, so he married her, George's mom. McMeanie held a grudge so strong for all these years that she made poor George pay for it in her eleventh grade math class. George wasn't the smartest tack on a wall, but he worked hard with what he had. No one is for sure as to what set her off that day. Some suspect that she caught George holding hands with Debra Minton in the hallway, reminding her of Mr. Wilson and Miss Jean back when. Anyway, as soon as they set foot in the classroom McMeanie set about her cruelty like a rabid dog.

"Students, we're going to do something a little different today. You know, whatever careers you undertake when you become adults, will require the basic principles of arithmetic... money! I'm going to point to you, and you will tell the class your name, what profession you hope to be and how much money you aim to make. Let's start with you!" McMeanie pointed her stick with the black rubber tip to the head of Debra.

"My name is Debra...."

"Speak up and stand up straight girl!" McMeanie smirked.

Debra popped up from her seat. Loud and strong, "My name is Debra Ann Minton. I would like to be a nurse for babies when I grow up. I believe they earn about a hundred and twenty dollars a week in the big cities." She beamed.

"That's a lot of money Miss Debra, one hundred-twenty dollars every week. Why I don't know for sure if that sounds quite right...for a baby nurse, I mean. What other profession do you think could make that kind of money in a week?"

Everyone squirmed in their seats.

"Well I don't know." Debra hesitated.

"Think about it, what could you do with those pretty lips and face you have? Hmmm? Boys like George seem to like it. What could you do that *all* the boys would like, Miss Debra?"

Tears started to well in the girl's eyes as she guided herself down to her seat, shoulders beginning to slump.

"No, Miss Debra, don't sit down now, we haven't finished! So what would you *call* a business that could make all the boys happy? Why, how silly am I. I just gave you a clue didn't I?"

"I don't understand, ma'am." Debra could hardly be heard in the death of silence.

"You don't understand? I'll give you the clue again. What would you *call* the business? Make maybe one hundred-twenty dollars in a day, pretty as you!"

Debra's head dropped to chest, while the tears streamed down the sides of her blushed cheeks. Her mouth moved, but the words could not be heard.

"What'd you say, Miss Debra? Speak up girl, we can't hear you?"

"A call girl." She whispered, as she melted into her seat.

McMeanie. An evil bully that could take the pleasure out of the simplest things. Like an angry toddler kicking sand on the other children's lollipops, making them cry. Her lips stained red from her own lollipop like blood.

I compared her to my sweet Aunt Alice, with little more than the daily act of kindness, courage to speak the truth of things, with a heaping spoonful of smarts, highly regarded and well loved by just about everyone in town. The oldest of the five girls, my mother being the youngest of them all, she began her teaching career in the family living room with her younger sisters, as my mother recalled. At the sage old age of twelve she would sit in the big chair with the sisters gathered around on the wood floor with homemade slate boards and chalk in hand. Reading and reciting were her favorites, aside from arithmetic. The kindness, patience, and love of learning that she displayed with her sisters carried over when she became a "real" teacher.

I followed McMeanie into the Mat, thinking this was my chance to see her in action first hand.

"Hi, ladies!" she called out, with conceit dripping from her lips. She loved the attention, but thought little of whether it was gained through bad deeds or not.

"Hey there, Sista' Neely." The ladies were still bent over their laundry as they threw her their unsynchronized chorus of good manners, as if to get past the ordeal of speaking to her.

My aunt, not afraid, nor willing to be impolite. "Mel." Auntie kept on folding, never skipping a beat, giving a sharp glance with her eye. A look so sharp, like a blade of grass fooled into believing it was still standing, not knowing that a mower had already run through it.

"Alice." She responded in kind, with her not-so-high-on-the-horse tone.

My aunt's lips curled at the sound of her name being spoken from between McMeanie's lips.

Whoa, I thought, as I eased back onto the bench behind me, searching with my fingertips to find the seat. I didn't want to miss a crease in her face, not a crack in her voice, not one blessed thing in this showdown.

McMeanie took her a place at the folding table across from my aunt, as the other ladies gave way. About ten feet long and five feet wide, there was plenty of room for a good seat around the crappy yellow laminate table. My Aunt Al continued to fold her pillowcases at the same steady beat as before.

Hmmmmm went the ceiling fans, along with the waggling sound of a few missing screws.

Sweat glistened in Miss Cecelia's sideburns like amber in a honeycomb.

"Shame about Mr. Samuel and his baby girl, don't you think?" McMeanie gloated.

Pang.

Everyone sucked in a breath just preparing themselves for whatever kind of venom would surely spew from that woman's mouth about that poor family.

Steady on the pink lily pillowcase, Auntie. I prayed for her, since I knew I would have been no good in her shoes right now.

McMeanie looked up from underneath the layered hoods of her eyelids, checking the pulse of the room.

"I heard around town that you had to be the one to identify their dead bodies, Alice. Poor thing, Miss Violet couldn't take seeing her baby and her love lying there dead in the sheriff's office. Or maybe…she felt guilty about something else. All those hours that Joseph spent at the lumber yard. Bringing it up to snuff can work a toll on a mind…and a body. Sittin' home lonely and all. Maybe she was angry with him that day and that's why he picked up the baby for once."

That strike made me wince.

"Maybe that brother of his, Benjamin, should have identi-fied the bodies."

Auntie dropped her hands with the pretty flower pil-lowcase clutched between them with a lifeless thump to the table. "How could you say such an awful thing?' A seething calmness is a dangerous thing to awaken.

McMeanie took a chesty breath in contemplation of what to do next. She knew she was no match for Alice Morgan. "I heard she nearly passed out in grief on the bridge seein' her husband's car dipped in the river. My cousin, Miss Fanny, came by this morning with a plate. Said that the woman could hardly speak, nearly frozen from grief, let alone able to eat. So how was it, Alice? Identifying those bodies and all?" McMeanie continued to fold her pile, smoldering with a great intent to exact more sorrow.

With a sigh of disbelief, Alice slowly looked up from her pile. "Yes. Miss Violet did ask me to identify her family. Poor child—"

"You would think she'd want to see them for the last time. I mean really!" McMeanie interrupted.

"Like I was saying, poor child, no woman should have to bear seeing her baby *and* her husband like that. To survive your husband is one thing, but to survive your child...well life's hard enough without one. I can't imagine. But only a black-hearted demon with wiry hair could speak of such horrible things about that family. What gives you the right, Mel? What gives you the right to be so cruel?"

With that, my aunt gently packed her clothes and a bottle of bleach and turned to the door. The sea of baskets parted for her to pass. I followed, trying hard to keep up and not to step onto her shadow behind her as she headed out the Mat.

"The right?" cried McMeanie. "My grandfather helped build that lumber yard, that's what gives me the right! It should have been mine to have. My legacy!" She slapped her chest hard with an open hand declaring her claim. "Mine!"

Auntie refused to look back at McMeanie, and I didn't dare say a word when we reached the parking lot. How could I? I was about to add more disappointment to the already chin-high pile of crap—more than one woman deserved at the moment and less than what I expected of myself.

No children of her own and a niece that was unworthy to be one.

I reached my side of the car. I waited for her reaction as she reached hers. I could feel my head and shoulders hanging low in anguish from where I stood. The light twinkled with bright colors from the prism created by the crack. Hardly something that one could miss. Then, leaning over the side of the hood with a curious frown she said—

"That sun sure is hot today. Come on Lizbeth, let's go home and have us something cool to drink."

After I shut the car door and snapped the seat belt, I looked to her, my mouth ready to apologize, feeling sad and ashamed that I had let her blame it on the sun.

"Auntie…."

"It sure is hot out this morning, isn't it Lizbeth?" she said, as she patted the back of my hand that rested between us on the seat. She smiled once again, checking for other cars, then backed the Dart out of the lot.

"Auntie…? About what McMeanie said…."

"Don't worry, honey, Melanie has always been jealous of the Samuel family."

Auntie drove slowly down Main Street. I rolled my window down and propped my chin on my arm, begging the wind to cool my face like a dog…wondering,

It was just a penny. But a penny's got a whole lotta power if you think about it.

You can pick it up and all the day you'll have good luck!

Then again…

In great numbers, it can bash the brains clear out of a man's head.

Five

I couldn't get McMeanie out of my head. She made me shiver; slapping her chest and all. I bit my bottom lip all through the ride home, waiting for the right time to ask.

As Aunt Alice slowly drove down the dirt road to our home, my bottom lip cautiously freed itself.

"Auntie, what was that about McMeanie claiming a right to the lumber yard?"

Auntie allowed the car to drift into the driveway. She took the key out of the ignition with a deep sigh.

"Miss Melanie is right up to point in the history of the Samuels and the Neelys owning the lumber yard together at one time. But John Neely, Miss Melanie's grandfather, not only gambled, but stole from David Samuel. David warned him that he might have to break their partnership if his 'ways' didn't change. Finally, the lumber yard couldn't take Neely's thievin'. It was hard to pay wages and purchase supplies. The two men had a nasty, nasty argument one evening as they were closing up shop.

"As usual, Neely brought his friend 'Mr. Moonshine' home to nurse him good-night. His neighbors heard him yelling at his wife. Maybe hurt her a little too, sadly."

Auntie took a quick glance at me when she said that part. "He must have fallen asleep with his bottle in bed that night along with his wife. The fireplace was still burning hot coals... the bottle must of slipped out of his hand somehow. Didn't take long for the house to burn down with all of them in it. All of them except Miss Melanie's mother, with a nasty burn down her arm and blind in both eyes to remind her of the near fatal escape.

"David Samuel did right by that child. Even though she had family that took her in, he sent her money until the day she died. But she was a proud woman. Rarely using a penny over what she needed, until she made the same mistake her mother had made...married a snake from a whiskey barrel. He was a handsome drifter that stayed with her for a summer, then headed south on the wings of a black tern. He took most of her money, but left her with one thing, a baby that was named Melanie Neely.

"Joseph continued to give Melanie some help years after his grandfather had passed—against his brother's wishes, one in particular. Of course she was ungrateful, bitter from a hard life. Wanting a share of the business because she deserved it. She never turned away the money Joseph gave her. I imagine she's boilin' up inside, wondering what's going to happen to her now that Joseph is dead."

"So Auntie, who is this brother of Mr. Samuel that's against McMeanie getting any money?"

She didn't answer, but smiled.

I began to question a few things about McMeanie. Maybe she wanted Mr. Samuel out so that she'd have the opportunity to take it over. What if she was on the bridge, a pistol in her hand? But why try to harm him, when he was always going to give her whatever money she needed?

What about the penny? Why would she take it? It seemed to me that whoever shot up the bridge took that penny. And the only reason to take the penny was to either conceal a secret or profit from its value. I wish I knew who'd been in and out of the sheriff's office while Mr. Samuel's body was lying there.

I told myself that this matter was up to the grown folks like the sheriff—but I couldn't help thinking about it. If in the meantime the penny would come my way, well then that's when I'd speak up.

God I would love to have a penny like that for myself.

Penny.

Penny, penny, penny!

"Lizbeth…Lena…come on down and wash up for dinner!" Auntie shouted from below.

After dinner I kept myself busy reading Auntie's collection of *Jet* magazines. I always thought there was something not-so-wholesome about a girl in the middle of the magazines with a bikini on, with an inch-by-inch write-up about how she attends this or that university and loves kittens.

By the time I set my head on the pillow, I could hardly finish yawning before falling asleep.

—————

First thing in the morning, we're awaken by the telephone instead of a rooster. Sheriff Bigly. Asking Aunt Al if she knew the name of that boy who'd seen the car go off the bridge from the Spring City bank. At least that's what I got from listening to Auntie's half of the conversation. Oh, and she didn't know.

Auntie nodded her head and rolled her eyes as I got myself ready for more surprise chores. She put the phone down, and her fists land on her hips. Uh, oh.

Next thing I know, we're in the Dart heading for who knows where.

Auntie decided that we deserved a treat without the agitation of Lena in the backseat. An ice cream seemed appropriate.

We pulled into the parking lot of the Mr. Softee ice cream parlor, with two lines of kids before us. White, black, short, tall, the rich, and the poor all waiting for a taste of happiness to run down their chin.

"I'll have a double chocolate chip mint," Auntie said as she handed me two dollars for our cones.

"That sounds good, Auntie, but I'm having the best ice cream cone in the galaxy...a scoop of chocolate, a scoop of peanut butter and finally, to top it off, a scoop of pistachio nut. Ooo-la-la." I sent a kiss off into the air from the tips of my five fingertips smooshed together.

"Well you might need another quarter for that, Missy." She dug into her change purse for extra change, just in case.

The tar-covered lot was steaming hot. I don't know how the kids without shoes could stand it. I did see one of them run over to the edge of the grass to cool his feet. But within a few seconds, he was right back in line with his friends. I could hear the rhythmic *pang* of a basketball being bounced. I looked toward the sound excitedly to see if maybe Terry or Tommy or even Chin-Chin were coming up the road for a cool treat. But no such luck. It was a couple of white kids getting in line.

But, just as if it fell from the sky, a red truck pulled up behind them. It took a few seconds before a figure came out from the cool air conditioning to brave the tar heat. I couldn't see him clearly since he was on the opposite side of his truck from me. He opened the back door and removed a big white cooler from it. He hitched up on its back wheels, with a short cord towing it, and began to stroll toward the shop.

While making his way across the lot, he got too busy reading a crinkled piece of yellow paper that he'd just freed from his jeans pocket to notice a kid crossing his path, and then, *crash!* He must of knocked that black boy clear into next week on his behind.

"Ow!" the boy cried rubbing his elbow and his butt.

A fall like that on blacktop can hurt like heck. Aside from leaving an ugly scar, it can easily get infected from bits of tar crammed into the flesh. The tall white man wavered between deciding whether to helping the boy up and juggling the cooler.

He chose the cooler.

"Come on, boy, get up. It doesn't hurt that bad. Spit on it and wipe it clean!" He shouted, then looked around for help or the boy's parents. Or better yet, if anyone had noticed he'd knocked the boy down. None came to the rescue, but I noticed.

"Follow me, boy!" He commanded.

"No sir, I ain't followin' you nowhere!" Like it never happened, the boy jumped up with one eye on the white man and the other searching for his place back in line.

"Who's that, Auntie?" I asked.

"Why that's Mr. Jake. The owner of the grocery store."

After a five minutes or so, Mr. Jake was bringing the cooler back to his truck with a little more effort. This time he threw it into the bed and took off. When the black kids were sure he was out of sight, they jeered and hollered at him. A couple did a little dance, kicking their feet up into the air with brown toes peeping through their worn sneakers. With thumbs in their ears and fingers wiggling, they stuck their tongues out at him, too. Then they laughed and laughed so hard they had to hold their bellies to keep from falling. I laughed, too, watching them have a good time.

"So *that's* Mr. Jake." I so noted as I got out of the Dart to get my own taste of happiness.

Six

What a pain in the butt! Whining so much about seeing Margaret that weekend, flapping her arms with knotted fists, stomping in circles like a chicken with its head cut off until Auntie finally gave in to Lena's demands. As a result, I became the innocent, well-mannered niece, but there would be a price to be paid.

———

Friday morning, I walked Lena over to Mrs. Coopers' house around ten a.m.

"Morning, girls! Good to see you, Lizbeth. You're not going to stay over too, by any chance?" I could see it in Mrs. Cooper's eyes, begging me, *please*. Me, babysitting the girls, while she heads out to shop in peace. Why couldn't Bob get off his lazy butt to do it? After all, one of the kids was his daughter.

"No, ma'am. I'm just here to drop Lena off, then I'm going with Aunt Alice to do the chores. Maybe Bob could sit with them for a while?" I asked, innocently enough.

"Oh no, no child. He's too busy with *things*, to do that!" She fiddled with her bouncy hair, still in a net.

"What kind of things?" I asked as I leaned over to see his scrawny body walk out from behind the doorway into the kitchen in his basketball shorts, worn holey tee-shirt, and blue flip-flops. He made his way to the table while scratching his beard with both hands like a raccoon cleaning up for breakfast.

"Oh, lots of things. He's looking for a new job that will pay for Margaret's college education someday. Much better than that old job at the sheriff's office. Right, Bob?"

That's when it hit me. This was the same Bob Jr. that the sheriff was talking about on the list yesterday. The "technician" that cleans up after dead bodies. Great! Then again, what was I going to do…investigate? I was just a kid looking for a valuable penny.

Bob Jr. was smacking his lips during his yawning, and blinking his beady brown eyes before he answered. Though he was about twenty-five, he looked no more mature than an eighth-grader with a scraggly beard. That definitely made me feel as though I had the upper hand on this guy. Boys are somewhat stupid in eighth grade compared to the girls!

"Yes, Momma. That's right. I could do a lot better than that ole' stupid job down there. Workin' me like a dog. Cheatin' me out of money I deserve."

Told you.

"Come to think of it, Mrs. Cooper, my Aunt Al said I could stay for a few, if you want to get breakfast ready for Bob? I'll keep them quiet in Margaret's room for the time being."

"Why thank you, Miss Lizbeth. Okay girls, follow Lizbeth upstairs to your room." She smiled with genuine appreciation as I led the girls up the stairs like the Pied Piper.

It wouldn't be hard to tell which room belonged to Bob Jr. I figured he was a slob by the way he was dressed at the kitchen table in front of his mom and his daughter, no less. Yep, it was easy all right.

"Now you girls sit here and play with the dollhouse. No cutting off Barbie's hair to make a wig, you hear! I'm going to the bathroom," I lied.

The beige and green-colored bathroom was next to Bob Jr.'s bedroom. If he had taken Mr. Samuel's penny, it might be in there. I could always snoop a little and use the bathroom for my cover if I were to be caught.

"Darn it." I hissed under my breath. The bedroom door was closed shut. I slowly held the blotchy gold knob in my hand, turning it ever so slowly. That didn't guarantee that it wouldn't whine like a skinned cat, but that's how I'd seen the spies do it in the movies.

Click.

My heart was thudding so loud in my ears I didn't hear the rattle of the door plate as I leaned against it, but I felt it, and it sent a shudder through my body that quaked to the tip of my toes. The door was barely cracked open when it became stuck by a bit of dark green shag carpet in the threshold. As I tried to tug at the carpet, holding the clapping plate with the other hand and pushing the door with my shoulder, I could feel my balance slipping too far into the door.

It was then that I heard footsteps rising up the staircase.

My spine wobbled in fear, which sent my balance so far off that if I let go of the knob I would tumble right through the door!

So…I let go.

Boom! I bounced into the door

Bang! I landed on the bathroom floor.

"Elizabeth?"

"Yes!" I answered rubbing my behind.

"You okay in there?"

"I'm fine. I felt a little dizzy that's all. A splash of water and I'll be okay. Thanks."

As I leaned against the sink to catch my breath, I could hear Mrs. Cooper talking to the girls down the hall. Bob Jr., apparently, was still smacking his lips to the tune of flapjacks and sausage in the kitchen.

One more try. If I could…

Knock, knock!

"Lizbeth, you still in there, sweetie?" Mrs. Cooper's voice pierced right through the dry wall and tiles.

"Uh, yes, Mrs. Cooper?" Can't a girl have some peace in the bathroom? Good thing I didn't have to go!

"Could I bother you once more for a favor?"

"Sure." Why not? If you can bother me in the bathroom, then you can bother me anywhere I suppose.

"Could you stay here just a little bit longer? I'll call Miss Al and let her know that I've kept you and I will drop you off wherever she'd like within the hour. Is that okay?"

Is that okay? Does the Devil's bare butt have a tail?

"Yes ma'am, but will Bob Jr. be staying with us?" Of course not, what would she need me for?

"Yes, he will. He has some things to do around here."

"Okay. See you later."

I wanted to ask *why*, but I thought that would be too bold for someone my age. Although it made my task a little more difficult, it was not impossible. I was up for the challenge.

For the penny.

"For the penny," I whispered to myself.

———

Ten minutes of my precious time had dragged by before Bob Jr. finally finished eating his breakfast.

Thump, thump…

Here he comes! I waited for his door to catch in the rug.

Boom! I heard his door bust open.

Some rattling around—keys, papers, a drawer slams. Then the most beautiful sound that left me drooling with anticipation…change.

I went downstairs to get us all orange twin pops (this makes sure that there wouldn't be any fuss over the flavor). But somewhere after handing them out, the devil tapped me on my shoulder, and I knocked on his door.

"Yep," he said.

The door was already cracked open, so I gave it a little nudge to poke my face in.

"Bob, I think I might have to leave a little sooner than Mrs. Cooper expected. Do you think that you would be able to watch the girls till she gets home from shopping?"

A body is a wondrous thing. Take the skin, for instance, the largest organ of the human body. It hides all the muscle and bones all sucked into a compact space, but it can't hide what the mind is thinking. And it can't sucker another body from knowing it either. Bob Jr.'s already tight shorts, puckered into his butt so quick, the vacuum could have been put out of business. His chest tensed hard, flexing his man breasts ever so slightly. He turned to me as he caught his breath, ready to speak.

"Uhh, yeah. I guess I could. Is your sister stayin'?"

This answer caught me off guard, but not enough to show it. Why would he care if Lena was staying?

"Yes, if I were to leave, but I'm not sure if I should leave. I did tell your mom I'd stay. Besides, I think your mom was planning on paying me a little something."

"Well I could pay you, anyway, then you can leave! I'll even take your lil' sista off your hands," he said excitedly. Like Santa was coming to town and leaving him a BB gun.

"I don't want to put you out and all...."

He suddenly dropped onto his bed like a dead man walking, then bounced up like a willow stick. There he was, standing before the drawers. He opened the second drawer, double the depth of the first, to shove aside his tee-shirts. A cigar box sat in the far corner in the back of the dark space. He eased it out like it had a cake in it, then set it atop of the dresser. I tried not to be too obvious in my excitement, so I stepped back into the doorway cupping my chest.

Something caught my eye. A jar of coins twinkled in the open drawer.

He ignored it, and instead rustled some paper bills out of the cigar box. In haste he counted aloud as he slammed each bill on top of the dresser. When he got past five I got scared. I'd never been paid more than five dollars...ever...for babysitting in my life. That queasy feeling started down low in my belly, telling me something was wrong. I tried not to stare at the jar of coins—at least long enough so he wouldn't catch me.

"Here, I'll give you fifteen bucks. My momma will never know you left. Here, take it."

He tried to shove the bills in my hands, but something kept them balled up tight against my chest. I backed away this time into the wall trying to get out of his room.

"You know, Bob Jr., I think I better do like I said I would to your momma. She'd be disappointed in me if I left you here with the girls high and dry. I don't want any trouble."

"It's no trouble, girl! I can watch the girls. I got the money right here. Take it, go on...take it!"

I shook my head. "No thanks, Bob Jr., I'll deal with your momma when she gets home."

Deflated, for which I couldn't understand for the life of me, he crunched the bills into his pocket, then threw the cigar box in the dresser drawer.

He's a strange fellow. I thought.

I must have stood there for a second too long looking about his room.

"Like my room, do yah? I know. I got a lot of real important stuff in here."

Real important *junk* came to my mind. He had a set of three hub caps (you need four, don't you?), light blue pickling jars of all sizes, some filled with marbles, buttons, and whatnots, screws, keys, you name it. Shoes, some as far as I could tell that didn't have a mate. Newspapers and magazines piled high in the corners of the room.

Then he came around my back like a sidewinder in the sand.

"See anything you like?" His throat throttled eerily, masking something.

As I shrugged my shoulders, I mistakenly turned my attention to the jar. He caught me.

"You see something over there, huh!" He held his eyes on mine as he slithered over to the dresser. He floated his hand over the top of it, as if he could sense the heat between me and the object of my desire. That jar of coins. If he stole *the penny*, it might be in that jar.

"This!" He picked up the jar with delight. Grinning, baring his teeth while he held the jar before his face like a torch. "A bunch of coins!" He laughed.

With one drawn step he was in my face with an outstretched hand. "Maybe you can have it…someday."

"I better go see what the girls are up to." I backed out of his room, leaving him to do his grinning.

When Mrs. Cooper hollered at the door that she was home, all us kids came running. She must have been feeling full of herself, when she handed me a five-dollar bill and a small box of chocolate-covered cherries.

"Elizabeth Parrot Landers, thanks so much for helping me out, child."

A lot of praise and money for a little nothing but watching some kids. Mrs. Cooper stood there staring at me while twittering with her fingers as I pried the box of candy open.

"I was just wondering, Lizbeth, would you and Lena be interested in sleeping over, so us grown-ups, some of my girlfriends from the factory, could go out tonight? We'd be getting home awful late, maybe get some breakfast in the wee hours, freshen up at home, then run on out again early in the morning to go fishing in the Chesapeake. What do you think, darlin'?" She rolled her lips waiting for my answer. It took me a moment to soak in my good fortune.

"Why yes, yes we would Mrs. Cooper."

 Seven

Once Mrs. Cooper called my aunt for permission, they decided to make a big deal out of bean sprout. What's better than having a live-in nanny for the weekend? A fourteen-year-old, responsible and cheap, live-in nanny. Auntie and Uncle Frank decided that they would go down to Manny's and dance all night too. Mrs. Cooper promised to make us a nice red fish stew Saturday evening when she got back. One of my all time favorites.

Hmmm, some pennies *and* some red stew!

Friday afternoon was uneventful, thank goodness. Even though Lena and I didn't have our bathing suits like Margaret, we took turns chasing each other with the water hose in our shorts and undershirts. After a couple of tuna fish sandwiches, we rode our bikes. Margaret on hers, while I took Lena on my handlebars, to the Ahoskie Little League Park. Lena loved standing on the swings, gliding through the air as if she were flying. I spent most of my time pushing between the two of them.

The day wound down like a ball of yarn. We finished it off by picking a pretty color to paint our fingernails.

By nine o'clock, Lena and Margaret were worn out and so was I. Mrs. Cooper had put us up in the spare guest bedroom.

She was also kind enough to set up a small black-and-white television in our bedroom. I had never missed an episode of *Columbo* before. It was a two-hour special tonight. And I would watch it in peace, in an overstuffed chair, with a big bag of barbeque chips in my lap and all the orange pop my belly could handle.

But halfway through a car commercial, my eyelids began to get heavy. I shook my head as a commercial for the next episode of "The Undersea World of Jacques Cousteau" played. They were in a ship that cut through deep waters like a knife, churning it into white foam during a night exploration. I leaned toward the television as a man in a black swimsuit sat upon the edge of the boat, relaxed, casually chatting in French with his back facing the open water. Then, without notice, he tipped back, blindly falling into the depths of the ocean.

Mr. Samuel never had a chance. The thought of him fighting his car to stop on the edge of the bridge washed over me.

I saw it all in my mind's eye.

Panic strikes him in the throat. His spine unexpectedly snaps to attention. His sweaty palms clinch onto the steering wheel far too tight. So tight that the beds of his nails are pale. He tries desperately to stop the car, braking with both feet, one foot crushing atop of the other. Wildly steering like a bumper car, crossing the double-yellow line too many times, he unwittingly charges a truss of the bridge. The fear of knowing is lying heavy upon his chest. BANG!

SCREEEEECH *cry the wheels of the car, locked in a heated embrace with the road until smoke billows from underneath the carriage.*

NOOOO! *His muscles are rigid in pain, trying to turn the now-locked steering wheel, heading to the right side of the bridge. A once-dry white cotton shirt now bleeds with stains of wear from his sweat-drenched body.*

Strange, it seems be taking too long for him to collide with the rail. Time deftly dragging its hand knowing what's to come. So long is the moment that he can afford to glance up to view his last tree-scaped blue sky. A lonesome tear cradles in his eye. Not for himself, but for her, his sweet little girl, Emma. She would never again coo at his smiling face while grasping his sole finger with her tiny miracle hand.

CRASH, *as the hood of the car rips open wide like a steely mouth from the lower jaw of the front grill. The blunt force digs into the windshield; the sound pierces his body long before the sharp pain of reality.*

"Ahhhh," a cry coincides with the crunch of the hood.

The car teeters for only a moment on the wooden ledge before tipping into a headlong dive as if on a rollercoaster. His stomach thrusts up into his chest, causing him to vomit in his mouth, then sputter bits of his lunch on his shirt. He reaches wildly to the backseat, frantically groping for something. His forefinger loops and snags the seat belt, but the vertical blow of the car hitting the water like fluid concrete snaps his finger clean off from the knuckle joint.

The blood-infused water rushes into the sinking floor of the car. Bubbling frothy mad, having to fight its way in to choke the air out. The screaming is becoming unbearable to his ears.

Emma is in the backseat.

His hands are tearing at the seat belt like metal claws, scraping curls of his own fleshy brown skin bloody underneath his nails. He doesn't care; he doesn't feel pain either, other than somewhere within himself that he's never been before. The thought of his beautiful child gurgling in choking pain; fighting for her last breath...too much to bear. "God, why couldn't I die first like a coward?"

Finally freed from the strap, his tears mingling with the splashing water that is now up to his waist, he turns again to grapple with the straps that were meant to bind Emma in safety. The thirteen-month-old baby is crying hysterically. Her round face glows too red for a paper-bag-colored child.

"DAADDYYY!"

Fighting frantically like a lunatic to release her, he stops with surprising calmness to reach into his front pocket. The river is flowing in steadily, as the front of the car bumps the river floor, rocking it from side to side until it cradles gently to its bed.

He holds his child close to his body to comfort her. So tight, he hopes that he has the strength to smother her before she swallows her last gasps with panic and fear, but rather knowing that he loves her dearly. The light of the sun from below is beginning to fade as well. A final prayer escapes from his once pursed lips to float aimlessly through the shifting waters, breaking their placid surface.

A cold shiver brought me back to reality. My eyes were wide open. What felt like forever had been merely a minute of bewilderment. Two hours later, I was fully satisfied with Colombo's amazing antics of annoyance, brilliantly uncovering the villain of tonight's episode.

I changed into my pajamas, brushed my teeth, and settled in for bed. I almost forgot that my sister, with her sharp elbows, was lying there beside me. On the opposite side of her was Mrs. Cooper's miniature Bible sitting on the nightstand. I figured a verse or two from Genesis would get my eyes drowsy. But before reading the verses, I had to do something in order to sleep soundly. I had the habit of creating a little alarm about the door of an unfamiliar home when sleeping over. Nothing has ever happened, mind you, but it was habit, and it made me feel better. Safer.

So I devised a mousetrap. No big deal, just some string tied around a brass bell on the dresser, shaped like a lady from *Gone with the Wind*, then wound around the doorknob. My grandmother had given that Lady Bell to me.

"This bell will protect you when you need my help," she exclaimed. "Just ring it!"

I read the verse, and then began to drift off to sleep. I felt my body sink deeper and deeper into the sheets. Deeper still, for not one dream had time to park in my vacant mind, before I was sound asleep.

———

Sometimes I would sleep so hard, that I startled myself by the sound of my own snoring. A trait I apparently inherited from my dad. I quickly turned over to my side to fall right back where I ended, when I heard a strained whine come from the hinge of my door. And as I did not know this house and its aches and pains, I tried to ignore it…at first.

Then I heard it again.

My eyes were bleary. I thought I was imagining things. The black gap opened wider, swallowing what little light there was in the room. The shadow of a figure appeared.

A male figure. I don't know how I could tell, but I could.

I kept blinking, trying to break free from the sleep and the shadow. Praying with my lids shut tight, that it would go back to my imagination. In disbelief, I laid there for seconds of for-ever, until the figure started to push open the door even wider.

Oh God!

I'm shaking so hard I can feel my teeth chatter. I clench the sheets between my fingers, drawing it in close between my knees and to my chest—a grip so tight I couldn't feel them.

I saw the brass lady race across the top of the wood dresser, heard her, scraping slowly at first, then *bang-clang* her head must have hit and scraped along the dresser top before falling off the ledge, hitting the floor with a sharp thud!

Ting-ting-a-ling, bam boom, ring!

It bounced around the carpet floor, to its final rest.

The shadow stepped back into the hallway, startled from the noise.

Was I dreaming? No I was not!

I would have run wild from the house if I'd caused that commotion, but I didn't hear a step run down the stairway. My eyes spread open wide, painfully stretching my face in search for another within the shadows. I prayed he was afraid like me, and had enough. My heart pounded like a sledge hammer against my chest in fear that the intruder was still here.

Then there he was.

As the form came closer, I wanted to recognize the face. Wanted to laugh about the joke in the morning, after I beat him senseless with the pillows on my bed tonight.

I couldn't tell who it was at first. The shadow steadily eased up upon me, quietly slow, thick like black fog to the foot of my bed. The little moonlight there was sneaked its way through between the curtains and caught a slice of his face. Bob Jr.'s face.

I sat up in the bed straight like an ironing board, waiting to hear what he had to say. He had to say something. Why else would he be in my bedroom? There was no fire. No sound of a siren, not the ring of a phone.

Why is he here, I screamed in my head?

He rested his hand gently on my bed.

"Bob Jr.?" My breath faltered when I said his name.

"Shhh, Lizbeth. I didn't mean to scare you. I just want to talk to you."

"About what?" I don't know where that breath came from.

He kept sliding up closer.

His hand slid up the sheet onto my ankle.

I waited for an answer.

He kept on coming, as his hand kept on riding to my knee.

I could feel the sweat rolling down my spine. I flinched tight in my now damp sheets.

What now?

"Just relax, you'll like it."

What did he just say to me? My ears had gone deaf from the blood rushing in my brain.

"What's wrong with you, Bob Jr.? I'm sleepin' and Lena is too, so you better get out of here!" My voice trembled. I turned to my side as if cuddling up to go back to sleep with one arm behind me flopped over Lena. My eyes burned on him, not allowing him a second from my sight. Maybe if I ignored him…

He kept on coming, with his hand just past my lower thigh. He rubbed his mouth and jaw with his other hand.

My eyes were still fixed on him.

Slowly, steadily, he drew up his fingers to drag my covers down. I snatched them from his hands.

"What are you doing? Didn't I tell you to get outta' here?"

"Shhh, girl. It won't hurt a bit but for a second." He attempted to touch my breast, but I slapped his hand away.

Slowly, his face came into full view from the light of the moon. My stomach shrunk in disgust for him.

"If you don't get your filthy hand off me, I swear…!"

"Come on now, girl. You know you ain't gonna hurt me and I ain't gonna hurt you! Just lay back."

He pushed my one shoulder back. I was scared, but I was full of anger too, and that made for a bad combination for me and him, too. I shook his hand free from my shoulder.

A deep grin rolled up to his bony cheeks.

Like a leopard he pounced upon me hard, knocking the breath from me. He'd caught me by both my wrists, twisting, pressing them back above my head against the pillow. Quickly he snatched both wrists into one large hand. He'd jerked me so quickly that I scratched a bit of my tongue between my teeth. I felt the warm blood roll about my mouth. I felt his hand riding up my thigh, fingertips coming close to where even I never dared to touch.

I tried to scream out loud, my mouth wide open, but nothing was coming out. I started to feel dizzy from breathing and not breathing—head swirling like an ice-slush that I'd sucked down too fast. Weak from the unimaginable strain of these things that I didn't fully understand, I almost gave up. Ready to give in to it. Who was I to fight?

Then he laughed at me. A sputter of his spit flew from his mouth to hit my lips. My stomach churned as my blood boiled fighting to wipe the splatter from my face. Without warning, an angry spirit took hold of my throat and squeezed words from between my gnashing teeth.

"You get out of here! Now! Now!" I said a little too loud for his comfort.

He chuckled once more, but not as confident as before. He must have seen something in my eyes that scared him, for the searing pain in my wrists eased up for a split second. Just enough time for my fury to rise, and my knee. I slammed it up into his groin as hard as I could. He fell back, almost falling to the floor, trying to hold his crotch at the same time like a crab flipped on its back and rolled off the bed to the floor. I watched his face twist up, his neck straining as he tried to choke his pain down. Some gurgling, painful sounds wrenched from Bob's mouth.

"Ahhhh!" A short spurt dashed out from behind his tears.

I don't know how I got there, but I was on top of him!

Fists flying like a madman, the first blow landing squarely into his blubbering lips. After that, my arms were flaring like a windmill, blind and out of control. I couldn't see what I was hitting, but I was hitting something. My fists hurt so bad I thought my fingers were broken. But that didn't stop me until I was worn out, sweat sticking my pajamas to my skin. I stumbled back to be held up by the night stand, thank goodness.

"Ahhhh, humf!" He was holding his lip with one hand, with the other caught between his legs somewhere. He let out a brief cry in pain, trying to muffle the rest in his hand, wheezing air in and out from his nose.

"I will scream so loud if you come near me or mine ever again!" Blood dripped from my bottom lip as I spoke. I looked back to Lena, still asleep through all the ruckus, sleeping smooth like a pond rock.

"Now get out!" I seemed tall as I stood up in the moonlit shadow that crossed him. My courage swelled when I heard Mrs. Cooper rumbling around through the front door to get in. He heard it too by the look on his face.

He slithered away like the snake that he was, tripping backwards toward the bedroom door. He stopped once he held the doorknob firm, then glared at me. Chilling me to the bone. Something told me that I could not live with that fear forever. I couldn't let him enslave a part of me forever. I picked up the ceramic pink piggy bank that sat on the dresser beside me for decoration and threw it at him.

CRASH!

It hit the wall beside his head. Chips of the piggy went flying into his face, while some stayed lodged in his nappy hair.

His beady eyes assured me that he would never try that again.

"I am going to tell your mama, Bob, Jr.!" I didn't care who heard me now.

I was shaking so hard. I still don't know how Lena was still asleep, but thank God she was. I wouldn't want her to have that kind of fear from a man, especially a weasel like Bob, Jr.! There are men, good men like my Uncle Frank, and our dad. Great men, strong men, loving and thoughtful.

I stood straight now. On my own will like a sentinel. When I heard his door shut, then lock, I finally let my legs go to collapse beside Lena. I sat up under the covers, for I don't know how long, until I couldn't stand it no more. My mind was whirling too fast for me think. Round and round for what seemed like hours, like a mouse running wild in a maze in my brain. I looked to Lena once more, and that's the last thing I remembered.

Who came up with, "When pigs fly"?

My face felt warm from the sun. I rolled over leisurely on my side to...when suddenly I jerked around to find myself in bed alone. Lena was gone!

I threw my jeans on over my pajama shorts, tried to take the top off so fast I popped some buttons. I didn't care. I heard them rattle across the floor and stepped on one as I ran out the door. Massaging my foot with my hands, I hopped down the hallway to the steps.

"Ow, Lena! Shoot, Lena!" I shouted. My heavy feet rumbled down the carpeted steps faster than I knew I could or should. When I hit the landing, I held onto the post and did a sling-shot to the kitchen.

"Lena!"

"What?" she shouted.

There they were—Lena, Mrs. Cooper, Margaret, and her slimeball father Bob Jr., around a stack of blueberry pancakes and fatty thick bacon.

"Come on Lena, get up! Let's go!" I tried to haul her up from her seat by her armpit.

"Ouch. Let go, what's wrong with you?" she snapped.

I gripped her shoulders hard and turned her to face me squarely. "Helena, I said get up from that chair now and get your things!"

Lena's face turned to stone. She knew I meant business. As she got up, I shoved her in the back which kick-started her into a run.

"Lizbeth! What's gotten into you?" said Mrs. Cooper, totally flabbergasted.

I curled my lips up tight like I was going into battle. "We're never coming here again as long as *he's* here! I'm telling my Auntie and the sheriff when I get home!"

I shook my one finger in Bob Jr.'s face, knowing that it was rude. I stomped my way up the stairs, catching up to a pouting Lena on the second-floor landing. The bed was still in a shamble, and I had no intention to fix it as I whirled through our things like a lunatic. Shoving toothbrushes and dirty socks together in my backpack in order to save time. Not caring that one leg of a pair of red shorts and my seersucker pajama top flounced about, waving good-bye to the bedroom. I kicked the door wide open with my foot, then nearly yanking Lena's arm out of its socket. We were clear to take off out of the house. My body was shaking hard with what I had just done.

What was I thinking? I did not think. I let my hot belly take control, which left my arms, legs and mouth to do as they pleased.

Then suddenly I heard Bob, Jr. creaking around upstairs in his shabby room—sounds of *crash* and *slam* echoed into the cramped hall. The shock nearly split my spine in two.

Coward, I said to myself trying to resurrect my own courage.

Though my arms were flapping like deadweight, I still had the ability to help Lena with her backpack, with mine dangling dangerously at the edge of my shoulder. I was just about to step off the landing and down the stairs, when Bob Jr. jumped out and blocked my escape, stopping me dead on at his door.

I felt my chest collapse at the sight of him.

If he hit me, I thought, Lena could still escape and run to tell Mrs. Cooper. Then again, he was her son. She just might agree to make that red fish stew out of *us*.

Then he shoved the coin jar at me.

"Here, take this. It's not much, but it's got more money in it than you think! Mostly quarters and dimes and a roll of pennies, I believe. It's worth a whole lot more than you've ever had, now take it!" he said.

"Take it, girl!" He shouted again, spittle in my face; he crammed the jar into my chest, shoving me back a bit, until my hands managed to hold on to it.

"It's not polite to shove people." I freed a hand to shove him back in his chest.

"Why did you take that penny from Mr. Samuel's dead hand when he drowned, Bob, Jr.?"

"I didn't take no penny," he said. "What penny?" I could hardly see his beady eyes now.

"Why did you quit your technician job without telling the sheriff first?" I asked him, like I had the authority.

"What...naugh, girl? I didn't come back to work 'cause I was interviewing for another job!"

"How would I know you were telling me the truth, Bob Jr.?"

"I'm suppose' to clock in when I come in. The time clock is on the wall. I didn't come to work the night Mr. Samuel's body came in or after that! Matter o' fact, I interviewed for the night shift at the steel mill in Spring City. The manager let me sleep over with the other crew members 'cause it was so late. Didn't make it home until the next afternoon."

I didn't have much to say after that. It would be simple enough for the sheriff to check his alibi.

"Now here, take these if you want pennies so bad."

With that, he released the jar into my hands. He slid back into his room on his belly like a snake into his hole, never turning his back on me with his glaring beady eyes. I didn't trust a word out of his mouth, but as soon as I got home, I'd check every coin one-by-one to be sure.

With a *bang*, I busted the front screen door open, pulling Lena through after me. She didn't fight me, just pouted at me because she didn't understand why I messed up her good time.

I threw our stuff in the basket, straddled my bike, and yanked her onto the seat behind me.

"Lizbeth, where are you going, girl?" Mrs. Cooper stood on her steps, weak like a wilted lily.

She knew. She had to have known all about what he would do.

But she left me. Left me to be gobbled up by him anyway for the sake of her grandchild and a good time for her!

I blamed her just as much as I did him.

"Please Elizabeth, don't tell Alice! I can explain!"

Her voice blurred like the ink on a water-soaked notepad with every thrust of the peddles.

"He really is a good boy," she added in a weary voice that resonated with disbelief in her own words.

I pumped my legs even harder with every word she spoke. I didn't want one word of hers to touch my back, clinging on to me. Like all would be forgiven if I brought them home with me.

Lena was holding on to my waist, wobbling like a rag doll on the back end of the banana seat.

"I don't know what happened there, Liz," she said.

"I know Lena. You're gonna call Mommy and cry a complaint to her and Daddy as usual," I grumbled hard beneath my breath. Her extra pounds took a toll on my legs, but I was so angry, so scared, that I could hardly tell.

"Nope. I think you were doing something right. You seemed kind of scared to me." She paused to let my legs keep pumping in rhythm up the crest of the hill, to then glide down with ease in payment for all their hard work. "Thanks, Lizbeth, you're a good big sister."

My throat flashed tight. I didn't know what to say to her.

———

By the time I'd dropped my bike on the lawn and run up the porch steps, Mrs. Cooper had already called my auntie. I don't know what words passed between her and Mrs. Cooper and I don't care.

What I do know, is that Aunt Al met us like magic at the screen door, arms open wide ready to swallow us in like she promised my momma, promising to protect us forever. I cried hard into her chest, as she held Lena and me in her arms.

Floods of worry and fear poured out on to her neat floral blouse as I locked my sister's soft little arm into mine.

She rubbed my back, trying to soothe me with her little hand.

And she did.

———

By mid-morning, I was finally back where I belonged…in my aunt and uncle's largest guest bedroom coveting my most precious possessions. Not the quarters, not the dimes, and I won't mention the nickels, but I loved my shiny copper pennies, even though *the penny* I sought was not among them. Exhausted, I deserved a nap. The breeze through the window was just right. My eyelids were too heavy; I could take it no longer. My head melted like butter on a biscuit into my pillow.

About an hour or so later, I yawned with an exaggerated stretch, happy to find myself at home in my bed. I jumped from my bed and headed straight for the gleaming jar. Lifting the heavy jar high above my head in all its glory, I twirled around and around until I became too dizzy to stand.

"Lizbeth, what's all that racket about, girl?"

"Sorry, Auntie." I shouted out. I flung myself onto my bed laughing, watching the blue-tinted glass jar rattled as it settled in beside me. I turned around on my belly, propped up by my elbows, with my ankles crisscrossing back and forth.

"What shall we do this afternoon?" I said aloud.

"Lizbeth," Auntie shouted.

"Yes, ma'am?"

"Are you dressed?"

"Yes ma'am."

"Let's go." I heard the clatter of her keys, scooping them up off the kitchen table. I jumped out of the bed heading for the door.

Eight

When Auntie finally stopped the Dart, we were in the parking lot of *Moore's Grocery & Feed Store*. Somehow I had gotten away with the 'grocery store chore' since I'd been in Ahoskie, but that wasn't unusual since I rarely went with my mom back in New York. But today, skirting a laminate floor with a shopping cart would be my cover in search of pennies.

It wasn't much, but it was the hub of Ahoskie, aside from Samuel's Lumber Yard. Just as I was two steps out the car and about to slam the door shut, Auntie's thick arm blocked my way to the store.

"Take it easy now, child. We're about to go into Mr. Jake's store and he doesn't stand for no foolishness." She tipped her head to me, and I nodded back that I fully understood. My heart was still thumping in my throat as I desperately tried to pace my way up the wooden steps.

As I pulled the brass handle of the screen door and crossed the threshold, I about jumped out of my skin.

Ring-a-ling, ring-a-ling, ring-a-ling, sang the bell hooked to the top of the door. It looked like the ones the fake Salvation Army Santas used to get those jingling coins out of your pocketbook. Although it was only about the size of my fist, with tarnish spots that would never shine, no matter what you scrubbed it with, it sang out bold like it had something important to say.

I must have landed six feet into the store, when I found myself standing before a tower of canned corn. If I had sneezed that would have been the end of it. I turned my head slowly to my left. I let my eyes do all the moving to scan the aisles of groceries. Turning my head once more, less cautiously, to my right, I saw a man standing nearly ten feet away behind the check-out counter.

Mr. Jake.

Just as I got my balance, Auntie almost set me off again.

"You go over there and get yourself a drink while I talk to Mr. Jake." She pointed so quickly I barely saw the direction her finger flickered to.

As I made my way over to the refrigerator, I inspected the store as best I could without tangling my feet up. When I finally made my way to the refrigerator, a sign as big as my face was nailed up against the wall above it.

KEEP THE LID SHUT UNTIL
YOU HAVE MADE UP YOUR MIND!
Management

I peeped between the dried goods and the corn tower watching Auntie speak to him in a soft mannerly tone. His face said nothing, nor did he speak. He merely continued to wrangle about the counter, looking up at her from time to time.

He wasn't bad-looking for a white man. His hair was like other white folks' hair, kind of light brown, but then again not. Parted off on the side and a little too long for a man his age, early thirties or so. Well built, but on the verge of being too skinny, like a plump chicken wing.

However, none of that mattered. Mr. Jake was a racist. All the kids said so, and that was that—

"Oh!" I gasped.

Aside from being a racist, maybe he could read minds, too! Because no sooner than I had put the *cist* on the end of my sentence, he looked me dead in my eye! Maybe mean white people could read minds. You never know. He wouldn't need it for white people; he's one of them regardless if they were racist or not.

As it was well reported at the baseball park, around the swings and on too many occasions by Tommy in particular, Mr. Jake had never taken to Negroes. Rosa Lee said that she went to buy a lollipop the size of her head one day, unknowingly, with less than the money required. She squeezed the two nickels from her fist on the counter, not quite sure if she had enough, and then snatched her hand back to her side. Mr. Jake slid the coins across the counter one by one to his shirt button just above the buckle.

"You don't have enough for this lollipop, girl." He shoved the coins back to her. "Go find something else you can *afford* to buy."

If he knew she didn't have enough from the jump, why did he bother to count them, then? Why didn't he just tell her she needed five cents more? Five more pennies that is.

By the same token, the kids complained about smelly Willy "Fingers," a twelve-year-old white boy whose family lived in the backwoods, who'd come to the store one day. Fool, he had the nerve to take a whole chicken out of the freezer, then shove it between his whities and his pants and then walk off with it. He tried to hide behind Mrs. Coolie, whose butt had a life of its own, as she walked down the grocery aisle heading for the door, but he wasn't agile enough. Mrs. Coolie grabbed hold of the door before he could slide out in front of her massive behind.

Ring-a-ling, ring-a-ling! I know that bell had to have screamed out at him.

Mr. Jake plucked him up by the scruff of his neck.

"You hold still, boy, or it'll be worse than what I've got planned for you!" he shouted.

Worse! He made Willy stand outside on the porch until the store closed with that chicken thawing in his pants. The smell nearly drove all of the customers away, so Mr. Jake had to send him home…with the chicken! Surely, nobody would eat that chicken knowing where it had been all day, but Jimmy got no whipping or scolding, not a call to Sheriff Bigly or his parents to know of. They probably didn't even have a phone, but that wasn't the point at all. Mr. Jake let him go because he was white. If one of *us* had done that, there's no telling what he would have done! Maybe taken out that shotgun he keeps behind the counter and put a round of buckshot in our behinds! *That* would be *worse!*

I'd read about things more horrible than that happening to blacks in the deep South like Alabama. I can't imagine being tarred and feathered. I thought that this was a tale that white people used to keep us scared. Another ignorant something coming from their mouths, like talking about how "Negroes love nothing better to do than whistle the day away and eat watermelon." But then I saw the pictures in the *New York Times*. My dad read that newspaper every day.

I remember one Sunday after church I peeped over his shoulder to see what held his face with such placid anger. That's when I saw the black-and-white pictures of a thin black man hung by the neck from a tree. Hands behind his back.

Limp, with his head resting upon his shoulder like a rag doll.

A roaring fire with men dressed in white sheets and hoods, carrying torches surrounding him.

I sometimes complained about the pictures not being in color in the paper. This time, I was grateful. But then....

Blam!

Out of the blue, Daddy slammed the paper shut on the kitchen table.

"Why can't I live in this world without the fear of someone killing me because my skin is brown? White to brown to blue-black. That's who we are. Something about our body we can't control—and wouldn't, since if this is what it means to be white, hurting and killing folks for no reason than our color. Every day. Week after week. Year after year. Lifetime after a lifetime. A white man out there to take my life from me, merely if he had the chance."

Sick and tired of waiting for my auntie, I walked right up beside her at the counter, to introduce myself.

"Hi, my name is Elizabeth. I prefer to be called Lizbeth, but Liz or Liza is fine by me too."

He didn't say a word, just looked at me for a full two seconds and asked the white woman behind me, "Will that be all?"

My mouth nearly hit the floor when he did that. My aunt read my face and promptly dragged me across the floor to the butcher section to wait for the steaks she ordered.

"Auntie, did you hear that? That, that man! Do you know what he is? He hates us, all of us Negroes!"

She shook me by the arm just in time for me to see him whip an apron over his head to sharpen a big shiny knife. He flashed his big bright hazel eyes at me for a moment, while yanking out the flank of meat. I knew he heard me and I didn't care.

Yeah, I bet you would like to split me wide open with that knife.

The car ride back home was awful, just like Mr. Jake. I pouted the entire way, right up to the house. Aunt Al cranked the car into "P" for park when we arrived at home in our driveway.

"I know you don't believe everything you hear out there on the playground Lizbeth?"

My lips curled in even tighter not wanting to admit that she was right about that. My arms were folded tightly across my chest being a stubborn sourpuss.

"There are things that we don't know about each other. What makes us happy or sad? Who has hurt us, and how. The painful and the wonderful things in our lives, which have made us who we are today. I imagine that goes for Mr. Jake too, like it or not."

"It still doesn't excuse him for being mean to me or hating all of us because we are Black!"

I pumped my already crossed arms against my chest in furtherance of my anger.

"Yes, you're right, it doesn't excuse him *if* those things are true, but it *does* give you an opportunity to understand why he is who he is. Don't judge him too quickly there, Miss. You got all summer to figure it out."

I rolled my eyes in time to see her get out of the car and carry the groceries inside. I stayed behind for a while, steaming in my stew. Fighting the tears that were cradled in my eyelids.

There I sat until they dried up.

Nine

It took me a day or so to shove my pride aside and give in to my need for an orange pop, and a small bag of barbeque chips. I could taste my fingertips already, with that salty tangy goodness, while churning my bike up the hot tarred hill to the grocery store.

When I arrived at the store I checked myself to make sure I looked nice. My summer plaid shirt neatly buttoned to the knob in my chest and my red Deck sneakers free from dust. I felt my stomach get goocy inside as I shoved the kickstand into place. It wasn't that I was afraid of Mr. Jake, I just wasn't sure about what to expect after the other day. No, I couldn't let that deprive me of my right to have a pop and chips like everybody else in town. So I squeezed my hands into fists, flexed them open and shut a couple of times then opened the door.

Ring-a-ling, ring-a-ling!

Couldn't that darn bell be busted for just one day?

Head bearing down, I set dead on to my target. The refrigerator, AKA the soda pop casket. This was not just any old soda machine. But a five-foot long, double glass-topped icebox. He had too much variety for a regular soda machine, and you could see what you *really* were thirsty for. There, each bottle lined up all tall and frosty, temping you to try them all. When I finally thought I had made the proper decision, I lifted the left side of the box to pick the coldest-looking orange pop in the row. But as I reached for it, something made me contemplate over the grape. My hesitation was well warranted, since the round glittering bunch of grapes on the neck of the bottle, fuzzed up white from the flush of warm air hitting them. Another dazed minute went by as I held the lid up, deep in thought.

"Shut the lid until you know what you want!" shouted Mr. Jake from behind the counter.

He stunned me so bad I dropped the lid from fright before my brain translated what he'd said. In shock, my legs scurried me over to the "tree" of bagged snacks to hide behind. At least I knew what I wanted there, and I could stand there for as long as I wanted.

"...and get from behind the snack tree! I can't see what you're doin' back there!"

I snatched a bag of green onion chips and then blindly bolted around the tower of canned petite peas. Not wanting to knock them over (dear Lord, please don't do that to me!), I instead shoved poor Mrs. Hoover's cat food and milk clear out of her hands.

"I'm so very sorry, Mrs. Hoover, I'll get that." I hurried myself after the cans of cat food rolling away on their sides, laughing at me.

"That's not a problem darlin'. Take your time. I'm in no hurry." She said, tapping my shoulder trying to slow me down.

I carried her entire list over to the counter to face the ridicule from Mr. Jake. I waited in agony behind her to pay for a bag of chips I didn't even like, and not a drop of orange soda. It was always my habit to try to get as many pennies as possible in change, and given the disappearance of Mr. Samuel's penny, I found myself swelling with greater zeal to possibly find such a thing. I calculated the cost of a piece of bubble gum and a bag of chips. Eleven cents…I had a quarter and a dime.

If I handed him the dime first and then the quarter, he'd think I'm stupidest Negro he'd ever met. If I gave him the quarter, he'd have to give me four pennies within the change. That would do the trick.

I placed the crappy bag of chips on the counter along with the bubble gum.

"What about that soda you wanted?" He grumbled, turning his back to me to lift a bag of feed over his shoulder the size of a small child, then tossing it down the chute to a truck outside. He glanced over his shoulder to see if I was still there, then gave me his back again to toss another child. This was my chance to run to the icebox, grab an orange pop as the Lord had intended me to, and snatch a bag of barbeque chips on the way back.

He faced me just as I hit the counter.

Breathing a little hard now, I slid over the quarter for my penny bubble gum, my ten-cent chips, and my ten-cent pop. All of which equaled twenty-one cents. He had to give me four pennies in change now.

He snapped open a small brown paper bag with a flick of his wrist, then placed the soda, the chips, and the gum in it. The register rang out after he hit some buttons, shoving the drawer into his waist. I stood there and watched him place the quarter into its slot, but then he did something amazing…not the familiar jangle of change from the penny slot.

He shut the register drawer and left a nickel on the counter.

I looked up at him under the hood of my brow. My feet cemented where I stood with not knowing what to do next.

Surely this man could add by now? I was due four pennies, not a nickel.

He turned away and went back to tossing the bags of feed down the chute.

Ring-a-ling, ring-a-ling!

Went the door as I ran out.

━━━━

As I rode my bike home, I noticed something. Something so obvious I flushed momentarily with embarrassment that the feeling had ended up pinned to my gut. This neighborhood, its people, wasn't really too different from my home in Queens. I mean, aside from the obvious—dirt roads, single homes on a lot big enough for five, wild chickens (I'd never heard nor seen such a thing in my life until now) and no streetlights—Aunt Al and Uncle Franks' neighborhood was made up of Negroes like my own. Of course being the Melting Pot of the World, we had a healthy dose of Puerto Ricans, Jamaicans, and a few Irish families that had been on the block around the corner since the 1800s, but it was basically the same. Instead of Mr. Jake, we had a Jewish family that owns our neighborhood grocery, the Stork Grocery store.

But then, a pitiful shade of sadness hit me. Unlike my cousins, I had to be bused to a school outside my neighborhood. Desegregation forced me to get up an hour earlier to be shipped out to a white school district, where I could have walked to the middle school in my neighborhood and always had time for breakfast.

Bused to a community, be mindful of the definition, that really didn't want me and that I didn't want either.

As I came around the corner to the last leg of my travel, I took my time coming down the hill. Watching the kids laughing so hard they could hardly run away in a game of hot peas and butter; Mrs. Laney hanging a mess of socks and undershirts on the clothesline, with an apron full of wooden pins, and one in her mouth at the ready.

"Lizbeth!" My Aunt waved at me as I rolled down the hill at my leisure.

"Hi, Auntie!" I waved back with both hands off the handle bars showing off.

No, this little town of Ahoskie wasn't too bad after all.

All except Mr. Jake. I bet he thinks I'm some stupid Negro. He didn't give me that bubble gum to be nice to me. Nope. He didn't want to give me any of his pennies. But why not? Was he just too lazy to open a new roll, or it possible that he had *the* penny?

Sure, Bob Jr. is as stupid as a cuss. But Mr. Jake, he's another story.

A smart one.

Ten

Uncle Frank was in need of a few yards of chicken wire to make a new fence for his booming gaggle. It seemed as though every time we turned around, another half dozen yellow puffs were finding their way out and underneath the porch. Skippy, the neighbor's orange tabby, started hanging closer to our home than usual, evidenced by the number of fresh feathers still caught in her whiskers.

No chickens meant no eggs, and no eggs meant no breakfast. And as far as Uncle Frank was concerned, buying them from the grocery store was out of the question. He wanted them fresh from the henhouse like he'd had as a child.

Something had to be done.

Getting tired of Uncle Frank's moaning, Aunt Alice and I took action. On a bright Thursday morning after an eggless breakfast, off to Samuel's Lumber Yard we went. You couldn't build a home or lay a brick without going by there.

This would be my first time at the lumber yard. As the local gossip had it, Mr. Benjamin Samuel, as the oldest living brother, had assumed the head of the family business after the death of Mr. Joseph Samuel. No one could say for sure what would happen to the lumber yard now. Some went so far to say that it might not survive after all these years. The Samuel family was full of brothers, sure, all talented in their own way, but not one came close to the capable Mr. Joseph. But if it were to survive, Benjamin Samuel was most capable to see to it.

Mr. Benjamin was touted as a jovial soul, always smiling and planning the family cookouts, doing what he could for others. But now, as the head of the lumber yard, he made sure his brothers understood that they had no choice in the matter. The lumber yard would be his and his alone to govern in Joseph's place for now on, including those decisions regarding McMeanie.

"Miss Alice!" hollered an unfamiliar voice.

The closer he got…well darn it if he didn't get better looking and more familiar. As tall as any man as my eye could tell, with primed muscles in his short-sleeved shirt. I cannot say for sure, but he was much older than me and younger than my Aunt Alice. I'd guess thirty-ish, since he was without one flaw as far as I could tell. Tiny curls of wood shavings lingered in his hair, making his head glow like the crown of Jesus. He looked a lot different than the man I saw at the bridge that night running to Miss Violet.

"Ben!" My Aunt Al immediately stepped out of the car to hug him long and pressed up hard to feel his soul. I was told once that there was a place for people like my Auntie: *In God's shirt pocket. Not far from his hand and close to his heart.*

A peck on his cheek. I flushed with envy.

"Ben, this is my niece, Lizbeth. Lizbeth, say hello to Mr. Ben."

I nodded my head, but I couldn't keep my eyes off of him. What could I say: glorious. All the boys back home were sporting glorious halos of an afro. This man didn't have but a quarter inch of hair on his head. The brown mustache across his top lip glimmered with wisps of red and honey. His eyes twinkled bright brown with golden wheat flicks.

I'd never seen such a being before.

"Lizbeth!" Aunt Al said softly but firm in her meaning.

"I'm sorry, sorry. Hello Mr. Ben, Benjamin. How are you doing?" I surely could have done better than that, but I couldn't get it together.

"Why *you* are the pretty girl that everyone has been talkin' about lately. Nice to finally meet you, Miss Lizbeth." He put his hand out to shake mine. I grabbed it like a hungry dog that doesn't know what to do once it had its prize in its mouth. I could feel myself glowing in perspiration being in his presence (not sweat since I'm a young woman who simply glows).

"Anyway," my aunt continued, "so very sorry for your loss, young Ben." She couldn't help from gripping his forearm again to let him know she meant every word.

"Mrs. Alice, thanks to you and the other folks in town, we're going to make it through. Don't you worry any." He shook her hand in both of his. "So what would you be needin' today?"

"You'd think that Franklin had been starving for the past week with our chicken coop fence being lame and all. He says he needs sixty feet of chicken wire and five posts. He could use a twenty-year-old hand too, but he'd never ask." She chuckled.

"Not a problem, Miss Alice. I'll have the order and a 'hand' sent to your home by tomorrow morning. Is that okay by you, young lady?"

Darn if he didn't get me again. I stood there stupid too long to be a mistake.

"Yes." Stupid me.

Later that afternoon Aunt Alice got an unexpected visitor.

Mrs. Cooper knocked on our door. As my aunt welcomed her in, I went into my bathroom, making a racket, then slipped with silent steps back to the top of the stairs. I crept in a little closer to the rail and sat on the second-floor landing waiting for whispers that were not meant for me.

"Alice…I—"Mrs. Cooper immediately broke off into tears. My aunt jumped and fetched her a glass of water. "Thank you," she said as she took a sip, and then placed the glass on the side table. Her hands were knotted in fists on her lap, finding the strength to try again.

"Alice, I want you to know…I went to put Robert Jr. out of my house that very next morning after the girls left, but…"

My aunt reached over and held her hand. "Go on, it's alright."

"…but when I went to his room he was gone. Gone for good; this time. I could tell by the things he took with him, and the things he didn't. The red lights that had hung from the ceiling since he was sixteen—all that was left were the hooks that held the wires. Boxes of junk he'd collected. Gone!" She swiped at the falling tears in futile, trying to shoo them away from her face.

Dirty dog.

"I'm so sorry, Alice. I'd hoped for so long…I never thought…." She looked to my aunt's face. What she saw, as I and many other have seen, was compassion abounding, but no fool!

"I knew Elizabeth would never let harm come to the girls. I used her to give me one day's rest! One day of peace, riding on a child's back so I could go fishing! How stupidly selfish could I have been, Alice? God forgive me. Alice can you forgive me?" Her eyes pleaded.

No other words were spoken between the two women. Aunt Alice rose from her favorite chair to pause, then sat weightlessly beside Mrs. Cooper on the sofa. She draped her arm across Mrs. Cooper's back and pulled her in close to her chest. Mrs. Cooper held on to my aunt like a child that'd lost her most beloved teddy bear.

The tears stung my sunburned face as I watched.

"He's not a bad boy Alice…he just couldn't have…he'd never hurt a soul," Mrs. Cooper said. "…could he?"

Eleven

The whole world cracked open like an egg yolk from its shell. The sun gleamed bright as it awakened from its solitary sleep, reminding me who's who on this Earth. Today, I had risen early for two things. First, to trade pennies for a dime from Mr. Jake. Second, to dream about becoming Mrs. Benjamin Samuel—in the next life, of course. He was way too old for me and I had a lot more education ahead of me, as dictated by my father.

It was twelve o'clock, high in the heat of the day. I needed my pop and barbeque chips. Once my bike stand was set on the porch of the grocery, I set my mind on getting it.

Ring-a-ling. Ring-a-ling, ring-a-ling!

The cool air felt good on my face. I didn't see Mr. Jake at his usual spot behind the counter. I knew he had to be in there somewhere, but at least I could get my pop in peace. To the left, around the middle aisle, and five long strides, I faced the soda pop coffin. Quickly, I lifted the lid on the right, reached in the casket, and snagged the orange pop. Yes!

"You sure?" a voice said.

"What?" I said, shaken by the sudden heat of his body behind me.

"You sure you want that pop?" Mr. Jake repeated, then walked away.

I don't know what got into me. "I'm sure!" I said, with half a snap in my tone. Half fear, half snap.

He didn't seem bothered by my response, anymore than shooing a fly away while plucking a dandelion. Bold as I was at that moment, I carried on to the snack tree. I took my time snagging the last bag of barbeque chips on the stand. Remembering the time before when I'd collided into Mrs. Hoover, I peeped around the tree to ready for a surprise attack when—

Ring-a-ling, ring-a-ling, ring-a-ling!

I would never have cared who or what caused the door to ring, but something was different this time. The smell of fresh magnolias lighted on the wind at the signal of the bell. It seemed as though everyone became entranced by the loveliness of this fragrance.

Even Mr. Jake.

I heard two cautious steps come through the threshold, then stop to shut the tattle-telling door. I could tell by the black shadows made by young children up against the sunbeams slipping through the window like glowing fingers. All they could do was nod at the figure standing there. Whether this was in pure disbelief or admiration, I couldn't tell and it didn't matter. All I know is that Mr. Jake was not immune to it either. What spell had been cast that he, of all of people, had all manner of meanness snatched away from him for that breathless moment.

A woman had walked in. A woman whose skin was a summer tan browner than a paper bag. So soft, I imagined, it looked like sheared velvet in the light. Her rosebud lips turned down, trying to hide behind her flawless cheeks. From the tip of her nose to the bun held tight behind her head, she was a thing of beauty.

It became awkward now. No one seemed to know the woman. At least no one would claim to know her outright. But me.

Miss Violet.

Good God, all mighty, I yelled out in my head.

"Miss Violet."

But it wasn't me who spoke so respectfully, it was Mr. Jake. Did he bow his eyes ever so slightly to her? This woman, Violet P. Samuel, surviving wife of Joseph and eternal mother of Emma, both dead when the car plunged into that murky river.

She must have been taken aback from the crushing reception.

"Mr. Jake," she said with barely a nod.

Turning to her right, she backed-out one of the rickety carts that had a bum wheel. It squealed like a baby pig running for its life from a cookout. Slowly she drew her shoulders back and headed past Mr. Jake, across the store. All of a sudden, everyone had to take a breath, since we'd all been holding it for the past minute, watching her. It about sucked all the air out of the place.

She made it down the bread and cereal aisle along with a loaf of Wonder Bread and a small box of Frosted Flakes. I admired her choices.

Around the back by the butcher block, she picked up a dozen brown eggs, cheese, milk, a couple of cans of tuna, and one large can of salmon. No one buys salmon unless they're going to make fried cakes out of them. I waited for her to pick up an onion and a stalk of crisp celery.

Yep, she was making salmon cakes.

I imagined for a moment that I would introduce myself and help take her groceries to the car. But as I took a step—*Christ!* I'd landed upon a cranky plank, which set a baby off. Crying and fussing in its stroller. The young mother shoved a bottle in the child's mouth to appease it, but it was too late. In a rush to get the child outside to calm it, the woman nearly ran Miss Violet over.

Miss Violet stopped where she stood, purse still swinging on her wrist, holding on to the cart for dear life. Her perfectly pursed lips began to quiver over her drawn chin. She bit her bottom lip and squeezed the cart bar until her knuckles were about to pop through her stretched skin.

Every eye was on her. Her own eyes darted to the door and then to the counter calculating what she would do next. Then with smooth agility she steered the cart around and shoved it into the counter before Mr. Jake.

Bang! went the cart.

"Sorry…very sorry!" Her soft voice could hardly be heard as she rushed out of the store. Even that darn doorbell rumbled about in confusion.

"Poor thing," someone mumbled.

We all stood dumb in our tracks, not knowing what to do. But suddenly a rattle came from behind the counter.

Snap! Went a large brown bag as the air cracked open its folds.

Mr. Jake stood over the abandoned shopping cart, shoving the groceries into the bag. He clearly knew what he was doing, since the last item on top was the carton of eggs. At least that's what I thought it was, until I saw a flash of something else drop from his hand into the bag.

Everyone in the store was holding their breath, not doing a darn thing to help him. But inside, we were cheering him on like deaf mutes! Finished, he headed out past the encouraging bell, hurrying him along after her.

Ring-a-ling, ring-a-ling-ling-ling!

Finally able to move my feet, I ran to the front window with the other kids, noses and sticky hands pressed to the glass to watch.

The gray exhaust fumes were already blowing out from Miss Violet's car by the time Mr. Jake reached the parking lot. The car jumped hard, with a *clump* as she put it in reverse. I guess Mr. Jake didn't realize it until he was smack dab in the middle of the rear bumper. My body tensed as I feared that he would be run over with the bag of groceries meant for the woman who had run him over still in his hands.

SRECCH! The car jerked to a halt but a hand's length from his knees.

It didn't seem to faze him though. He came around to the passenger side and knocked on the window. Miss Violet was gripping the wheel tight. She released her right hand and leaned over the seat to pull the lock up. Mr. Jake took a hard swallow, by the tide of his Adam's apple riding his throat. He opened the door and gently placed the bag on the floor in front of the passenger seat. He looked her dead-on into her eyes for a long moment, shut the door and never said a word, at least none that I could make out. As he headed back to the store he didn't turn back to wave, say good-bye, nothing. She must have been shaken like the rest of us watching, since she sat there a good minute with the gray smoke still blowing from her tailpipe before driving off.

As I watched him coming up the steps, I felt my shoulders relax on their own.

Jesus! Mr. Jake, running to *give* groceries to a Negro woman. I'd of never believed it, if I hadn't seen it for myself. What was happening? He's not what I thought him to be....

Of course I didn't have the nerve to ask him for ten pennies in exchange for a dime after that. He'd look at me like I was a darn fool! At this point I really don't know what I'd say. The fact is that he'd done something really nice for her. Something that he would do for his own kind.

Ring-a-ling, ring-a-ling!

Mr. Jake shut the door behind him real easy like. Our eyes followed his every movement. As he was making his way around the counter he had to endure a sea of kids, including myself, that stood like stick figures in awe in what he had done. He took his time, careful not to move any of us aside in any way but kindness. When he finally made it to the register, he went back to business.

"Will that be all, Mr. Cane?" Mr. Jake said.

"Why yes. Yes, that will be all, Mr. Jake." Mr. Cane, a frail elderly black man who walked with a bamboo cane with a silver tip and hook, started to place the few dollars on the counter with his bony wrinkled hand. Just like my grandfather, he had probably been taught painfully at a young age that you don't touch the skin of a white person ever. Not even the accidental brush of handing something to them.

As Mr. Cane began to count the bills on the table, Mr. Jake placed his cupped hand out to take his money. This startled Mr. Cane so that he stepped back, nearly falling to the floor but for his cane. Mr. Jake grabbed his hand to steady him. Right then and there, they came to a silent understanding. Though their faces showed no sign of expression, it was there. I saw it in their eyes...something for a spit of a second, then gone.

Mr. Crane cleared his throat, "I gotta' start all over again to count my money out."

"Take your time, Mr. Cane."

Mr. Jake put his hand out again to take Mr. Cane's money. "One, two, three...."

Mr. Cane said his good-byes to everybody in the store as they countered him with their cheery *good-day to you too*, and then out the door he went with his parcel.

By now all the kids had shuffled back to their mamas in line, except for me. And darn it if Mr. Jake didn't catch me before I could get my fingertips on the doorknob.

"Gal!" He shouted as he pointed to his front window smeared with gooey hands and dirty noses. I couldn't deny it. I had some claim to that mess too. He bent down below into the counter shelves, and came out with a rag and spray cleaner.

"Here." He said as he handed the cleaning supplies to me. I opened my mouth ready to protest, but I couldn't, in all fairness.

I scrubbed and hot breathed the window with pride until it gleamed bright with "Moore's Grocery and Feed Store" once again. For twenty minutes or so I whistled along to the rhythm of the bell as folks went home with supplies to cook their meals and feed their chickens. When I was done, I said nothing to Mr. Jake, nor he to me. I tried to raise the anger of hate within me against him, but I couldn't. It just didn't seem right to even think he could be involved in Mr. Samuel's death after that basic act of humanity, that act which was against all that he really was: a hateful man.

So I simply set the cloth and bottle down and left the doorbell to do its business.

As I got on my bike, I thought of Miss Violet, and I vowed to myself that I would find that penny. Whether it be the cause or the clue to the mystery, I would find it. For the first time in my life I felt...well, strong. Strong beyond the limitations of my color or the weakness of my sex, that I could actually make things right with little more than my willingness to help Miss Violet.

Twelve

All night long I thought about Mr. Jake, Mr. Crane, and Miss Violet. It reminded me of the stories I'd read of slaves. More like house slaves. Just a notch above a domestic pet, but still too low to sleep in a decent bed, or to be free of fear, to sleep without worry.

A slave I am not, nor will I ever be. But if I were, if I had lived before the Emancipation Proclamation had rolled off the beard of Lincoln, I surely would have been killed early on. Not die a natural death from suffering in the field, but tortured or hung because I wouldn't behave. I'd speak my mind, take baths in the river when I was dirty, and eat whenever I was hungry. And no white man would ever touch me. Never.

Big talk for a "gal" who couldn't say no to cleaning a white man's window, but I truly believe I would not have made it past the age of fourteen!

———

That Saturday Aunt Alice suggested an outing. "How about you and Lena taking a ride with me over to Mr. Cockney's farm? There's something I want you two to see."

Sure. Chickens, cows, and a few fat, hairy pigs, rolling around in smelly slop. Yep, that sounded like a lot of fun.

The ride over there was less than twenty minutes long. I don't know how my aunt knew to take a turn down the split dirt-path, because there wasn't one single sign to say *when*. Just a rusty mailbox hanging half off the hinge on its post. The overgrown vines, bushes, and pine trees canopied the way, making it seem more like a tunnel instead of a road. I'll admit I was a little nervous as we bumped our heads several times to the car roof. No gravel. No tar. Just dirt and rocks and a strip of half-dead crab grass caught between two tire-worn paths.

When we finally came to the clearing, I expected to see a home straight from *The Beverly Hillbillies*, and that's the one before they moved to California. You know, the kind where the wood slats were so worn from rain wash and heat that you couldn't tell what color, if any, it had been before. Where the wood porch bowed just where the steps came up to the front door. Better still, it would be missing a few boards, thus appearing like an old piano missing some of its keys or an old man spared a few of his teeth.

Well, it turned out to be nothing quite like that at all. In fact, just the opposite. There were roses nearly floating in the breeze, planted neatly before a grand porch, dotted with finely manicured dwarf bushes. Two round and fat magnolia trees stood, posted on each end as if guarding the house. Wild blue creeping hydrangea clung to the porch post, running a line across the rain gutter, like pretty lace on the hem of a summer dress. But the home—my goodness, you'd never see such a thing in Queens! That was made clear by my gaping mouth as we drove up the brick paved driveway.

"Well, what do you think?" My aunt smiled in delight.

"Wow!" Lena's mouth remained open until I tapped her underneath her chin.

The magnificent three-story house stood before a background of majestic oak trees and grass so green and tantalizing, you would've believed it to be carpet. The clapboard home had been recently painted snow white with coal black shutters, which pronounced the oversized windows. The massive wood front door was painted red with gold fixtures crowning it in glory.

I could not respond to my aunt, except to shake my head in disbelief.

"Hey there!" a thin male voice shouted from the woods.

A brown stick figure resembling a praying mantis with blue overalls and a straw hat waved at us as he hurried up to greet us. The closer he got, I realized he was quite tall and much older than I first thought. His wrinkles had wrinkles. The yellow shirt he wore beneath his overalls was short-sleeved with thin white stripes running through it, with more wrinkles. His bony elbows had a layer of skin as thin as an onion peel.

"Lookie here, lookie here! Miss Alice and two young visitors! Who are you and what are your names, gals?" He put out his boney fingers to Lena first, then to me to shake.

"I'm Helena."

"Mine is Elizabeth, sir. You can call me Lizbeth if you'd like."

"And you can call me Lena, if you'd like!" She said.

Copycat!

I continued to shake his warm hard hand to find that he had a grip as mighty as my dad's. I wondered if he could beat me in arm wrestling too.

"Miss Alice is our aunt. We're from New York City." I tried to hide the pride that I had in saying that.

"Ho, hoooo, city gals, are you?" He threw out his belly like he was one of Momma's Negro Santas in her precious china closet.

I had to giggle at him.

"I was thinking if anyone could cheer Lizbeth up, it would be you and this place. And by the look on her face, I think we're almost there."

I was smiling so hard that my cheeks began to ache. "This place is…it's amazing, sir."

"Oh come on now, let me show you something that's really amazing!" He made a quarter turn to his back, and down the path he headed where he had first appeared. There, past the white flowering four o'clock bushes, was a horse-drawn buggy.

"You ever been on one of these before?" he asked.

"No, sir." "No, sir." We admitted in unison.

"No! You're big city gals and you've never been on a horse and buggy ride around that fancy park?" He looked at me in disbelief, then Lena. Like I was lying. I gave him a wide-eyed shake of my head to let him know I meant what I'd said.

"Well come on then. But before we go, I heard that you're interested in numismatics?"

"Me, sir?" I pointed to my chest.

He shoved his hand down deep in his pocket as if he was digging for gold. His perfectly gapped teeth gleamed when he struck his mark. The peculiar old man leaned over, grinning, having his fun with me while I waited for the treasure to appear. Out came his clutched fist, then he held it under my chin.

"For you, city gal," he said as he open his hand wide.

There in his weathered palm were three coins. I didn't recognize but two of them. First was a twelve-sided three pence, Elizabeth II 1958. That was fine, but hey, it was a British coin. The second was, as I called them, an everyday penny. So bright, you'd think it wasn't real…but it was. It was cast in 1962. No wonder, it was just a spit younger than my sister.

But he wasn't done yet.

A large copper coin, obviously not American, called my attention. But to my surprise, it said United States of America, ONE CENT 1849. My God! And it had a cut in its side. I almost passed out, but for swallowing so hard that my teeth would have gone down too. It was the size of a quarter. I'd never seen such a thing in my life.

"These are for you, gal. Since I had these coins rattlin' around the house doin' nothing, I thought that they could find some use at yours."

He yanked my arm near out of the socket to place them gently into my hand. Not to pain me, mind you. But to appreciate what I was being given.

Three coins.

Dropped into my palm, like heavy rain.

"I know you're huntin' for somethin' real important, gal. But sometimes you gotta' ease up on the chase. It'll come to you in time, just like these coins. You don't have to do a thing, but 'be' you. Otherwise, you can end up chasin' your own tail, bitin' it, if you're not careful." His watery eyes gripped my soul firmly.

"Thank you, Mr. Cockney. I can't believe you're giving these to me. I don't know what to say."

"Nothing to say, city gal, but what you said. Now let's go do what we came to do. Ride that carriage." He poked out his bony elbows to escort us to the carriage.

This must have been how Cinderella felt on her first ride in the pumpkin, only without the flies and the sound of poop plopping from behind or the smell.

"Come on sista' girls. Let's take a ride to my field."

We took off down the path through a short wooded area.

Mr. Cockney jumped off the buggy and headed toward the fence. As I took in the most beautiful fields of golden rods and blue sky, feathered in with clouds, I could hear Mr. Cockney muttering to my aunt. When he came by my side, I saw that he had a sickle in his hands.

"Not a whole lot of people do it like this anymore." Proud of himself, he slung the tool over his shoulder with ease. "I grew up swinging this instrument, if you will, on this very farm with my grandfather. Let me show you how it's done."

I stepped back, holding Lena's hand, far enough, calculating that if it slipped through his fingers, we were still a good distance away from losing our heads. I tapped my aunt's arm gently as I eased back, to persuade her to do the same. She did.

"Once you get into the rhythm of it, it's not that hard at all. It's like a pendulum. You know what that is, city gal, don't yah?" He swiftly cut through fifteen feet while I stood my ground.

Swoosh, swish, swoosh, swish....

"Yep! Not so bad at all, really, as long as the blade is sharp."

The sun was starting down by now, the glittering glow of the wheat buds shimmered against the trees. I thought my eyes were playing tricks on me. I blinked once, then twice more. At first, I thought they were vines, long thick black vines hooked in the neck of the sickle. Except they jiggled a bit more than a vine would, and one end was thicker that the other. Like a head.

"You can see that I keep my head straight, let my waist and arms do the work, then...HEY!"

Mr. Cockney had freed up some of the vines all right, and now they were flopping around his neck. He scooped them up in mid holler, flinging them into the air, then realized that they were snakes! Black snakes; he had dipped his sickle through a nest full of them. All knotted about and thick like thieves.

"Good gracious!" my aunt whispered in shock.

"AHHHHHHH, get off me! Get off me!" Mr. Cockney dropped his sickle like it was lead, then ran like he was on fire.

Too stunned to move a muscle, I watched him run right into the forest. The snakes had already fallen off about twenty feet into it, but he didn't notice. He just kept on running with his arms flapping wildly into the air like a mad gorilla. Later on we heard that he'd run clear to town still screaming for the snakes to get let him go!

I heard a sweet giggle come from beside me.

"Auntie?" I reprimanded with a playful slap on her wrist. How could she laugh at someone who was clearly in mortal danger? Lena gave a giggle that I let her get away with.

"Oh Lizbeth, I would never...he's fine, honey! Those were black snakes. They don't bite; they eat the field mice not tough old Negroes! Besides, half of them fell off from fright when he started hollering like the Devil was chasing him!"

I had to laugh too. I laughed so hard, my stomach knotted up until I had to bend over. All of us ended up falling out on the grass, rolling around, almost wetting ourselves...when—

It occurred to me...those harmless snakes might be sitting here with us! Mad that we laughed at their family members being scooped up with a sickle! Bite us right in the butt with all they've got if they wanted to. They still had teeth, no matter how harmless they were!

I sat up...and my body froze like an ice pop. Lena must have read my mind.

She was up first, leaving Auntie and me to jump up like two hotcakes in a frying pan.

Thirteen

One thing is for sure, people down here don't call in advance to let you know they're dropping in. All that is required is a knock on the door and you're in.

Knock, knock!

See, just like that!

I was writing a letter to my parents from my bedroom, a few days after the adventure with the snakes, when I heard Auntie's footsteps coming from the kitchen to answer the door. I waited for the front door to sound, or Auntie's honey voice or that of the person who'd come calling. I held my breath so I could make them out clearly.

Whineeee, went the door.

But Auntie didn't speak.

Why would she hesitate? Maybe it was danger, or fear of such. Either way, I bounded down the steps to see.

Just as I hit the landing, heart pounding, I saw them. Auntie and *her*. Holding onto each other, at least that's what it looked like. I found myself moving in closer to be sure.

"Auntie? You okay?"

I'd never seen my auntie weep before, but that's just was she was doing. Finally, stretching out her arms like a butterfly's wing from a cocoon, she revealed the precious visitor to me.

"Oh Lizbeth…. I'm more that okay, honey," she said, presenting *her* and wiping a tear from her smiling face.

"Hello Lizbeth, I'm Violet. Violet Samuel. Nice to meet you." Her slender arm extended a small delicate hand to me.

I took it. "Yes ma'am, nice to meet you too." Surely she did not remember me from the grocery store, but that made no nevermind to me.

As my aunt dabbed her eyes with a tissue she snatched from a cream crocheted covered box, she held Miss Violet's hand to guide her to the sofa beside her. They spoke tenderly to each other. Mimicking each other's smile, trying not to slight the other with too much cheerfulness.

"Excuse me, Violet, let me get us some refreshments from the…"

"I'll get it, Auntie!"

"What dear?"

"I'll get your refreshments, if you don't mind." I tried hard not to stare at Miss Violet.

"Okay, then. How about you get us some ice tea, those little sandwiches I showed you how to make, and the chocolate frosted cake I made Monday?" She smiled so hard at me, I thought her cheeks would bust from pride. "Take your time, Lizbeth."

I was so excited, I had to insist to my feet that they walk like a lady, not run to the kitchen like a wild tomboy.

After gathering the ingredients in the kitchen for our little party, I placed them on the counter closest to the living room in order to spy on their conversation. I say "spy," but actually I was learning things—about friendship, courage, about life as a black woman. Rude or not, I was preparing the meal, thus giving me a small right to participate, just this once at least, in this small way.

I was sure that after my services were used, they'd send me to my room or outside to do some imaginary chore, so I decided to keep my mouth shut, voiceless in their adult conversation. Besides, what could I offer anyway?

Auntie, Miss Violet, have you seen those multi-colored sear-suckered bell bottoms in the new Sears catalog?

Or maybe…

The kids from the baseball park and I are considering having a bake sale in the picnic area next week in order to buy new seats for the swings. What do you think?

Riiiight.

I presented each delicacy one at a time on Auntie's precious china. She was giving me an opportunity, and I didn't want to screw it up with cucumber slices stranded on their napkins. They both thanked me every time I came in through the living room to deliver the delights. So when I placed the last tray of plates, forks, and napkins on the coffee table, I turned on my heel and headed for the back door.

No need for them to embarrass me outright.

"Where're you going, Lizbeth?" Miss Violet's finger lifted ever so slightly from her lap to halt me in my tracks. "I thought you would be joining us after making this lovely treat?"

"Me?" I said.

"Why of course, Lizbeth. Don't be silly child. You're a young lady now." Auntie patted the arm of the chair cattycorner to her. Sitting across from them, I realized they were dressed rather nice. Both in skirts and cotton blouses. Miss Violet in a pink sleeveless and Auntie in a white short-sleeved blouse. I, on the other hand, wasn't dressed as lady-like. Looking myself over, I saw that I was sporting cuffed denim shorts and a green tee-shirt with *Adidas* across my chest, white ankle socks, and sneakers.

The best I could do was to cross my ankles.

"So tell me about yourself. How do you like it down here?" Miss Violet asked sipping her tea.

What in the world would I have to say to someone like her? For a moment I hardly knew what to say, bumbling around my words, slow, shrugging my shoulders in mid sentence. But then she kept on asking me questions. Questions that interested me, that I could answer. I waited for her to tire of me and find an opening where she could direct her adult attention politely to Auntie.

Nope, she kept right on conversing with me. Books, movies, school, even shopping.

"By the way," she said, "have you seen the new Sears catalog? I just saw the nicest pair of multi-colored seersucker bellbottom pants that would look great on you!" She waited for me to respond, smiling in anticipation.

I giggled.

An hour passed and Miss Violet hadn't moved from her seat. We spoke of each other's dreams and hope for the future, for ourselves, our expectations of Negroes, and our country. I didn't know I knew so much.

"So who do you admire, Miss Lizbeth?" as she took the last sip of her ice tea, setting the clanking glass of ice on the table.

"Well, besides my dad, who's just like Dr. Martin Luther King, I'd have to say Shirley Chisholm." I stopped for a second to think about my answer. "Yes, I would definitely say Mrs. Chisholm."

"Go on."

"For lots of reasons. She is the first black woman elected to Congress, the first major party black candidate to run for president of the United States, and the first woman to run as a Democrat for the presidency."

"I can see why you admire her so." She nodded approval.

"But that's not the most incredible thing about this woman."

Miss Violet turned her head in question.

"She survived three assassination attempts on her life. Three! The same year George Wallace was shot to spend the rest of his days in a wheelchair. Then she did the unthinkable…she visited him while in was in the hospital! Here was a man that thought *we* were all stupid, and should stay stupid, and deserved no better than nothing to make them feel better about themselves, even Mrs. Chisholm. But she wishes him well anyway. That's someone to admire."

I got so worked up saying my little speech, I nearly gulped down my orange pop.

"More ice tea or orange pop anyone?" Auntie interrupted.

"No thanks, Auntie. Would you like some more, Miss Violet?"

"No, no thank you, Lizbeth. I would love to spend more time discussing the world with you, but I bet Miss Alice has to get started on dinner and I'm just in the way of things. I best be on my way." She barely lifted up from her seat, when—

"You're not in the way!" I jumped up from mine and dashed a look at my aunt for support. *Please Auntie, don't you dare let her go!*

"Absolutely not, Violet. I've been waiting to have you over for dinner, and won't hear nothing of it except you'll be washing up before it's served!" Aunt Al walked straight away to the kitchen like, *that's that.*

"Besides, my little sister Helena will be here in a little bit, and she'd make my life miserable if she found out that I let you go before she got home. Much more than she usually does!"

She sat back into her chair. Her smile appeared to be uncomfortable. Something wasn't right. Maybe if I changed the topic. I chose my words carefully for what I was about to ask.

"Do you have any little sisters or brothers?" I slid over to Auntie's spot on the couch. It was still warm from her body and a lovely way to be closer to Miss Violet.

Her face, her lips, her smell.

For the first time all afternoon, she looked sad. She collapsed her fingers into her lap to think. First in her heart, then in her head before saying it aloud. I could have kicked myself for hurting her.

"Yes, I had a younger sister, Lizbeth. She was younger than me by one minute and thirty-five seconds." A safe smile emerged from her face.

At first I didn't understand and then….Thank God I said it in my head and not for her to hear. They were twins.

My head dropped in shame. I just hurt one of nicest people I've ever met in my short life. She reached over and gently lifted my chin with her finger tips.

"Don't be ashamed, Lizbeth. It's been many years since she passed away. Funny, it doesn't feel as bad as I thought it would be to talk about her." She took a deep breath, and a soft smile emerged from her face.

"Even so, Joseph had so many brothers and sisters I could hardly complain. I'd known them since I was a little girl. When I used to play with Thomasina at the Samuel house—she was a year older than me—no one would even notice that I wasn't part of the family. And when it was suppertime, Mrs. Samuel would holler out the door and nearly get knocked over from all the kids running past her.

"Go wash your hands, boy. And make sure you clean under those dirty nails, Joseph!' she'd say.

"He was always working on somethin' with his hands. I'd secretly watch him hammering away on some birdhouse or other. Thomasina would catch me peeping at him and tease me for it. I nearly cut my thumb in two while peeling apples for a pie once." She giggled at the thought.

"As we got older he started noticing me, just a little. He'd never speak to me, but his older brother Ben would sometimes talk to me. He even asked me to go to the senior prom with him, but I said no."

"Why would you say no to Mr. Ben?" I had to catch myself to keep from showing too much interest in him.

"He was a little older and all the girls in school wanted him. He had his choice of plenty. Their pretty faces swarming around his golden smile and charming ways. But then there was Joe. Just plain and simple Joe. I liked him well enough.

"I never forgot him, even though he had been in the Army for years. He came home one day for good. I danced with him at the Candied Yam Festival and that was it."

I held her hand without a thought to my age or position in her life. To my surprise she held my hand tight; both our hands compounding into one place of power. Squeezing with all our might into one. I was determined not to cry. Not one tear, but then....

Her hands began to tremble in mine. The heat from her body radiated to the touch. Tears were already streaming down her cheeks, wrapping around the soft curve of her chin, down through the hollows of her throat. Her mouth opened. *God.* I thought. I waited for the room to explode from the cries of such pain that I would die from it piercing my own heart. Instead, nothing came out. The red bow tie lips were stretched wide, strings of saliva bridged them together. The mucus from her nose rolled with the vanity of blood across the crest of her top lip. I wanted to shout for help, but I couldn't. Auntie must have sensed that the air was too thick for no reason, thus running in with a cold dish rag in her hand.

"Come on, baby doll. I've got you. It's time to let it go." Auntie was so quiet it scared me. She shoved me out of her way and held the shoulders of Miss Violet like she was about to throw up. The cold rag was slapped around the back of Miss Violet's neck with a *thwap*.

Miss Violet tried to stand, but she lost control of her arms. While her body swayed, her neck flopped back, now she could hardly breathe. Squealing to the ceiling above, nature made her flop her head forward, allowing her a gasp of air. Losing her balance, she descended toward the coffee table like a rag doll. Before I could react, Auntie snatched Miss Violet by the collar of her cotton shirt and shoulder. Still she fell, knocking over all the cups and trays of food upside down and to the floor, barely sparing her life from the deadly blow of the pointy silver salt shaker through her eye.

Then the wailing began.

"I WANT MY BABY BACK. YOU TOOK THEM TOO SOON FROM ME. YOU TOOK THEM TOO SOON! I WANT THEM BACK! AHHHHHHHHHH. I WANT HER BACK!

"AND, AND, I HAVE...I DON'T...I-CANNOT-UNDERSTAND-WHY!-THIS IS HAPPENING TO ME. GOD NO! MY BABY! No, no, no, no, no...."

She sobbed heavy tears that choked the last of her words. Auntie rocked her like a newborn baby in her arms.

Back and forth.

Back and forth.

I wished at that moment my momma were here to rock me. So I sat on the other side of Miss Violet, put my arm around her and rocked too. Rocked until the yelps and cries to God flushed from her body in exhaustion.

The time did not fly.

The pain did not flee.

We were helplessly bound together until one of us confessed to being worn-out.

Sapped of strength, I crawled away on hands and knees from her and Auntie, up the carpeted stairs. I stopped on the half-landing to watch them…to watch her grieve from a distance. Though it was evident that tears were falling down my face, I did not cry. These were tears of another kind, a thunder that was rolling inside of me.

There I sat until Miss Violet collected herself and Uncle Frank drove her home.

I don't know how long my family let me be on those steps.

Miss Violet's visit had done something to me, for me. It made me angry, but also made me strong. *Mighty*, might be the word for it. I had paid close attention to her every movement; from her lips to the dipping of her chin, to the dimming light behind her eyes. I saw it.

Over and over I saw her face in my head, as when we'd first met.

Glowing.

Just like the warm sun falling low over Ahoskie.

I was determined to help her.

To find that penny.

Fourteen

The Saturday after Miss Violet nearly lost her eye to the silver salt shaker, the first of July, was to be a day of great importance. And although Auntie had been talking it up all week, I had ignored the fact that it was her turn to host card night until I got up for breakfast that very morning. This would be my first to attend, plus my Great Aunt Ode was supposed to show up for the first time too, therefore preparations had to be made. Great preparations. Greater than the use of a fork and knife for breakfast. Thus I was hustled out of the kitchen, fingertips burning from a hot cornbread pancake folded around a link of sausage with a slice of cheese, and into the Dart.

At ten o'clock that morning, Moore's Grocery was fully packed, like sardines in a can. I was fearless whenever I walked in there with Auntie. Not that I was afraid of Mr. Jake or anything, I was just more myself whenever she was around. By eleven, we were walking out the door, with arms full of goodies she'd never buy otherwise.

"Oh Lizbeth, honey, I forgot one more thing," she said, just as she flopped behind the wheel with an exhausted sigh. "I need a large bag of salted cashews for your Great Aunt Ode. She just loves those things, especially when I heat 'em

up in the oven. Mm, mm, mm. Could you get some for me?"
She shuffled through her purse to hand me three dollar bills.
"Here, this should be plenty, and go ahead and buy yourself
something other than a orange pop for once," she teased.

I slammed the heavy door shut behind me prepared to take
my time, since Auntie stepped out of the car to gossip in the
parking lot. Seemed as though the tide had rushed out of the
store just before I walked back in, as empty as it was. Mr. Jake
was straightening things around the store for the next wave of
last-minute hostesses. Although the bell rang out as I came
into the store, he didn't glance away from his work to see who
it was. He must have seen me coming through the window.

Mean old coot! I mumbled underneath my breath.

Anyway, try as I may, I couldn't stay away from that soda
pop icebox. Just beside it was a freezer full of tempting ice
cream pops and 'sicles. I considered for a moment what Aunt
Al had advised me, and determined that an ice cream cone
with chocolate sprinkles was the order of the day. As I shut
the lid with my left hand with the cone in my right, I heard
the bell ring soft and shiny at the door. Magnolias blossomed
under my nose.

Miss Violet was there.

There was only one other soul besides me in the store at
the time, and that was Mr. Whiskers, the county cat. Known
by all, but noticed by few. Well, two if you count Mr. Mean
Old Coot!

I don't know why, but I slid beside the tower of petite
canned peas, haunches still and ready like a mouse, trying not
to wake the sagging floorboard. I hid quietly to watch them.

Miss Violet cautiously made her way down the bread aisle.
She didn't bother to pick up a basket or cart, so I knew she
wouldn't be shopping for much nor have time to discover that

I was there. I slowed my breathing down as she came within arm's reach of me.

She stopped at the butcher block, clutching her patent leather pocketbook with both hands at her chest. Never looking back at Mr. Jake, she waited for him to oblige her. Mr. Jake's eyes lit up, only for as long as a bug's hair, when she walked by.

Without a word, he came from around the counter heading toward her. He stopped for a moment to take his apron off a nail that hung high by the cured meats. Lord knows why it took him nearly forever to loop it over his head, kicking up a tuff of hair, and then tie it around his waist. When he finally made it behind the butcher block he brushed his hands down the front of his apron, measured, like he was holding back, and then eased them gently on the block.

The two of them stood there for a moment more, without a word between them. A hush seemed to lie thick like a blanket waiting for something to lift it. What were they doing?

"I wanted to thank you for the groceries the other day," she said, so softly I could hardly hear her speak. Her eyes would meet his for only a second or two.

Her elbows unlocked like a toll bridge, allowing her to rest her pocketbook on the counter, hands still clutching the straps.

"I, I tried to add up the cost to pay you, but I...."

Mr. Jake lifted a hand. "No. No, that won't be necessary." He responded equally softly as he placed his hand back on the counter where it belonged. Somehow, his voice soothed her, allowing her to release her hands from the fretted pocketbook, to let them rest on the counter across from his. The sunlight beaming down from the widow's peak window caught them.

Suspended them.

While the particles and bits of air glistened around them like fairy dust, there they stood, in this unlikely common ground for the back and forth of grief. So what happens to the grief? Does it melt away? Or does it settle low, so very low that room can be made for happiness— where they, together, can connect and share that space.

I was in awe of them.

Touching, though they never touched.

I hadn't met too many women like Miss Violet before. Sweet and serene, pretty and smart. A day's entire lesson on how to be the perfect Negro woman in America. For a moment I swelled with pride as I thought of how she'd entrusted me with her pain. It was fleeting, dissolved in an instant for self-ishly reveling in her sorrow.

And then, I thought about her...and Mr. Jake, it made me...well...queasy. I can't say I know why. But as I spied upon them, I felt a flush of hot blood run down my spine, then the spread of a spasm of burning fingers around my ribs. A thud in my heart made me want to cry out in a flash of anger.

My belly burned as I realized that I was jealous.

But how, why? I didn't have one bit of attraction to him. Like I said, Mr. Benjamin was more my cup of tea.

Jealous over a man that didn't like me a bit! That paid no attention to me, even when his doorbell did!

Everyone liked me—me the City Gal! Even Miss Violet liked me!

Then like a brick that dropped from the sky, I realized why I was jealous. The sweet magnolia scent. The red rosebud lips surrounded by her paper bag brown velvety smooth skin. She didn't need to nor did she try; he liked her and he couldn't help himself. She was the exception, the one that left the rest of us Negroes behind.

I tried to make peace with my soul that I was not an exceptional person like Miss Violet, nor would I ever be. I buried that hurt feeling like crow. I shoved and shoved....

Suddenly my wonderment shifted into guilt, some kid spying in on their lives.

"Are you gonna' eat that ice cream, or you are you gonna let it melt all over my floor?" Mr. Jake shouted at me.

I ran to the counter with the quarter ready in my hand to give to him. On second thought, I dropped it flat by the register and ran out the door.

Ring-a-ding-dong-clash-bang!

I swore to all that was good, that I was going to cut that bell loose one day.

Oh crap, I forgot the cashews.

Fifteen

"Hey y'all, are you in there?" a woman shouted through the screen door.

I was in my bedroom dressing Lena and myself for the card party. I changed from the day's outfit into something new, a matching set of multi-color, seersucker pants and matching sleeveless top—the one Miss Violet and I had liked in the Sears catalog. Lena had the same, except hers was mostly pink. I posed in front of my closet mirror to check myself. I turned and turned again, searching for that feeling I get when I'm pleased with my outfit. Maybe I wasn't standing tall?

No, that wasn't it.

Was it the shoes? No, they were flat sandals with a wide strap just below the wiggle of my toes with a shiny gold buckle on top. They matched the color of my seersucker pants perfectly.

I knew. I knew. But I was too stubborn to admit it.

I knew I would never pass for the likes of *her.*

A roar of "Hi" and "Hey there, stranger!" nearly blew the roof off.

Lena and I peeped around the bend from the stairway to see what all the hooptidy-doo was about.

A woman stood there, all but five foot nothing, a tiny crisp of a thing, with her hair rolled up in gray knots pinned about her head. I couldn't see her face, but her voice—scratchy though, rich—dipping into a deep well, snatching up some gravel, then flying high clear out to the stars. A bottle of golden brown liquid was tucked inside the pocket of her blue-and-white cotton apron edged with white wavy lace.

That woman, Great Aunt Ode.

"Where's the youngins? My nephew's children from New York?" She parted the room like Moses. Aunt Al stepped into the eye of the gathering with her arms open wide to smother the twig of an aunt.

"They're coming, Aunt Ode. You set yourself right here by the fan, until we get started."

We came down the stairs and stood, holding hands in the archway of the kitchen and the dining room like a grand prize from "The Price is Right."

"Goodness gracious, look at them!" she exclaimed. Her withering arms and ravaged fingers reached us, ready to pinch hold of our two cheeks between them. The crowd laughed and clapped in glee, patting themselves on the back for participating in this amazing sight, along with their courageous participation in eating a dozen pigs-in-the-blanket.

She was no more than an arm's length away when a whiff of her slammed upside my nostrils. Whiskey, bourbon or Indian piss, she stank like…like what rhymes with well! I couldn't figure out whether it was coming from her body, her mouth, or both. My inexperience told me it was her breath. Reason being, she hardly had a tooth standing in her mouth that wasn't a lab experiment gone wrong. She was chewing on something lodged in the back of her jaw. Chewing tobacco, as I was later on told. Turned her teeth into a green and brown moldy mess.

I cringed as she took hold of my cheeks to kiss me. I didn't feel bad about twisting up my face since she probably couldn't see it. Her glasses were as thick as Coke-bottle bottoms. The closer she got, the more I didn't want to see. Little curls of white hair sprinkled her chin. A couple of them dared to be bone straight after all those years. As she planted the kiss of smelly death breath on my face, I found myself eye-to-eye with her. One of those eyes was blue. Hazy though, like a filmy veil of milk that wouldn't wash away.

"Oh, look at you girls! Just like your daddy, you are!" She reached for Lena to give her a kiss, but Lena would have none of that. She gave Aunt Ode a block that would have made any fullback proud. Thank goodness, she was young enough to get away with it, by the laughter from the crowd.

"Come on everybody, let's get it on up in here!" Uncle Frank shouted. He threw his hands up in the air holding on to Auntie's, then turned and gave her a big kiss smack dab on her lips. The party had officially begun.

Three tables, set up with chairs, cards, and colored chips were ready to go. Each large enough to seat eight players. There was a bucket in the kitchen with every bottled and canned drink one could imagine, even orange soda pops for me. My main duty for the night was to keep the nut bowls full. It sounds simple enough, but to keep those salty tongues happy took a patrol worthy of Patton himself. Cashews, peanuts, almonds, and those tiny nuts with a red skin all in separate bowls for three tables and standbys in the waiting.

As soon as I got a moment, I turned the television on. One of my favorite James Bond, 007 movies was on *From Russia with Love*. So whatever it took to watch Bond and keep those bowls filled, I was up for the challenge.

My favorite part of the evening was the music. Music only Negros could love, so I thought. Sad, pitiful music that only we could appreciate because we had lived it, were living it, and *gonna* live it forever. This music drenched itself into your bones. Made you cry even though you didn't need to.

But then I heard it. The loud-mouthed whisper of gossip. You can tell the difference between it and the innocent murmurs of good will.

"I was there, right across the street a bit ago when he and Joseph were arguin' 'bout somethin'. His face got all red and knotted up. Heh, heh, he don't like us fo' sure!" They laughed with the man wearing the diamond pinky ring.

He who? I wondered.

"Lizbeth, I need some napkins over here please." Uncle Frank rumbled with a chicken wing in his mouth.

The churning smoke had put me in a light daze. "Comin'." I shouted.

As the evening wore on, Aunt Ode's little bottle of brown liquid emptied, and had stretched her pronunciation of words long beyond my high school intelligence. Cards snapping hard around me. Smoke filling my lungs, burning my eyes. I got up from the TV to serve them, every now and again, with a tray full of cold peeled shrimp and fried chicken wings. The glowing praise I would get for waiting on them was beyond reckoning.

More sly gossip burned in my ears from the man with the pinky ring. He was getting louder by the sip of his cup.

"But a couple of years ago, I do remember some rumblin's about some money that was stolen."

"Who'd he steal it from?" said some woman, squinting her eyes while she took a deep drag off her cigarette.

"Don't know. I think there was another involved too—his

partner in crime, so to speak. Hey gal, whatcha' doin' over there? How about passin' me some of those *scrimp!*"

"Yes, sir," I said, but what the heck is *scrimp?*

"What I do know," said the man with the pinky ring, "is that it was big enuff for the District Attorney to come down and square things. Heard tell that Mr. Jake hired himself a lawyer even."

"What happened after that?" Same skinny woman with the cigarette.

"Come on, Jessie. You know how it is with white folks. They hushed it all up with a handshake and a bag of money!" Pinky ring man had a point there—laughing like a gaggle of geese.

But I didn't find this funny at all.

"Which a' you fine fellas' gonna take me home ta-night?" Aunt Ode declared. "It be you, or maybe you, Johnny Boy?" She swished about pointing a bony finger with someone else's drink in her hand. Johnny Boy took the drink respectfully from her and made a joke about not being able to drive if she gave him one more.

But once in a while, something wonderful would happen without will.

A comforting kiss.

A lingering hug.

A drunken conversation about how the sun didn't deserve its praise over the moon.

A cackling laugh could lead to tears within a flick of an eye.

Johnny Boy's keys did a little ditty on his way out. Aunt Ode's eyelids began to droop, and so did she. Jerked herself awake, opening her brown eye for a second, then went right back to a light snooze on the living room couch.

"Lizbeth, go get your great aunt a blanket and two down pillows from the cedar box, sweetie."

I obliged Auntie, moving quickly, hoping that I wouldn't miss the part where Bond sits around the fire with the Gypsies watching the belly dancer.

Aunt Ode had hollered and played as long as her eighty-something-year-old body could hold on to. Can't blame her though. She had walked from her house to here for one, which was at least two miles, and who knows where she'd been earlier that day.

Later, I learned she hadn't had a driver's license in over forty years, and pride wasn't about to let her ask folks for a ride. If she got a lift on her way, great! And if not, she'd wriggle her toes into her most comfy flip-flops and off she went. She was a busy woman, with too many things to do, I guess.

When I came back with the camping materials, she was already leaning over like the Tower of Pisa on the couch.

I had little experience in these situations. None really. I looked to Aunt Alice for instructions, but all I got from her was a look of intolerance, as if I should know. But she was right, I was acting trifling. So I poked Aunt Ode gently in the shoulder with my fingers until she went the rest of the way down into the couch, landing just where I had placed the pillows.

To my surprise, I heard her pocket jingle and a handful of change spewed out from one of her apron pockets. I forgot myself, leaning over her to scoop them up from the couch. But just as my fingertips grazed the bronze metal, she popped my hand like she was cracking a freshly plucked switch across my thin legs.

"Ouch!" I yelped. I thought she was dead drunk asleep.

"What chu doin' there, gal? Huh? Tryin' to take my little bit o' change are you! Or maybe you just can't help yourself. It does sound beautiful don't it? Gets you excited. Like gumballs rattlin' down the shoot, fightin' to be the first one to pop into your mouth."

Those were her last words to me as she went back to sleep again. I flapped the blanket over her, and then tucked it underneath her chin like a child. My hands lingered as I smoothed the blanket down her arm to her paper-thin hand.

Though I was still tingling from the sight of the pennies that poured from her pocket, I didn't worry about them at all, for I knew she would be there in the morning. Keeping them warm and safe for me to dive into tomorrow.

Lena had long since passed out in her bed, still in her party clothes. I eased back into the La-Z-Boy just as the Bond movie ended, and I let the soft music of the stereo lull my eyes shut. A woman was singing. Her name was Nina, Nina Simone, I believe, moaning how she loved some *man*.

I loves you Porgy, don't let him take me,
Don't let him handle me and drive me mad.

From the depths of her dreams something stirred Aunt Ode. Maybe the heartbreaking lyrics the woman sang.

Something bad. Ode started bubbling with fits. I paid her no mind until she started the shouting.

"No, no please Manny. Ahhhh, God Manny, I loves ya' Manny, please don't! Don't let 'em takes me! MANNY! Kill me first Manny! Kill me first! Why, sweet Jesus? I loves you, Manny!"

I ran over to her to shake her.

"Aunt Ode, wake up!" I said.

"NO!" shouted Aunt Al. "Leave her be, Lizbeth. Just leave her be!"

I couldn't wake her, but I didn't have to leave her be.

So I held her, something my mama would have done for me when I had bad dreams.

"It's okay, Aunt Ode. It's all right now. Nobody's gonna hurt you now. Please Aunt Ode."

…Don't let him handle me with his hot hands…

A tear weaved its way patiently through the tiny wrinkles down her face. She was so frail in my arms, I wept too. Wept because I didn't know what to do. Because I couldn't, didn't understand what depths of pain could wound one so deep, to cause this kind of lifetime woe.

Even in her sleep. I didn't want to learn.

She'd mumble, toss and turn her head wildly sometimes. Then whimper like a baby. She scared me, but I was compelled to stay.

When she finally calmed down, I squeezed her hand tight, hoping she knew that someone was watching over her.

The music wailed on.

If you can keep me,

I wants to stay here with you forever,

I've got my man.

Twelve o' clock, and the voices were raising high through the roof. Laughter bounced carelessly off the walls, with mouths so wide open I could see their molars. Slits for eyes. The music blared the rhythm so strong that your feet tapped from the rumble of others. Eventually somebody got foolish enough to dare my Uncle Frank that he or she could still tear up the floor with the jitterbug better than he could. More laughing and more clapping, half the bodies bumping into each other, splashing their drinks to the floor, all shaking what shouldn't be seen shaken.

There I stood in the farthest corner laughing, with one hand covering my mouth and the other across my belly, desperately trying not to bring attention to myself. Any young person like me caught doing so would have to pay the price of *let's see if you can do any better.*

But I was caught anyway, and of course I could do better, though the price to be paid was to teach them how to do it! I must admit, even though my sandals provided no protection against Mr. Moe's two clubfeet, I did have fun being the center of attention, along with making out like a bandit with the dollars they paid me.

How my Aunt Ode was able to sleep through all the noise will always remain a mystery to me. I assumed that the liquor was at the root of it. I was wrong.

After the dancing as I sat by Great Aunt Ode's side; Aunt Alice made a seat beside me. Three generations to pass along a tale of beauty and despair.

Aunt Al told me the truth this night.

"Ode was a beautiful woman in her youth. Beautiful, sassy, talented, and smart as all get out, all bundled up in a sprite girl. She was 'the one' in Ahoskie expected to become somebody. Somebody great, put all of Ahoskie on the map. The first in her family line to attend college on the prayers and coin collection of the town church. But the Devil wasn't about to let her go that easily. He had something else in mind, in the form of Manuel Cummings—Manny.

"Mean as cuss. Dumb as a brick. A smile like pure sunshine, and with one blink of an eye she was blindly in love. Manny. Why did he smile at my aunt all those years ago?" Like a yarn weaving its way through the blaring music, Auntie's soft voice was clearer than ever before, drifting through to tell a tale of another tragic love. I made myself comfortable to listen.

She was all set. A senior at Ahoskie High School, Odell Mae Roosevelt. Straight A's, class president (all of twenty-five

117

students), and 1909 prom queen. Had every boy in the county praying to lie beside her for eternity. Manny was no different.

Moonshine was easy to get back then, whether you were fifteen or fifty in the back woods, as long as you had a dollar. And Manny always had a dollar. Hot nights and cigarettes in the backseat of his car. Sooner or later it was going to happen.

Odell was more than willing to give up her dreams, the town's dreams, for the love of Manny. So he took her. Took her slow, and nice, and easy. He melted her like molasses on hotcakes between his fingers. She married him upon the doctor's confirmation that she was due next winter. Wore a bright lemon yellow hat with baby breath and daisies for her wedding that Sunday.

That's when it happened.

Not one month after they jumped over the broom, Manny invited some of his boys over to celebrate. Jugs of moonshine passed around the small house they rented on the edge of town. Hot fried chicken popping fresh on the stove.

Five men. One woman.

"Ode, we getting' hungry here now, woman! When you gonna' be done in there?"

"Oh hush up, Manny, I just got these rolls here to rise in the oven, and then you all can eat!"

"Did your wife just tell you to 'hush" man? My woman don't tell me to hush. What is you? Some pussy or somethin'?"They all laughed their sweaty nasty laugh. She heard it in her gut.

"Okay fellas', I'll be right there." She stirred that pot as quick as she could, but she couldn't stop it. Why couldn't they just let it go?

"Man, my wife could never talk to me like that without gettin' a busted lip!" Bowline grumbled, chewing on his tobacco, then spit on the wall. Manny was not much on thinking. A hot head got him in trouble too many times to account for, but that didn't stop him this night.

"Ode, come on out here. NOW!"

"What you talking at me like that for, Manny? I—"

Slap! Ode fell to the floor in shock.

"What you do that fo'?" The warm blood was already trickling down her chin. Her beautiful eyes welled from disappointment. Slowly, she leaned up against the wall to pick herself up from the mixed gold shag-carpeted floor.

"You still talkin' and not gettin' my food out here, girl?" He rose to his feet, hovering over her with red glassy eyes.

"What's wrong, Manny? I love you, honey. Just sit back down with your friends and relax." She made the innocent mistake of turning her back to him.

"Did she just put her ass to you, man? I can't believe this shit, Manny. You ain't chit, man!" Bowline spat at him.

He hated Manny for having her. He too loved Ode, but it had turned. Twisted back with hateful jealously, odious vengeance, then he turned to stone. She had spurned his affections for her years ago, without a flicker to a fly. If she had been asked about it, she would not have recalled this injustice that had occurred at the age of ten.

It was intolerable after all these years. Now was his time for vengeance upon the innocent couple. He could taste it, smell it—sense the smoldering rage that could turn into a blaze of fire within Manny with just a whisper.

"Hit her, Manny!

"Hit her! Hit her hard man!"

"Make her bleed, like she made me bleed for her!"

"Git up, Ode and get my food, woman!" Manny shouted. He looked around, checking the faces of the pack with their yellow teeth baring, and lips drawn back ready to take a taste. He kicked her in the side for good measure.

"Manny don't, the baby, Manny, God, the baby!" The pain burned deep within her belly through her chest. Her breathing became labored. Tears poured from pain.

From the sadness. The knowing of what's to come always hurts the most.

Ode scuffled as quickly as she could on all fours toward the tiny kitchen. A carpet nail snagged the stockings she had bought that day for a dollar. It nipped a bit off skin from her knee, but she didn't dare make a squeak. Just as she reached the coolness of the blue laminate floor of the kitchen, her neck was jerked back by the collar of her dress. It choked her like a cutting noose, hauling her hands up from the floor. He whipped her around hard, burning her throat like a rope, back to face the pack. The sweat stung the fleshy wound as it mingled with a hint of blood. She sat with her bottom on her heels, limp, tears streaming down her face. Her nose running with blood and snot. Her clothing drenched, plastered tightly to her skin.

"Please…" her chest heaving, begging him to stop. "…please don't…do this. I love you…why you gonna do this, Manny?" She whimpered like a scolded child.

Thwap! The back of his hand pierced the air, his ring landed, cutting deep into the bone of her jaw. Blood sprayed out freely from the wound, like the water from a sprinkler. Red dots bubbled into half moons, as they hit the floor, leaving the remainder to melt into her clothes.

A quiet hush. The wolves turn to their prey. Eyes hungry.

Ode tries to hold the tear back.

Clenches her teeth.

She begs God to stop her heart from beating too loud for them to hear.

The tear drops. The beat is heard.

Together. One by one. Ripping and tearing her apart. The hollowed cries hammer the night air. But the blood keeps coming.

Hot breath grunting, bodies sticky with blood and sweat, confused with noises. Ode lies still from the thrashing. One bloody eye peeps open from a slit made from the skin stretching too far.

"…please…"

But the blood keeps coming.

———

Aunt Alice was still a baby in her mother's arms when they visited Aunt Ode in the hospital the day after the beating, though she told the tale as if it were she who stood at the foot of Ode's bed with daisies in her hand.

"The nurses hushed low when family came around, but that didn't stop them from talking," said Aunt Al.

"Lord who would do that to such a pretty thing? I hope they string them up and cut their Johnsons off!" one said.

"They caught 'em the day after, still drunk as skunks, and sleeping in their own piss water. No matter what, there's nothing that the law could do to bring that girl back to her right self. It's just not fair the way things are."

"Does her family know that she'll never be able to see out of that eye again?"

"That's just one of her worries. Her jaw is broken in two places, and cut so deep into it that the surgeon had stitch fifty inside before out. Took half her grown teeth out. Broken ribs, punctured lung, a blood clot in her brain…" The head nurse took a sigh of angry regret. Buckled her lips like she wanted beat the crap out of somebody.

"Tore her up so bad inside that she lost her baby and will never be able to bear another again."

Ode spent just nearly a week over at the county hospital in the trauma unit. Just over a month in the psychiatric ward.

The only good thing from it was the death of Bowline and Manny. A few weeks later they crashed into a tree one late night drinking clear moonshine as usual. No charges had been forthcoming as yet. They figured they were home free. They were mashed up and mangled pretty bad. Manny lived for two days not knowing where he was or who he was. Bowline, he managed to survive much longer. A month or so, eyes wide open, not able to speak. Pleading with his eyes for the doctors to kill him, he was in so much pain. He died in that pain.

My auntie placed her hand on top of mine, which was already settled on top of Ode's. Spent from the story she'd told.

I never heard such a horrible account in my life, probably never would, and I would never question my Aunt Alice again.

Sixteen

I got up surprisingly early Sunday morning after card night, leaping from the third-stairway step, landing with a *boom* to the living room floor, practically flying in the air—only to find the couch empty and the blankets folded neatly in her place. Heavens knows where Aunt Ode could have gone. She could be walking down a dirt road singing praises to her Jesus. Sitting at the table of a friend for a late breakfast. Always invited without need of an invitation. Or, amazingly enough, the family vagabond might be found at home, rocking in her favorite chair on the porch with a spittoon beside her.

It was a little after ten o'clock. I could tell by the sliding of the sun—a skill which my Uncle Frank had taught me—when I went out back barefoot into the soft blades of grass with a shoebox in my hand. Not far behind the house was a small stream, with a portion of it shaded by a huge dogwood tree. I figured I might as well hunt for a few frogs to keep me busy. As I crept up to the bank, the leaves moved.

"Hey!" I yelped, fumbling back.

I watched the lump of leaves continue to shuffle slowly to the bank too. I followed beside it. Something poked out and

123

took a look at me. With its mouth wide open, bearing one dangerous hook I knew what it was. A snapping turtle. And as my cousin Tommy had explained to me once, if you walked up on one big enough and mean enough, you might find your big toe missing in his mouth!

"Lizbeth!" That was my Aunt Al shouting for me.

"Yes, Auntie?"

"Would you like to take a visit to Miss Violet?"

"Yes ma'am!" I hollered back.

I looked back to the turtle and my toes. "Thought you were going to have brown toe for a snack, huh?" Although I shook my finger at him all brave like, I backed away from him slowly, and then dashed away.

"Comin'!"

That turtle got me thinking.

What if whoever took that shot on the bridge was hiding in the forest...waiting. Everyone in town knew when Mr. Samuel headed home evenings. And like that snapping turtle, the shooter waited for Mr. Samuel.

Waited for him to drive right into his jaws.

───

Turns out, Aunt Al had promised my body to Miss Violet for the afternoon. So off to her house I went on my bike, thrilled at the thought of seeing her. But wondering if that sadness would take her over again.

Her house wasn't as big as Auntie's, but it was brimming with warmth, and loved just as much. Two pink blossom crepe myrtle trees greeted you on either side of her centered porch steps, with the reddest of rosebushes stretched out beside them. I half-expected that violets would be dancing freely in the garden. I decided right then and there, just before taking another step to press the ivory doorbell, that I would have violets in mine some day.

An impressively large mahogany clock stood tall from the floor, which inclined me to sit with my spine pressed straight against the gold velvety couch in Miss Violet's living room. It had tricked me into thinking that it would be the most comfortable, luxurious piece of furniture I'd ever sat upon. It felt like a brick of solid sand, crunchy-like too.

"Can you wait a while longer while I get things ready, Lizbeth?"

"Yes, ma'am." I looked up only briefly to connect with her eyes, enough time to see the brightness returning in them. Any longer than that, I knew I'd be caught lingering too long at that beautiful face. My eyes followed her to the kitchen.

The sunny yellow and white room had an ironing board ready at the window. Warm air billowed through the eyelet-laced curtains, flicking the board every once in a while. She tested the iron with a tap of a moist fingertip. Popping hot and ready.

As the steam puffed like an engine from the iron, Miss Violet pressed hard against the little scrap of cloth beneath it. A spray of starch sizzled as it hit the cotton skin. Over and over she pressed hard until the collar of the dress lay stiff as a popsicle stick.

I finally became antsy waiting for Miss Violet on the uncomfortable golden sofa. The cloud of steam, with the help of the starch, lingered in the air aimlessly. It tempted me to make my way to her.

"There," she said, pleased with her work. "She'd like this one."

I crept into her view so as not to startle her.

"Lizbeth, I'm sorry. I don't know why it takes me so long to press such a little thing. Such a very little thing." She held up her work strangely. Without admiration now.

"Excuse me, if you don't mind me asking, Miss Violet, but who are you making this dress for?"

She folded her lips softly between her teeth, and then spoke.

"I started in the habit of making my baby…Emma's dresses, for her since birth. Every single one. Even the one she…" She gathered her strength by the rise in her shoulders.

Waiting for the starch to set hard into the fabric, she opened a closet door, full to the brim with flowered cardboard boxes. Each labeled with a season and the year. The scent of mothballs clung to the air within the small space. Her questioning finger glided across the dated boxes, trying to decide which would shelter this dress.

"Since the accident, I thought it would be nice to donate most of them to the church. I heard that a young woman is having twin girls. I made a couple of sets in here that would work just fine for her. Twins can be expensive, you know." She smiled with her little teeth showing.

She took a stack of five boxes from one corner of the closet and set them on the kitchen table. She lifted one of the boxes, and the air sucked the lid down like a body's chest. When she removed the lid, three layers of dresses were in full display. She took the first out of the box.

"She'd have grown out of these by now." Her mouth contorted as though she'd swallowed a bitter taste. She held a box inscribed *10 months old.*

Layers of lavender-scented paper sat beside the iron to her left. Her delicate fingers lifted the red and white cotton dress with stitched-in cherries on the white collar that she'd been working on. It was still warm from the iron's heat. She let the pads of her thumbs rub circularly against the fabric thoughtfully, patiently. As if loving the sweet cheeks of a child. She smiled woefully and then pressed the little dress against the board spreading her fingers wide in completion.

"You don't sew dresses for—" It was too late to shut my mouth.

"Oh, I just finished up a few that I had started for Emma." She paused. "I know it's silly. I doubt that I'll be making another again."

"Why not, if you want to?"

I saw a faint tear die at the crest of her eye as she began to fold the puffed sleeves behind the bodice of the tiny dress. With every fold, she pressed hard to make it stay put, as another tear fell as if to set it in place.

I choked back my own tears as I watched her from the door. What sort of monster would take a shot at a car with a baby in it?

Satisfied that the dress understood that it was to stay still, she wrapped the lovely papers around it, and then presented it gently to its box. There she stood, with one hand laid upon the dress, until she had buried her pain deep within the box too.

Three deep and the lid was placed atop again. A vacuum sucked the air in, with a *swoosh*, and the deed was finally done.

"Oh, Dearest God," she whimpered as softly as she could. Two tears plummeted to the edge of her chin, hurtling to their end on the board.

Her chest heaved in rhythm with her pain. She trembled when she released the air from her lungs. I prayed, as I watched her, that she did not fall, for I could not have moved from my place in the floor to help her.

I wanted to hold her to tell her how sorry I was for her loss, and that it would simply be all right. But I couldn't, because I did not want to tell her a lie. I didn't know for sure, and that was the truth.

"Please, Miss Violet. Maybe you should keep sewing these beautiful dresses…if it brings you some happiness."

"But that won't bring my family back, Lizbeth."

"But maybe…" I shrugged my shoulders, "…it will give you the courage to have a new one." And maybe I talk too much.

Slowly, she gathered herself. I should have taken this as a signal to run back to the golden lying couch, but I didn't.

"Sorry, Lizbeth," she said as she swiped a tear on the run with her wrist, then smiled brightly like any true mommy would. She handed me the cardboard box, then gathered up the other four, then handed me another. "Can you carry that okay?"

I nodded that I could, then followed her out the door to the car.

By the time we reached Sister Haney's house, the head church Deaconess at the largest Baptist church in the county, the clouds began to boil. A low rumble caught my attention just as gray clouds lumbered across the bright blue sky. As the air stirred, curls of air kicked up leaves and scattered bits of twigs brashly across the lawns.

"You stay in the car, Elizabeth. No need for you to get wet too." Miss Violet shut the car door and then turned to peep back through the car window with a broad smile to confirm that it was all right.

"Miss Violet! You okay, honey? It's getting' wet out there!" shouted Sister Haney. She'd opened her screen door, popping her little round head out to see what she could.

"I'm coming!" Miss Violet hopscotched the slate squares with her best sweater caped over her head, clutching the boxes precariously in one contorted arm, then up the rickety porch steps to the round-headed Deaconess.

"Hi there, Missy. Come on inside and get yourself dry!' A juicy fat hand reached out from around the screen door.

"I'm fine, Mrs. Haney. Here are the…well…here they are!" Miss Violet looked to the boxes in her arms, and then shoved them into the arms of the big-headed woman behind the screen door.

The rain had begun to fall in heavy drops. I sat there watching them, and the rain, and the darkened sky, and listened to the rush of water against the paved street. It was muggy, but soft…the air smelled of pine needles. I delighted in the cozy moment of the time alone.

The rain was beating down hard now. She ran back to the car, her sweater stretched over her head, the rain pummeling her without regard. Her taut face welcomed the droplets as it camouflaged the tears running down her face.

I saw them anyway.

Tears are heavier than raindrops, you know. It's the resentful salt that can't help but show itself. Besides that, when Miss Violet got into the car, she wiped the wetness from her eyes rather than from her face.

We drove silently for the few minutes it took to get back to her home.

As the time passed, so did the fretful clouds. A rainbow gleamed across the sky while trickles of rain continued to fall. The Devil must have been beating his wife with a leg of lamb, as the wives' tale goes.

The gravel crackled as we crept up her driveway. Thank goodness I parked my bike on her screened-in porch. That's all it would have taken to start it to rusting.

She didn't ask, but I followed her in. As she held open the door open, she looked back at me and brushed her hand across my cheek.

"How about some lemonade and shortbread cookies, Lizbeth?"

"Sure!" I clapped my hands then shoved them in my pockets.

"Come on then!" She nearly blinded me with her smile. Next thing I knew, she'd grabbed me by the arms. Her hand feathered my cheek and pulled me into her body. I felt her lips; lingering on my forehead in a kiss. Cautiously, I wrapped my weak arms around her waist.

We sat on the porch sipping that ice-cold lemonade from Bell jars, rocking in white wicker chairs. By now, the sun was blazing hot, burning so that I could see the steam rise up from the grass. The white moths were out, flickering about the tall flowers of Queen Anne's lace. The *clink* of melting ice in my glass made everything fall into place, for that moment. I felt like a grown-up, sliding the buttery cookies across the plate to my mouth. Yet I had so many questions bound up in me to ask, though I didn't know how to.

"Rest yourself here for a while. I'll be back soon."

She liked my company, and I knew that.

I heard a chair being drawn out, and then scooted back in with the heaviness of a body upon it. The low hum of an engine gearing up then pumping wildly. I pitched my head over to look through the screen door inside. There she sat, behind her sewing machine.

I eased back into my chair and let it rock me.

I bet my Great Aunt Ode was doing the same about now.

The engine of the sewing machine finally stopped. It stopped for more than a minute or two. Then…

"Lizbeth!" she yelped, with excitement in her voice.

I ran quickly to be by her side. There she was, standing in the glow of her window with a tiny dress between her hands.

"It's beautiful, Miss Violet," I said.

"It is, isn't it Lizbeth? It's just beautiful." She smiled with ease at her work this time.

She had a small mirror against the ledge of the kitchen counter. We smiled together in it, like we were taking pictures in a carnival booth. We laughed out loud at each other's funny faces, snapshots of what we felt in our hearts. I watched her closely, then noticed how beautiful her hair was. Not nappy like mine. But smooth as glass, yielding to her Cherokee profile.

"What's wrong, Lizbeth?"

"Nothing Miss Violet, I was just admiring your hair." I dropped my face to the floor, not wanting her to see my envy. She picked up my chin gently and looked into my eyes.

"You, young lady, have beautiful hair too, you just don't know it...yet!"

"Miss Violet, you don't understand, I have kinky, nappy, peasy hair, and nothing is ever going to change that! Ever!"

"And that's a good thing!"

"A good thing?" I gave a questionable look to her sanity.

"Yes, and I'll show you. You sit right here at the kitchen table while I get my things."

"What things?" I asked. She was already gone by the time the words flew from between my teeth.

She came back with her arms full of ointments, straightening comb, curling hot comb, bows, clips and rubber bands.

"Is this going to hurt?" I asked.

"As much as you believe it to. Remember, in beauty there is some pain." She stood behind me, gripped me by the shoulders, then went to work.

First she shampooed my hair.

Then she conditioned it for twenty minutes under a pink portable dryer.

She washed the conditioner out, and then poured some hot oil in her hands to massage it into my scalp. That felt soooo good!

Carefully she parted my hair into sections and braided each one. Oh Lord, this was taking so long my butt began to get tired from sitting. Then it came to the hot iron. She set it on the open blue flame of her stove until it was just right.

Then the hard part began: pressing my kinky hair as near straight as it would ever get with a metal torch at my scalp.

"Stop fidgeting, Lizbeth, we're almost done." She giggled behind me. "There, have a look."

She handed me a tortoiseshell hand mirror, which was unexpectedly heavy. I slowly peeped into silver glass then jerked back and nearly dropped it at the sight of the girl facing me in the mirror. I didn't have faith in what my eyes were seeing. My hair was bone straight, smooth as black ice, pulled back into a donut shaped bun. I was floored that my hair looked so beautiful, just like Miss Violet's, except she gave me little spit curls that bounced about my cheekbones, and two more brushing at the nape of my neck.

"Well, what do you think?" She asked with wide eyes.

"I can't believe it. It looks…it's just beautiful, Miss Violet. Thank you so much!" I hugged her about the waist with both arms still holding tight to the reflection in the mirror.

———

As I rode my bike home, I reviewed the list of things Miss Violet told me to do and not to do in order to keep my hair looking fine.

Keep a scarf tied around my head just before I go to bed (try to sleep on your face if you can).

Wear a shower cap anytime I'm near water. That meant when I washed my face, took a bath or shower or running through a sprinkler trying to keep cool.

And most importantly, try not to perspire, but...especially when I ride my bike.

Darn it! A bead was runnin' down my eyebrow already!

Seventeen

"Okay everybody let's get packing. I told Grandma that you two would be spending some time with them this week. Give me a break from running after you, Lizbeth."

"Me?" My face crunched at that statement.

So away we went to spend a few summer days in early July at my grandmother's sweet little house. The same place Aunt Ode lived—whenever she stumbled in, that is.

It was a simple Cape Cod type of home with a fairly sized porch. Ode hadn't had a job since that summer of the beating, aside from picking a little tobacco for payment in-kind. Thus, as the matriarch of the family, my grandmother took her into the family home. They were all born there. All ten of ten kids. Eight were long since dead. My grandma and Ode were the oldest and the strongest, I suppose.

I'd imagined that they'd survived this long to school me and Lena. Love doesn't know when it is time to quit.

I remembered what my grandma told me that all the boys within a mile of her home were related to me by blood, making it quite clear that I wasn't to get to know any of the boys in town, in any way, other than by a handshake. That didn't help me much, since the town was less than five miles long from one end to the other.

I loved being outside, even in New York. My parents had to call me in at dusk for fear I'd sleep outside on the park bench, waiting for next on the handball court. Girls were always allowed to play with boys, since where I came from, we were just as talented and just as tough! I had assumed that the country girls may have been tougher, but they couldn't be smarter. I was wrong on both counts.

Yep, they had tough, calloused feet and hands. They didn't mind getting up at the crack of dawn to do some chores before school, and even during summer vacation! But not city tough. Fist to fist, if a stick or brick wasn't within arm's reach. Greasing-up your face and taking off your pierced earrings was a requirement if you didn't want to have scratches on your face or the holes in your ear make a rip in two.

This wasn't the first time I visited my grandma, mind you. I could hardly stay away from my cousins, Tommy and Terry. They lived right next door, a quarter of an acre away. I loved playing with them, especially basketball. They were tough on me, but no more than necessary to keep up. My other cousins, Chin-Chin, Red, and Boyd were great comrades too. Problem was they lived a mile away. Thus, upon every visit, I knew we would be playing basketball. No socks, tee-shirts that at one-time had sleeves, scraped knees, and smelly boy bodies. God, it was fun.

So when all of my cousins begged me to play in the summer basketball tournament, be the only girl on the team and get a free tee-shirt just for showing up—heck, I was in! There was no way that I would get onto the court. I knew that even though it wasn't said. Tommy, nor Terry, could not afford to cater to my lack in skills, and I surely could not bear for them to lose because of it. But as long as I sat on that bench beside them, I would be as proud as a peacock.

The Dust Bowl, our nickname for the basketball court, was brimming with brown bodies and sprinkled with fine tan dirt. My cousins were the best you could see in town. Imagine having Dr. J, Earl The Pearl Monroe, and Walt and so on, all together on your home-town team! Yeah, that's what I'm talking about. I was the Queen Bee. I heard the kids mumble their names and mine right behind us as we made our way through the crowd.

Glorious!

It was a round robin tournament set up for six teams of kids between the ages of fourteen and eighteen. My shoulders stood tall in my bright orange tee-shirt. I was proud to wear it, and I didn't need to play.

But my cousins had ideas of their own.

"Okay everybody! Bring it in here!" Tommy, the oldest, shouted for the boys to huddle around him. They all admired him, looked up to him. I stepped back to let the boys place their hands in the center for the cheer. Terry caught me by the short sleeve and pulled me in right up to the center, then slapped my hand on top of the tower of shades of skin, to be protected by Tommy's large hand like a cherry on top. While we were huddled, the man who took care of the park gave the court a light spray of water with a hose in order to keep the dust down.

"Chin-Chin, Terry, Boyd, Red, and I are gonna start things off!" Tommy said, with his eyes peering at us from below. He was the tallest, but by him squatting down low like that, we were looking down at him for once. The sounds of cheering was deafeningly, but I could hear my cousin clear as crystal.

"Let'sssssssssss GO!" We shouted in crescendo as we raised our hands high above our heads.

"Lizbeth, you keep the score and mark the fouls for us, okay?" Tommy asked as he gently smiled at me.

"Sure thing, Tommy!" Smiling so hard you could see my molars.

The whistle blew and the game was on!

Sweat was glistening down Tommy's dark skin and chest like a bucket full of water hit him within the first five minutes. He made two baskets right away. Gracefully he passed the ball half-way down the court to Chin-Chin who was waiting in the key. He caught the ball then pivoted left, then right just before….

Tweet! "Three seconds!" The Ref shouted.

"Awh, come on, Chin-Chin. Stop winking at your girlfriend, man!" Tommy winked at him to assure Chin-Chin that he was pulling his chain. He was looking at his girlfriend, though.

It was coming down to the end of the second quarter. Red made the prettiest lay-up I'd ever seen just as the buzzer sounded. The score was twenty-five to eighteen, in favor of the Tangs. That was us, the orange team. Mr. Jake had plenty of Tang on his shelf and figured he could pawn the extra jars off on the Negroes. I don't know how or who did it, but he was our sponsor. Bought our shirts, donated all the drinks, plus raffled off a giant jar of Tang for the spectators. I looked around for his white face in the crowd. Wouldn't be hard to pick out.

He didn't show. Why would he? So many black folks here, he'd be too scared to show his face since the murders. Then it hit me.

He likes Miss Violet. He has no interest in the lumber yard. Maybe he was on the bridge to confront Mr. Samuel and fired that shot. Maybe he was glad Mr. Samuel was dead!

"Lizbeth! Hey girl, you daydreamin' about some boy?" Red laughed at me.

"Yeah, boy! You!" Everybody laughed even harder.

We did our cheer and five Tangs strutted out into the Bowl like gladiators for the second half. Two new players appeared for the blue-clad team, the Berry Delights, sponsored by Berry's Barber shop, numbers thirty-two and fifteen. Fifteen was my number, thanks to Earl The Pearl Monroe of the New York Knicks. I found myself rudely staring at this new number fifteen.

"What you doing looking at that boy, Lizbeth?" my second cousin Red asked, sitting next to me on the bench.

"I'm not lookin' at that boy!" I declared in my Southern-infused accent. I lied.

"Uh-huh, yes you are. Let me tell you somethin', gal, he's your cousin too. Maybe fourth down the line related by marriage, but he's your cousin too!' He punched me in the arm and grinned with a toothpick between his lips.

I shook my head at him as if he was crazy. I'd heard about this boy before, but I hadn't seen him until now. There he was, a forward with one good arm, while the other looked like an eraser tip just below his elbow. Falling in love with a one-armed boy wouldn't bother me none. He was gorgeous. It was the fourth cousin part that made me leery of looking at him.

Red read my face. "Little cousin, you're asking yourself, 'What the heck is he doin' out there?' He was better than Tommy until he lost his arm, if you can believe that! Now, he's maybe number five in town…one behind me." He chewed his toothpick once more, and then threw it aside in the grass.

Sure enough, Red was more than right. That boy could play. That boy's name was Daniel Rainwater. He was a sight—a tall red-bone with light hazel eyes and coal wavy black hair.

His eyelashes were as long as my own and his lips were so red they looked as though they were painted.

"Lizbeth!" Tommy shouted. "Lizbeth, get your butt in here!" He shook me by the arm as he sat down beside me.

"What?" I thought he had lost his mind.

"You better get in there before we get a tech, girl!"

"Me! No, its okay, Tommy...."

A technical would allow the Berry Delights a free shot from the foul line!

"Get in there, girl! You can do this!"

"Tommy!" I stood up like a zombie waiting for further orders.

"You'll be all right. Now go on in there." He shoved my hip to set me in motion. Chin-Chin was already giving me a high-five before I could step onto the court.

"Number fifteen, let's go!" The referee barked at me. Good, because that's what sparked my legs to get going.

"Come on in, Cuz. We're all family out here. No one is gonna hurt you and everyone is gonna help you! Promise." Daniel smiled brightly at me and nodded, as well as the other members of the Berry team. Pride from the love of family washed over me at that instant. Something that I had never experienced before. The crowd roared when Terry passed the ball to me to bring down the court. Chills ran down my arms rising into little pimples. I felt my chest swell up within me.

"Come on wit' it, gal!" I heard my Aunt Ode cry out. I giggled at the thought of the small bottle of brown lightning in the pocket of her smocked apron dress weighing her down.

I made it down the court to the top of the key. The blue shirts seemed to move too quickly for me to make a pass to the orange.

"Liz, Liz!" someone shouted, but it was too late by the time I turned to pass the ball. I decided that I'd drive to the left to the hoop. I stepped right, then shifted to make my way, but there he was, in my way, Daniel! He reached out to steal the ball from me, but I was too low for him to complete his mission. I brought the ball up to my chest, but he held on to it as well. The whistle blew.

"Jump ball!" The referee shot his hand straight up and shouted.

How was I supposed to out jump a boy who had almost a foot over me? I could hear folks in the crowd chuckling about my obvious predicament.

I didn't like it. Besides that, I thought he liked me. He did smile at me, didn't he? I burned as the referee made preparations in all earnest, like we were All Stars! We faced each other as the referee held the orange globe in the palm of his hand before tossing it up into the air. Daniel's one good arm was turned to the center to tip the ball.

Tweet!

I knew what I had to do. But could I pull it off?

We both leaped into the air; I saw Daniel flying high above me, his hand almost touching the ball on its descent. I hesitated just long enough that on his way down I came up and hip-checked him just enough that he could not control the ball with that hand. Time dripped like molasses in winter. I could see my outstretched fingers reaching for the ball. Daniel, an amazing athlete, began to turn his body in mid-air, trying to regain his balance and snatch the ball. I knew at that moment that I was about to fail. But something happened.

Daniel landed squarely to the ground—then fell backwards!

Just enough time for me to snatch the orange globe from his hand. Realizing that this was a miracle never to happen again, I passed the ball to Terry on my left, and split Daniel to go to the right. Terry passed the ball to Chin-Chin, who was at the top of the key. I knew this play like the back of my hand. Terry would pass by Chin-Chin; Chin-Chin would fake the pass to me as I passed him on the right of the key, and then pass it back to Terry for a beautiful lay-up.

I could feel Daniel racing behind me, trying to catch up, but it was too late. Terry was across the court with his hands out, ready for the pass. I ran fearlessly, mimicking Terry's pattern across the key, knowing what was to come.

"Liz!" Chin-Chin hollered. But then the something crazy happened...he passed the ball to the wrong side of the key.

He passed it to me!

I didn't have time to say "no thanks" or even think it. The ball hit my lead hand hard with a *Bap*. I looked up to see the hoop already towering over me. Terry had drawn the forward that would have been able to slap the ball out of my hands, but he was as surprised as I was, and his feet were committed to standing where they were. Somehow my body took over, and let the ball go just before I ran out of bounds.

I was behind the backboard. I couldn't see the hoop, but I could see their faces. All of them. The crowd in the stand, both benches of orange and blue, the referee, and the players on the court. I stood there, for what seemed forever.

Bounce...bounce, bounce! I could hear the ball dance around the hoop.

And then it happened. The gray shabby net spit the orange globe out.

The crowd roared.

Aunt Ode roared.

My teammates swarmed me. High-fives and pats on the back. Hit me so hard someone had to lift me up from the ground by the back of my shirt. A brown arm extended through the crowd. It took me a second to realize that it was Daniel's arm. I grabbed it with all my weight. He lifted me up like I was a baby doll. A bright, toothy smile met me as I stood.

"Keep playing like this, Elizabeth, and I might have to marry you one day!" he exclaimed.

"Can't do that Daniel," I said as I jogged to the bench.

"Why not?" He said with consternation across his face. I'm sure he thought that I was as shallow and ignorant as the other girls who would not date him because of his missing arm.

"I'm out of the game…and you're my cousin!"

He laughed belly hard with his hands on his hips.

I liked his smile, that Daniel Rainwater.

Eighteen

We won that game against Berry's Barber Shop, but we lost the tournament. Third place wasn't bad for the only team with a girl, for one, *and* who let her play, for two. Our team didn't care. After the games were over, we had a family Fourth of July barbeque that put most any other celebration I'd ever attended to shame. I'd never seen a whole pig before—cooked, that is. The women cooked that pig from stem to stern, from the snout to the tail and every part in between. Fresh fish fried in a huge black cauldron, bubbling up to the surface full of the peanut oil, golden brown and crisp. Chicken necks were broken, then their bodies briefly boiled in hot water so the feathers could be plucked off with ease. Smothered, fried, barbequed, Cajun—aluminum pans brimming with every delight.

I sat myself down in the circle of chairs among the younger women to help prepare the side dishes. Clearly, by the muffle of their laughter, I had interrupted their amusement at something or someone.

"So, Missy Liz, you had yourself some sweaty fun out there today, ah-huh?" Jean, the bride-to-be of my oldest cousin, Ned, thought she was funny. By the tone of her voice, this was not going to be fun.

She had a pretty face, but on the chubby, rather sloppy side of life. Funny thing is, when I first met her I thought she was so sweet. But now on this wonderful evening, I noticed the lopsided breasts with the rolls of flesh rising out of her bra like yeasty dough, the bumpy skin down the right side of her neck, the two ugly moles that stood tall enough to tempt me to pluck them like seeds on a willow branch.

She cranked her enormous arms, lifting herself up from her chair to shuck another bushel of corn. I noticed her husky knees stayed together when she walked, with her feet spread miles apart from each other. Why hadn't I noticed these imperfections before?

I broke from my trance to find her glaring eyes upon me, looking for an answer.

"Yeah, yes I had fun today." I continued to shuck the few ears left in my basket.

"For a city girl you sho' is cut from the straight and narrow of the cloth, ain't cha?" she said as she sashayed her two rotund balls of butt back to the tiny metal chair. It yelped in pain when she backed into it. A sneak attack is how I saw it, or the chair would have run for its life.

I made some kind of disinterested face and kept on shucking.

"Let me tell you somthin', Lizzy, you ain't got nobody here fooled! You think you are all high and mighty 'cause you from the Big City—well, you ain't! I'm just as good as you with your red hot pants and halter top."

What the heck, I thought, watching that flawless chubby face boil into a sour mash of hatefulness. I looked around at the other faces in the circle of metal chairs. A variety of confused expressions as the girls looked to their leader. A poke of fun had turned into something entirely different.

"YOU," she pointed with an ugly finger, "ain't...got nothin'...on me!" Tears were streaming, blistering down her face. Falling too quick for a new wound to cause such a commotion. She stood too tall for a woman who had been beaten and too low for a woman who hadn't.

Her voluptuous breasts heaving hard in her purple cotton blouse like she'd just run to get the last bushel of corn. Now she was tearing those poor ears apart. Ripping into the kernels with her fingertips, while the blood of the corn oozed. Her fiancé saw what was happening, and made the mistake coming within her sight.

"You mangy dog!" she hollered as she threw the innocent ears of corn at his head.

"Lizbeth! Lizbeth! Come over here child!" My Aunt Ode had been spying this scene all along. If she waved at me too long, I feared that she might fall off the porch, being that the liquor bottle in her pocket would put her off balance. I shot up from the sticky plastic seat with no complaints.

Thank you, Great Aunt Ode!

I was well out of my league, and she knew it.

"Lookie here child, that gal there is in a lotta pain. She knows your cousin Ned is no good fo' her. But she can't help herself, you know what I mean. There's just somthin' about a man that ain't no good for you...and you know it, but you can't help yourself. Strange as it is, I was once like that too." She bobbed her head up and down to affirm that the madness that she spoke of was true.

I looked over to my "mangy" cousin to make sure the beating he was receiving from Jean wasn't heading back my way.

"Yes, yes, yes, it's true! I *knowed* that you'd never believe it, but it's true! I was pretty like hu' a long, long time ago... prettier even."

She leaned in low to me as she cupped her hand to the side of her mouth so others couldn't hear our secret.

"'Cept I wasn't as juicy as she is." She cackled a laugh that stirred her into frenzy. I had to catch her, as she almost fell out of the flimsy chair. "Whoa there, hah-hahhh! Thank you, gal!" She slapped her knee into a kick, nearly choking on a wad of tobacco.

"I understand that, Aunt Ode, but what I don't understand is why she's so mean to me today. I thought we were friends, family and all." I pursed my lips in thinking that I had admitted too much.

"Oh, gal...." She became somber and stroked the side of my face like a buttercup. "She sees in you what we all had once seen in ourselves—innocence, a faith that all dreams can come true. That what's good really matters in this world."

I thought I saw a tear in the crinkle of her eye, but instead, she honkered up some snot and spat into the spittoon. Wiped her mouth with her sleeveless arm.

"I love you, Aunt Ode." I spoke these words quiet and deliberate. I meant them. She needed to hear them.

She held my hand and squeezed it tight on her lap.

"I love you too, gal."

I kissed her on the cheek with both my eyes wide open.

"Hey, gal!" She wiped her nose again with the other shirtless sleeve. "Let's go look at my pennies. Al said you'd want to see!"

She yanked me up by the arm and led me into Grandma's house. Her bedroom was rather nice for someone who slept in it as often as the cat crowed. The peachy cream walls made you feel light and warm at the same time. Trinkets were hung from everywhere—from the voluptuous lamp by her bedpost, the mirror across from her bed over a heavy dresser, the closet door, and even the large window that faced the garden in the backyard.

I was mesmerized as she rummaged around a beautiful chestnut-colored trunk beneath her window.

"HAH!" she yelped as she raised a clear blue pickle jar, almost as big as she, above her gray head, cluttered with coins full to the rusted tin cap. She handed me the jar to open the tight lid.

Jesus! I thought. *How did she twist this so tight?*

"Oh gimme that, gal!" she laughed, and snatched the jar from my hands. With a flip of her bottom apron in one hand and the jar in the other, she tapped it upside down on the dresser, then twisted the cap off with a *pop*. Immediately she doused her yellow chenille bed cover with a spray of silver- and copper-colored coins.

"Go ahead!" She motioned me to dive in.

First I separated the coins by colors. That was easy. Then I separated them by size within the color—quarters, nickels, and dimes, and one 1963 silver dollar. That left only pennies swaddling on the other side of the white cover. Lots of pennies. As I started to sift through the mound, my aunt tapped me on the shoulder.

"Here gal, use these to take the rest of them coins home with you." She presented me with two crystal blue Bell jars with tin lids, and pointed to the pile of silver on the bed with her bony elbow.

"But Aunt Ode…"

"I know you don't have a hankering for the silver, but I want you to have them too. I never had anything that somebody else loved so bad. Feels good."

She bent down on her knees to the other side of the bed facing me. Together we took our time scooping up the copper coins by hand into the jars as we talked.

Gathering up every single coin from the bed must have exhausted Aunt Ode. She decided to lie down on her bed, "and get a little shut eye." As she slept, I snuck outside to admire the copper and silver gems against the moonlight. I ran to the log bench that sat underneath a bushy tree, just far enough from the heart of the party, with low hanging branches to hide me. I had established that the penny was not there, but was looking for other oddities, when a figure loomed out of nowhere.

"What are you doin' there, girl?" asked McMeanie.

"Well I was…I was just…." I knew what I was doin. I just didn't want to talk to her about it. About anything!"

"I know what you're doing out here, girl, don't play with me!" A steaming McMeanie gritted through her teeth.

I shivered for a second at her attack.

"I know you stole that coin jar!"

"I did not! My Aunt Ode gave it to me because I collect pennies!"

"Don't lie to *me*! I'm no softie like your high and mighty Miss Al! I see you sneaking around town and I know you're up to no good. Sneaking, lying, thieving—"

Suddenly Aunt Ode busted out the backdoor. A knotted-up brown fist swung at McMeanie, but missed. Uncle Frank pounced in out of nowhere and saved McMeanie's life as Aunt Ode tried to claw her eyes out. It shook the snot out of McMeanie for sure, as it nearly did me, though that she-Devil simply pranced to her car and speed off into the dark until it swallowed her up.

It made me queasy, though, seeing how McMeanie could attack me with accusations full of such hate and spite.

"You all right, gal?" Aunt Ode put her arm over my shoulder, hugging over to the bench.

"I'm okay, Auntie, thanks to you."

While she rubbed my arm to soothe me, it occurred to me that if the one and only child of the dead Mr. Joseph Samuel were gone, she might decide she would be secure to inherit the whole lumber yard. If Mr. Benjamin wasn't around.

She had the Devil in her enough to do it.

Nineteen

A few days after the cookout, Aunt Al informed me that Tommy, Terry, and I were going to the movies, but no one said a thing about a drive-in movie in the boonies! I'd never seen or been in such blackness in all my life. If it wasn't for the headlights of Tommy's car, I wouldn't be able to see my hands to scratch my nose. The thickness of the forest is what made it pitch black. Pine trees packed together, running full to the sky, until only patches of crystals were left glinting in the darkness above me.

It was getting a little spooky in the backseat alone; I almost climbed up front with them. But I couldn't live with them calling me scaredy-cat for the rest of my days, so I started chatting away about anything that came to the top of my head.

"You guys failed to mention how Daniel, the boy with one arm, got that way. Was he born without that part of his arm or what?" I squeezed my elbows between the front bucket seats and onto the console, wiggling until I got comfortable, resting my chin on the heels of my hands.

"A bear ate it." Terry answered as casual as brushing his teeth.

"Come again?" I thought he was pulling my leg.

"That's it...right there is where it happened." Tommy pointed across Terry's chest, driving with one hand on the wheel. As the car light swerved across the trees I saw a dirt path as wide as Jean's fat butt, and then it was gone.

"Yep, Mr. Rainwater used to go out at night to wrestle bears."

"Wrestle bears!" I said, with a dubious look on my face— which was out of sight from my dubious cousins. I popped up straight in the backseat, then scooted right back between them.

"Yeah, Lizbeth. Black bears live out here in the woods," Tommy exclaimed, as if I was the one talking crazy!

"I know that, but that wasn't the part I was talking about. It's the wrestling the bears part, that I don't believe." I know I'm the city gal, but not a stupid one. "What does Daniel's dad do besides wrestling bears?"

"Nothing...he's dead. That dirt road we passed a minute ago, that's where the last bear he wrestled killed and ate him!" Tommy said.

My mouth perched open slightly. Joseph Rainwater, half Cherokee, half Negro—all crazy. The father of four boys and two girls with his Negro wife Naomi. They lived by reasonable means with forty acres of farmland and a barn of horses as wild as he. It dawned on me that Mrs. Rainwater was the one that sold her beautiful soaps and teas at Mr. Jake's store. He couldn't keep enough on the shelf for all the orders, thank goodness.

"Mr. Rainwater was determined, on his son's soul, that Cousin Bear would fulfill his family destiny. Cousin Bear's fur, thick and black, would be his once again, as it had been, bringing bounty and blessings." Terry spoke as though he was telling a Grimm's fairy tale.

"It's not funny, you guys!" I hit Terry on his shoulder.

"On that cold, damp night, Mr. Rainwater walked the trail of his ancestors to meet the Black Bear. Wrestle with his cousin as his nation had done lifetimes before him. But this night, he brought Daniel, as he was the oldest boy. As they sat by the fire, the smoke billowed high, radiating in warmth and protection. He chanted. A chant that was not familiar to young Daniel. Fear fell to the soles of his feet when his father spoke." Tommy said, trying to scare the life out of me. He did a good job.

"*You now, are the man of our family, son.*'

"*But father!*' Daniel answered.

"At that moment the Black Bear made his appearance to them. I know it's true," said Tommy. "I made Daniel show me the spot.

"On its hind legs it ROARED! Roared to summon the earth and the sky to this place, moment and time. The beast showed itself through the thickets of bush to my cousin, our cousin Rainwater. The roar quaked the earth and all that surrounded them!" Terry added.

"*I am here brother!*' cried Rainwater." Terry about scared me to death when he boomed out this part of the story.

"The beast roared once again, and then thrashed his paw against the face of Rainwater, ripping his head clean off, leaving the stump of his neck. Daniel stood there motionless as it devoured his father whole right before his eyes."

"Daniel had been instructed by his father to stand still by the fire no matter what he saw.

"*Receive the fate of the kinship,*' Rainwater had warned Daniel.

"But he did not listen. Mad with fright and angry as hell, he attacked the black bear, standing tall with only a burning stick in his hand," continued Tommy.

Raising his arm up to the roof with an imaginary torch, Tommy nearly killed us swerving the car into the edge of a ditch, ramming into a well-camouflaged hump to get back onto the road.

"Just like that, the bear snatched his arm off just before the root of his elbow! Left him with that stump to remind him who's who. At least, that's what Daniel told me."

If this story was true, my tears were well worth the payment. If it were false, I cursed those who laughed at me while I shed them.

Poor Daniel. No mere mortal woman would ever want him.

***

I'd never been so glad to plant my feet on solid ground as when we arrived at the drive-in. Even if it included the crunch of popcorn beneath them. Still swaying from the thought of blood and body parts flying through the air, by a bear no less, I nearly wretched a few times inhaling the buttery fumes.

"What do you want to eat, Lizbeth? A hot dog? Oh, a chili hot dog with hot peppers, onions and cheese! Yeah, I'll take three of those!" Tommy was rubbing his hands together in delight.

"I'll take a Coke for now. I need to settle my stomach."

"From what? My driving wasn't that bad!" said Tommy.

"Oh I know, poor little city girl couldn't take the story of Rainwater having his arm torn off!" said Terry. They laughed belly hard at me for a minute while I tried to get my bearings straight.

"Well, I bet I could tell you something that could make you sick."

"What?" They looked at me like I was a weak kitten.

"I saw the body of Mr. Samuel after the accident on the

bridge." Not exactly true, but a little white lie shouldn't keep me from heaven. Just to be sure, I'd remember to ask for forgiveness the next Sunday.

First their eyes popped out of their sockets in shock, and then drew back into their heads, until they were slits of embarrassing disbelief.

"There's no way you saw that, Lizbeth. Why you gonna' tell a tale like that?" questioned Tommy.

I started to feel my oats when I saw the near-fright on their smart faces.

But then I saw *him*. His brown leather shoe cocked on the silver rear bumper of his truck. Laughing out loud. The center of attention, surrounded by men, but mostly women, buzzing to be a part of him: Mr. Benjamin. For a second I thought he saw me, between his flirting and flicking a kernel of popcorn into his mouth. He did it with such ease, barely settling the yellow puff on his thumb then—vanishing into his mouth.

Did he just wink at me?

I felt my hand boldly waving back, high into the air. While in reality I barely lifted my elbow, slightly shifting my hand back and forth.

"Who you wavin' at, Liz?" Tommy looked about the crowd. "Oh, you sweet on Mr. Benjamin, aren't you?" He laughed.

"No way. It's just *hi!*" I shot back.

"Don't worry, Cuz, you're not the only girl that's fallin' for him. Quit your drooling, and let's get those hot dogs!"

I punched him in the arm for teasing me as he walked off.

I wondered which one was *his* girlfriend?

"Come on, Lizbeth!" Tommy shouted.

"Comin'." I got stuck on Miss Violet and Mr. Benjamin that night on the bridge. Her fighting him like mad as he tried to console her, her finally giving up, easing back into his arms like a rag doll. Obviously he cared deeply for his sister-in-law and her loss. Miss Violet had already told me that, in her own way.

I took two steps toward Mr. Benjamin and his fan club. "Hey there, Mr. Benjamin. Do you remember me? I'm…"

"Hey, Lizbeth, come on over here. 'Course I remember you!"

He shooed his fans away like flies hovering over an apple pie, all except one woman. He introduced her as Maylene. Maylene was the tallest black woman I'd ever seen. She was taller than Mr. Benjamin by a good couple of inches or so. Her face, not the prettiest in the world, but jeez, her body had round parts and curves that made me uncomfortable. Her clothes had to be homemade. Nothing in the Sears catalog would ever fit that woman.

"Baby, I'm hungry," she moaned, then batted her eyelashes at Mr. Benjamin.

"Sure baby, here you go. Oh, and get Lizbeth a…?"

"No thanks, I'm fine." I hoped Tommy got me that Coke I asked for.

Mr. Benjamin handed her few a dollars, then she shoved them deep into the V of her red-dressed bosom. She licked her lips fully in preparation to plant a kiss on his lips. A shiver went through me when she did. As she rocked her hips, side to side like a giraffe in the heat of the Sahara, she finally left us heading toward the snack booths.

"So whatcha been up to, Lizbeth?" he asked.

"Hmm, I saw Miss Violet the other day at my auntie's house. She was, you know, kind of sad." I looked him dead in the eye to see what he was thinking. The happiness seemed to evaporate right through the top of his head from my words. What cruelty had I come up with now? He put his hand lightly upon my shoulder, then eked out a sullen smile.

"At least I know she's in good hands with you and Miss Alice. I've called her a few times. She doesn't say a word other than hello, all the rest is her breathing. I guess I'm too close a reminder for her. I beg her to talk to me, shout at me, curse me, but nothing. She says nothing. I heard something once. I pressed the phone hard to my ear and squeezed my eyes shut. Then—there…there it was again! Like a kitchen faucet that wasn't shut tight enough, a drop. A tear that dived into a black hole of the phone." He held his lips with his hand.

"I loved my brother, but when he married her, I loved him even more for that. Might say that he was loved more than a man could possibly deserve, but nothing compared to the love of Emma." He went into his shirt pocket and showed me a picture of his deceased niece. The photographer had her propped up in the center of a field of fake spring flowers, wearing the same popcorn sweater she had drowned in.

"Baby, do you think you could give me a couple mo' dollars for a bottle of Schlitz? That cheep beer isn't good for my intestines, you know."

"Sure thing, baby." He shoved the picture back into his shirt pocket before she was upon him with her hand out.

What was there left to say? "Good night, Mr. Benjamin, I better go catch up to my cousins before the movie starts."

"Good night, Lizbeth," he said. The woman coiled her arm through his and gave me a look as I walked away.

Twenty

A few days away from my home-away-from-home took me out of my routine, but a trip to the lumber yard with Auntie would fix me right up. Mr. Benjamin would be there; at least I was hoping he would be.

"Auntie, what do you think of Mr. Benjamin?"

"What do you mean?" Smiling at me with something curious in her eyes.

"Does he date a lot of ladies?" I looked out the kitchen window as if this conversation meant little to me.

"Maybe you should ask him yourself. You'll get to see him soon enough!"

She tried to pinch back a giggle, but I caught her. Darn it!

"I saw him last night with the tallest woman I'd ever seen." Auntie looked like she was about to bust.

"Really, where? At the drive-in?"

"Yes, Auntie. Even a little too tall for Mr. Benjamin, if you ask me. Maybe he would prefer someone like Miss Violet, or maybe someone like her?"

She looked me up and down, and then turned back to drying the dishes.

I wore my finest play outfit. But I must admit, I did feel a little uncomfortable wearing it. Miss Violet wouldn't be caught dead strolling down to the lumber yard wearing this. Dungaree shorts and a red, white, and blue-patch halter top. There was just enough plumpness to my breasts to notice them, but they were still too small to fill the cups. My aunt looked me up and down as we hit the screen door.

"Where are you going?" she asked.

"With you to the lumber yard! Remember, you asked me! You wanted me to make sure that you didn't get carried away in ordering stuff you need for the house."

"Oh yes, I remember. It's just that I became a little confused by the sassy outfit you're wearing. Are you going someplace else that I don't know about?" She tilted her head like a pup with a question on his mind.

"Nope, just going with you to the lumber yard as far as I know, Auntie." I contemplated on running up stairs and changing my clothes, but there wasn't enough time to do that now.

"Let's go then."

I followed behind her to let the door stammer shut. I felt big drops of perspiration drip down from the pits of my arms, causing my arm to stick to my side. Though I had deodorant on, I covertly took a whiff of myself to be sure.

The smell of fresh cut wood hit my nostrils before the sawdust hit the tires. I loved that smell. Nothing could go wrong with that smell. Sweet and raw. Pungent and fresh. As alluring as the salty spray of a sea breeze. I rolled my window down and stuck my head out like a dog with his tongue lapping at air.

Auntie was able to park in her usual spot without driving

around forever. That was a good sign. We might not have to share Mr. Benjamin's time with other customers.

"Hey there, Miss Alice, Miss Elizabeth!"

Working already.

"Benjamin. How you doin', honey? I got a plate ready for you at the table when you come around."

"I know, Miss Alice, but if I ate every single plate that a woman offered me, I'll be as big as a barn in a week!"

They laughed a little, and I laughed too much. I had no idea what they were laughing about.

"So what is it that you all need today?"

I stood there between them with my wrists crossed behind my back. Tommy told me that I looked quite grown-up when I stood like that.

"Franklin finally agreed to build us a car garage." She pulled out a tangled piece of lined paper from her pocketbook with sketches on it, then handed it to him.

I followed them inside the office building, which was humming with an air conditioner and several ceiling fans strategically placed. So I would wait, forever if need be, for Auntie to do her business while I, in the luxury of a wooden swivel chair, kept my eyes glued to Mr. Benjamin's every movement.

"So, Miss Elizabeth, how has your summer been so far here in Ahoskie? You raised quite a stir at the basketball tournament. The only woman that played, and the only one to score. Must have been something special. I'm sorry I missed it. I had some housekeeping to do." His eyes softened, breaking away from our gaze. "I had to get some things together for the service tonight. Thank God it's finally happening. There's just no excuse, holding things up like that. No excuse…" His voice trailed off at the end.

Thank goodness his phone rang. I swear I was about to cry for him.

"Hello, Samuel's Lumber Yard, Ben— Oh." He tried to whisper into the receiver. "I'm telling you for the last time, I am not going to give or sell you half the interest in the yard. Not now, not ever. Have a good day!"

Bang went the phone.

"I'm sorry about that ladies, but that…! Lord have mercy!"

Elbows resting on his desk, he ran his fingers through his hair in anguish.

"Anyway, I didn't get the chance to ask you last night, but did you ever get to meet my brother, Joseph?" he said.

I shook my head.

"He would have liked you. I know he would of." He stood to open the curtains to let the sun bounce into the dark room. There was *a sadness* about him, aside from the obvious deaths of his family. Something that I couldn't quite understand. He tried to hide it, but he couldn't do that, not from me. I wanted him to be happy. It suddenly came to me that maybe if he visited Miss Violet, he might get himself to feeling better. Maybe now she would be able to share her pain with him. But then again, maybe never. Maybe his face reminded her too much of Mr. Joseph.

As he walked us back to the Dart, like any gentleman would, he shut my aunt's door as we said our good-byes. But something came over me.

"I've been searching for Mr. Samuel's penny!" *Was I out of my mind?*

His face would have bleached white if it wasn't so golden brown.

"I'm sorry Mr. Benjamin, but I… just want to help find out what happened!" I dropped my head in shame of my big mouth.

"No, Miss Elizabeth, don't feel bad." He leaned his head against the frame of my aunt's empty car window. "I appreciate you trying to help. But the medical examiner says it was just a terrible accident, I think it's best that we just move on," he stated bravely.

"Well we can all appreciate that, Benjamin. You need anything, you call me. You hear?" Aunt Alice clenched the steering wheel and turned the key to the engine.

"Yes sir, Mr. Benjamin, you hear?" I said as I waved from the car window.

We may have been twenty feet out of the driveway.

"What in the world were you thinking, Elizabeth, when you said that?"

I couldn't answer her, since I really didn't know.

One thing about Ahoskie, I didn't have to wait in line over the swing like I would in New York. A major fight could break out over who had nexts on a prime swing. Meaning, not hitched lopsided over the pole, broken chain, or a seat so worn that the plastic cut into your legs.

Lena and I were on the prime swings at the baseball park that afternoon when I saw this boy coming across the road with a fishing pole and a bucket. A couple of kids ran up to him to see what was in it. Ooooos and ahaaahs came from each mouth as they peeked into the tin hole.

"Who's that?" I shouted to the swinger beside me.

"That's Dean. He goes fishin' just about every single day. Rain or shine. Light or dark." She popped a bubble from her pink gum, which splattered from her nose to her chin like fresh paint.

Graciously, like the kings' servant, he did a promenade through the swing park to show off his catch.

Finally his parade came my way. The girl next to me on the swing, the one with the dusty legs and half braided hair, did all the introductions.

"Dean, this here is...what's your name again?"

"Lizbeth. I'm living down here with my Aunt Alice and Uncle Frank Roosevelt." I put my hand out to shake his. I felt a little silly with my hand hanging out there, waiting for him to wipe his bucket hand with his jeans.

"My name is Dean Major Jenkins. I fish wherever there are fish, and I'm darn good at it!" As soon as we shook hands he lifted his bucket to show me the proof. I was waiting to see only enough water in there to keep them floppin' around fresh like dead men waiting for execution. But no, he had as much water as they needed to swim around happy until they were supper. Fried or otherwise. Maybe that's why the fish liked him so much?

"I guess that's why I haven't seen you around since I've been in Ahoskie." I looked him in the eye since I could tell he was younger than me. "But I think I heard about you."

"When was that?" he frowned.

"Around the time of the Samuel accident on the bridge a few weeks ago. Remember?" I kept on swinging with my toes dragging through the dirt, ready for him to move on to the next admirer.

His head dropped to his chest as if to check on his fish in the bucket, but I knew better. "What'd you see?" I asked.

"Just the car go into the river. I had to hurry up and get home for supper. But I would have helped, if I could."

"I'm sure you would," I said. "You sure you didn't see anything else?"

"Sheriff told me not to say nothin'."

"So you did see something!"

"Maybe. I yelled out, but whoever it was didn't seem to hear me. Just ran away through the fields."

We said nothing for a moment.

"How long are you going to be staying?" he asked.

"The rest of the summer, along with my little sister here."

He nodded at her. "Maybe I'll see you around, Lizbeth. Go fishing with me sometime?"

"Sure thing, Dean." I jumped off the swing and headed home as he continued with his parade.

Twenty-one

Swinging at the park really got my craving going for barbeque chips and orange pop so bad, that I started doing all kinds of things to keep my mind off them. Crazy things. Like, I'd chase the baby chicks all around the fenced-in yard until I ran out of breath. Roll down the little hill in the back with Lena, bumping into each other and laughing so hard we'd nearly wet ourselves. Lie on our backs in the sun, closing our eyes until we could see through our thin red eyelids.

"Lizbeth!"

Thank goodness, Auntie needed a bag of cake flour, Crisco, and unsweetened bars of chocolate for the Samuels' service at the church that night.

I would never admit this out loud, but I was looking for a reason to go back to the grocery store. I couldn't tell Auntie, but if I got the wheat penny with the bump on Lincoln's nose at the store, I planned to tell Sheriff Bigly about it, and about Miss Violet.

As many times as I'd been to the grocery store, this was the first time that I noticed a small faded black-and-white photo behind the counter. It sat way back, swinging back and forth on the thin nail of a tack. I only noticed it now because Mr.

Jake wasn't standing there as usual, and the breeze from the door shook it. The black was fading to brown, and the white an ugly tan. From what I could see, it was Mr. Jake and some white woman. She was a pretty woman. Dark, long, wavy hair. She had both her arms wrapped around his neck and a heel kicked up behind her, with a smile as wide as a waxing crescent moon. I couldn't stop staring at it. I wasn't surprised by the fact that she was white; it was the smiling that she did. And he did, too! But who was she?

"What do you want today, gal?" Mr. Jake about scared the white off my teeth.

"I, I…"

"If you don't have nothin' better to do than to stare at my shelves, maybe you need to get on home!"

"I need a bag of cake flour, Crisco, and unsweetened chocolate for my auntie!" I could feel the heat rise through my face.

"And what's that in your hand?" He pointed.

I had an orange pop and the chips clenched in one hand, with five single dollars rolled up in the sweaty fist in the other. I fought back the tears that begged me to release them. I slammed my money on the counter. Before I knew what was happening, Mr. Jake had my auntie's grocery list on the counter looking at me. Swiftly, he packed the brown bag and handed me the change. I must have stood there too long pouting at him.

"Go on, then!" he said, thrashing a hand toward the door and that darn bell.

I ran out of the store and bumped into that stinky Willy Fingers. That white boy who'd been stealing Mr. Jake blind. A scrawny raggedy, smelly, thieving white boy who this time dropped two cans of creamed corn to the porch when I bumped into him. We both watched the cans roll down the street like crazy firecrackers on the Fourth of July. I half expected a whole chicken to fall out from underneath his pants.

"You stinky thief! If I was white, I could steal too. But I don't. If I was white, maybe Mr. Jake would treat me right, too. But he don't and he won't. Because I'm a Negro!"

I leaped onto my bike with tears already racing me home. I looked back at him, expecting him to be sticking his tongue out at me, but he didn't. He just stood there with his arms sagging by his side. I almost ran into a meter staring back too long. I looked back again pumping harder. Still, nothing from him.

But all that I could feel was hate. Angry, fitful hate. Fighting until its arms were weak from the beating it gave me.

I hated how white folks hated me.

I didn't like hating anyone.

What I hated most, was how it made me feel.

I flung myself onto my bed when I got home. I screamed hard and loud into my pillow so that no one could hear me.

The service for Mr. Samuel and Emma was scheduled for six o'clock at the Christ the King Church. Auntie said that we could wear what was comfortable, as long as it wasn't shorts or jeans. No air conditioning was allowed on weekday-evening events. Church funds had to be spared in trade for smelly bodies.

When I stepped through the opened doors that flanked me, a natural hush came upon me. The lights were dimmed so low that it would have been hard to see the red cushions on the benches but for the multitude of white candles. Candles of every size were everywhere, glowing an easy warmth throughout the congregation. It was beautiful, yet sad. Auntie held my hand while Uncle Frank towed Lena along. I could hear a low hum in the air.

Maybe the angels were singing little Emma to sleep on her way to heaven, I thought.

"Auntie…" I whispered. "Do you hear something?" Auntie turned her head to me with confusion. "Oh that, it's the air conditioner."

"But I thought…."

"Yes, me too. But apparently Sister Haney put her foot down on the Board's neck mighty hard. Said she would pay for the extra electricity needed for tonight's service herself. Said that she wasn't about to watch Miss Violet wilt with grief and heat tonight. Bless her soul." Auntie patted me on my leg. I was proud of my decision to wear one of my best dresses tonight for Miss Violet.

***

Pastor Reynolds had given a sermon about the wondrous world in the hereafter for young Emma, leaving the entire congregation gulping in a well of tears. All except McMeanie. She was heading out the door before the rest of us stood up to say our last good-byes. What was she up to? What could be so important to leave in such a hurry without giving her condolences to Miss Violet?

Twenty-two

Dag-gone-it!

The very next day Auntie sent me to the grocery store to get two cans of petite peas. Tried as I may to get out of it, she wouldn't budge. How could she do this to me?

"Please Auntie, don't make me go there ever again. I hate that man, and he hates me!"

"What you gonna do? Ride down to the Piggly Wiggly another two miles away?"

She was right about that. But couldn't she simply drive the Dart, and get the groceries without me going into that store again? Why was she being so…so, stubborn?!

Why didn't she hate him like I did?

Ring, ring!

As Auntie picked up the phone, I headed on out the screen door to ride my bike to the park. Maybe she'd forget about those dumb 'ole peas!

———

God help me, Auntie did not forget, and I had to go to Mr. Jake's store that very afternoon for two cans of petite peas. That damn bell rang like it was hungry for its dinner.

Ring-a-ling, ring-a-ling, ring-a-ling!

I headed straight to the icebox, snatched an orange bottle, for my payment, and then headed for the tower of peas. Around the tower, I hit a dead end at the butcher block and nearly bumped into Miss Violet's behind.

"Excuse me, Miss Violet."

"Lizbeth! I haven't seen you in a while. I was hoping that you would come by again and help me with the packing." She curled her lips in a crimpled smile trying to be brave after last night.

"Sure, Miss Violet. I'll come by tomorrow afternoon." I bent my head down as to not look Mr. Jake in the eye behind the butcher block. I waited by the counter with the cans of peas and the pop by the register.

Here he comes.

I put a dollar down and waited for my brown bag and change.

He gave them to me without a word. I snatched the bag and stomped my way out the door. Lord, I couldn't believe it was over, but that's all it was. My blood seethed with anger.

I ran to my bike and dropped the bag into the basket before me. My back twitched for some unknown reason, a second or so, though I tried to ignore it, my eyes shot up to find three white boys surrounding me. Big boys like they were in high school. I recognized one of them.

"That's a nice bike!" the stupid-looking one yelled at me, the one I recognized. He was the son of one of Aunt Al's tenth-grade math teachers, Mrs. Yarnell. She came over one day to discuss school business for next fall, and for a slice of Auntie's lemon meringue pie.

"I need a bike like that. Mine is gettin' fixed right now, and I need somethin' to replace it. I think that this bike will do me just fine. Don't you, boys?" he said. They nodded their heads like donkeys.

I didn't say a word. I just sat there on the purple and silver sparkled banana seat. My feet naturally lifted to get on their way, but he jumped in front of me, holding the handlebars still while I wobbled off the seat of my bike.

"You ain't going nowhere with *my* bike!" he said.

Thank God my blood was already steaming from Mr. Jake. Now it was coming to a full fury.

"This is my bike!" I said. The other two boys crept up closer to me. If Tommy and Terry were there I bet they wouldn't have been so brave. But they weren't.

The fat boy shoved my shoulder several times, until I fell off my bike to the dirt. I got up strong, but I wasn't sure if I could do this. My eyes searched for a black someone to help me. Not a soul in sight.

"This is my bike!" I screamed.

"I like this bike and it's mine now!" He straddled my banana seat like he was a king.

"It's mine!" I cried.

"I don't think so," another dirty face said. "This is a nice bike. Where would a Negra get money for a bike like this?"

"My mom and dad!" My gut burned in rage that I even answered him.

They laughed and hooted out loud like the stupid fools they were.

"What's your name, Negra?"

"The Queen of Sheba!" I shouted.

They laughed a little until the dummies realized I was being smart.

"I tell you what, Queenie, I like this bike and I'm gonna keep it."

"No you're not! This is my bike!" I cried. I took one step forward to claim my property when the double-chinned fat boy shoved me in my chest. The sandy dirt kicked up a little into my throat, causing me to choke for a minute. My tears streaked a trail down my face. Defeated in round one, I decided I had nothing to lose. If it was a fight they wanted, by God… that's what I would give them.

"HEY!" someone shouted from behind me. I didn't recognize the voice, but it didn't matter as long as I was getting enough time to gather up some courage or someone to help.

Click.

That sound caught everyone's attention. Necks turned toward the grocery porch like cranes.

There stood Mr. Jake—with a shotgun in his hands!

"Elizabeth?" he shouted.

I heard him, but it took me a moment to speak.

"Elizabeth!"

"Yeah?"

"You all right?"

I cleared my throat "Yes, sir, Mr. Jake."

"Come on up here then!" He swung the nose of his rifle toward the porch to emphasize *here.*

There I stood. Too stunned to understand what was happening. He clearly wasn't one for waiting on interpretation.

"Elizabeth, did you hear me?" He was panting hard. You could tell by the rifle moving up and down, with the butt of it bound to his side.

"Yes, sir, I'm coming!"

At that moment, I was blown wide open. I didn't care about my bike. No, the bike wasn't it at all.

Mr. Jake had called me by my name, Elizabeth. He'd never addressed me as nothing better than *gal*, and not in a familiar way.

Before I could get a foot on the steps, I heard my bike fall to the ground with a *clank*. The fat-headed boy was now standing over my bike, shaking like one of the giant dryers at the Mat. Clearly he was not about to take my bike now, but I was now concerned with him peeing on it, since a wet streak was running fast from his crotch down the side of his leg.

"Hey!" I hollered. I felt Mr. Jake grab me by the shoulder from behind with one hand, with the rifle cradled in the other.

"Get away from her bike, boy, before you piss on it!" he said.

The fat-headed boy scampered away, bumping into the boy that had shoved me to the ground.

"We…we was just foolin', Mr. Jake. We weren't gonna really take her bike." The other two mealy mouthed boys agreed in the background.

"I'll tell you boys what. You're not comin' nowhere near this store for the next two weeks." Mr. Jake paused for a second and looked at me.

What did I do now?

"And you are never to bother this…Elizabeth…again! You hear me? Now go on home while I call your parents! Run now, see if you can tell them before I do!"

I stood there frozen; seemed like forever I watched those boys scurrying down the street. The fat one ran so hard that he tripped and landed on his big belly. When he was finally able to roll himself off the ground, he started whimpering like a baby trying to catch up with the others.

But I didn't care about them; I just didn't know what to do with myself.

I started to cry.

"Come on inside," a gentle voice said. Mr. Jake opened the screen door and led me inside the grocery store.

I don't remember hearing the bell ring, though I know she did.

Behind the counter was a wooden chair with a green velvet cushion. He sat me down in it.

A line had formed by now at the counter with no complaints. Miss Hattie was ready to be rung up, but Mr. Jake held up his hand as if asking her to wait a minute. By now my tears were flowing freely down my face. I hiccupped on the ones I tried to force down my throat, trying to suppress a full blown cry.

He came back around the counter with an ice cold orange pop already opened with a damp tissue in the other hand.

"You sit here for a while and watch the store for me, okay?" he said.

I managed to nod my head.

He went on about his business ringing up Miss Hattie and the other customers, not saying a word other than the usual. I sat by his side, barely able to see above the counter, sipping my favorite soda.

By the time Miss Violet came up to the register, I had settled down some. She placed her basket on the counter only to drop her eyes dead on me.

"You're a brave one, Elizabeth," she said, as if she really meant it. That was a first for her to call me by my birth name. I wondered if she knew what that meant to me.

"I don't know if I was really the brave one, Miss Violet. Mr. Jake." I stopped to see what I could read off Mr. Jake's face. He continued to bag the groceries, but he flashed a glance at me, then Miss Violet.

"Mr. Jake is the real brave one. I just stood there screaming at them...that I was the Queen of Sheba."

Miss Violet giggled at me.

"And that was just enough to make them think twice before messing with you. All I did was let them know that you meant it." He smiled. Sweet Jesus, Mr. Jake smiled. My giddiness made me lose all control of my senses.

"That was the greatest thing I've ever seen Mr. Jake, ever! The way you pointed at them with your gun, well what else could they do but be so scared as to pee in their pants! Almost peed on my bike, that big fat pig! And you told him to get away from my bike before he did. You're the best ever!" There, I'd done it! Having blown all the pride that I had left within me, I wanted to melt away deep into that green cushion.

"Thanks, Elizabeth, but I suspect if it weren't for you, I wouldn't have been so brave. Your parents must be some kind of great people."

I nearly died when he said this, although it was true.

"Well I think both of you were mighty brave," said Miss Violet. She went down into her purse and pulled out two nicely folded squares of tissue paper, one blue, the other pink. "The two of you have been so kind to me, I've been meaning to give you both something. It's nothing much, but it's what I do best."

She handed the pink square to me and the blue to Mr. Jake. He and I looked at each other with sweet surprise, if there were such a thing for him. He unwrapped his first, a pure white handkerchief stitched with bold capital letters, J.M., in midnight blue in one quarter of the hankie. Perfect dots of the same color bordered the edges of the square, with small brown ones in between the pattern. The beauty of his cotton piece excited me to hurry up and open my own.

I had expected that my initials would be glorified in pink, the handkerchief trimmed in pink polka dots. Yes, it was what I had expected, stitched to perfection, but there was not a dot on the border of the cotton square. Instead, tiny red roses with a green stems were delicately sewn in a soft wave around the edges. They blossomed here and there in the creases of the letters. I'd never seen such magic made with needle and thread before.

"I better go now, the line is getting long." She took the change from his hand, and then hurried it into her purse. "And Elizabeth, *you* are one to be admired." Then she was gone.

Before either of us could manage to say a word, the door chided us.

Ring-a-ling, ring-a-ling, ring-a-ling!

We folded our little gifts back up into the pretty-smelling paper as best we could in order to replay the moment over and over again later, when we were all alone.

After a while I got fidgety sitting there, so Mr. Jake sent me about the store to get a bag of flour or whatever for customers at the register. Surprisingly enough, I knew just about where everything was.

Before long it was six o' clock, time to close up. Mr. Jake had called my auntie to let her know where I was. As he was putting the meats away in cold storage, I took it upon myself to put away the dry goods. I watched him hang up his apron, stained brown here and there from the meat, then shut the lights off in the back. I was a bit nervous, not about being alone with him, but about the events of the day.

I wondered if Mr. Jake would go back to being hateful to me again. But how could he after the handkerchiefs that Miss Violet had made for us?

And what did I think of him now, after he'd seen me cry like that, and then letting me sit in his chair with an orange pop in my hands he'd given to me?

Back behind the register, he counted the money, placing the bulk of it in a black bank bag, along with all the change. The balance of it he shoved in his front pants pocket, then rested a few dollars on the counter.

He slid them toward me. "Ask your Aunt Alice, if it is okay with her, that I see you here at nine a.m. Monday morning."

I looked at the money, and then looked back at him. For the first time since we'd met, right square into his bright blue-green eyes. I slid the few dollars back toward him.

"I really owe you for today, Mr. Jake. You can start paying me next week."

He put his hand out to me. I took a deep breath and we shook on the deal, me grinning from ear to ear. I swear I saw him smile back.

"I'll see you Monday morning!" he said.

I could barely remember riding my bike home that evening. People were honking, shouting *hey* at me from their cars. Did they know what had happened today at the grocery? I stood high on my bike peddles, gliding free down Main Street with the wind blowing in my face.

I nearly broke my bike tossing it to the ground, running up to the porch door, busting to tell Aunt Al, Uncle Frank, and Lena what had happened today. Uncle Frank hugged and kissed me then threatened to get those boys himself tomorrow. Lena was still holding my hand as we passed the handkerchief around the kitchen table admiring Miss Violet's craftsmanship.

" Did he pay you?"

"Yes. He called me Elizabeth today!" I answered incredulously.

Auntie nodded at me with pride.

I nodded back, confirming that she was right. She was right about not knowing a person and his story, about judging him by the words of others rather than to judge the man by his actions. I found myself feeling ashamed to have suspected Mr. Jake as the man on the bridge. What he'd done for me could never be the action of a man who'd do harm to another. I sat on the porch dreaming how it would be Monday.

Ring-a-ling, Ring-a-ling

The bell would greet me in the morning.

Twenty-three

Uncle Frank has a sweet tooth that's always craving; it's hard to imagine how he's kept his real teeth this long. As he passed us servings of chocolate cream pie, I noticed Auntie was not nearly as cheerful as the rest of us.

"So what are we having for dinner, Auntie?"

"Oh, I suspect something special for you. It'll take all night, but if it's fried chicken, macaroni 'n' cheese, with cabbage and golden potatoes on the side that you desire, I'll get to cooking it right now." She smiled and caressed my cheek with her hard hands.

"Listen here, Lizbeth, you are not to work at Mr. Jake's this late anymore unless I say so, okay?"

"Sure, Auntie. But is something else wrong? Did I do something wrong?"

"No, Lizbeth. It's just that, well, I didn't want to scare you, but the medical examiner had to change the death of the Samuels to murder because of the bullet Sheriff Bigly found in the bridge. That's why the service had to be postponed until he had the chance to reexamine the bodies. I don't like what that means."

"Auntie, it'll be okay. I'll be okay." I leaned away from her warm body to look up to her face. She patted my hand and went to work on my special dinner without a word.

If you've never been to a Southern Baptist church, you're missing a pure sight. It smells and feels even better after a hard rain, when the sun comes out full and bright. You can sense the freshness of the world through every pore of your body, shivering full of hope, faith in man, and all the glory you can fit in your heart. The glow of the stained glass windows excites you before entering its doors. A full acre of the whitest gravel you've ever seen against the backdrop of a tremendous white steeple church and a fan of pine trees stretched across the world without end.

But hold on, it takes preparations to worship here on a Sunday.

Up at eight-thirty in the morning for a ten o'clock service, I headed for the kitchen for breakfast (a big one). Uncle Frank had already bathed and was in his favorite navy blue robe. He had a fat cigar in his mouth that wasn't lit. It was Sunday, after all! Smothering the morning paper in his left hand, while shoveling fresh eggs and sausage into his mouth with the right, he asked for an extra link of sausage or two to keep him going when he prayed.

"I can't ask God to forgive me if I don't have the strength to do the asking!"

He wasn't paying too much attention to his grits that formed hard and cold from loneliness on his plate, so Lena and I used this as an excuse to tickle him. There was nothing more painfully fun to our Uncle than to tickle him around his sides and armpits. He'd squeal like a girl getting her hair braided for the first time.

"No, no stop it girls, stop it!" He gasped for air in between the laughter. "Okay, okay, what do you want from your old Uncle Frank to stop?"

Lena and I looked at each other for a hard second.

"Ice cream!" we shouted in unison, but we kept on tickling him until he said…

"Yes, yes!"

"Right after church?" Lena demanded with her little hands wiggling about his side.

"Yes, yes, yes, just please stop…tickling me!" he cried.

Satisfied that we had accomplished our goal and some, we sat down to finish our breakfast.

"Don't you go changing your mind, Uncle Frank, or else!" Lena wiggled her fingers at him.

"I won't! I promise!" He broke into his hard grits nervously.

Aunt Al was fluent in what Lena and I liked: pancakes! All day, all night, her pancakes. As big as your head and as fluffy as a pillow. I should know; every now and then I'd chewed on mine the night before dreaming about them. We downed the gooey fluffiness until our bellies ached.

But the scrumptious meal had come to an end. It was time to get dressed.

———

I had brought only two dresses here from New York (Lena had oodles but still found her way into mine), along with my shiniest black patent-leather shoes and matching pocketbook. A dab of Vaseline, with only weekend wear, would keep them looking fresh for quite a while, but my aunt had decided that I needed two more dresses in my closet to last the summer. Just like that, she got me two new dresses: one light green with daisies for trim; the other peach with spaghetti straps.

Three months, and four dresses for each month. Thus by the next month, the first one would seem brand new to everyone.

"Oh, look at you, Missy Elizabeth! You look so pretty and all. Where'd you get that dress from? I bet it's one of those dresses you brought down here from New York. Huh?" That was the general question I got every Sunday.

What'd I tell you?

———

By the time the Dart crackled its way onto the white gravel, parking positions were already set. The first one there usually set the tone. And this was usually Deacon Jones. His burgundy Cadillac was not to be mistaken for any other. With its cream interior and roll-down top, there wasn't another in the county like it, maybe even in all of North Carolina. He was the one who opened the church doors, set out the offering plates, and stacked the programs.

We always arrived at the right time to see all the hats collapse through the front door of the church with all their glory. Amazingly beautiful hats. All colors, shapes, and sizes. Crowns of Glory. Some on the verge of ridiculous, if they'd asked me. But glorious just the same.

As bold as ten peacock feathers perched on top, to a simple crown of baby's breath peeking about the rim. Every color the mind hadn't imagined and then some. Made to order at Linda's Hair & What Not or purchased out of the Sears & Roebuck catalog. It was a majestic parade of pride. All that they'd lived through and seen—the joy and the pain, the sun and the rain.

Even as a slave, if a woman could weave a straw hat together, gather up some fresh flowers or a simple ribbon, she would wear such a hat with great pride. Why? Because the Bible told them so. It commanded that women cover their heads while worshipping in the house of the Lord. Imagine a field slave, fingers swollen and raw from picking cotton from sun up to sun down, so painful, but she hardly even notices because she'd just given birth to a baby in the barn late last night. A soft rag tied between her legs. But for tomorrow, Sunday the day of rest, she will wash one of her two garments in hot water and pig lye, making her hands burn like her skin would roll off into the tub. Then set her straw hat beside it for worship tomorrow. Admire it until she fell asleep.

No wonder the women wept before entering the church doors.

You could touch the energy, if you were brave enough to stretch out your hand to God. And although I was not brave enough, the pumping and the thumping of the choir willed me into thinking I could. The more the choir shouted, the more the flock cried aloud. I looked to the ceiling to make sure of my escape if the roof were to collapse upon me. Not that God would allow such a thing smack-dab in the middle of service, but men constructed His house, not the other way around!

"Lord, Jesus!" many shouted.

"Yesss Lord, take me!"

I didn't like the way that sounded.

Praying.

"I shall not want!"

"You might not believe in the Devil, but he believes in you!" Scared me to death for the first Sunday or so. The Reverend kept on shouting and stomping, jitterbugging on a Holy Roller coaster ride. Sweat poured down his face, as he uselessly tried to dab it away.

Before long he had the entire congregation flying high in frenzy.

Higher! Higher! Higher!

Until the energy erupted, with women weeping, babies crying, and sinners praying *in tongue*. Cripples passed their canes to the center aisle to be tossed at the foot of the pulpit like kindling for fire. Grown men in suits standing up with their hands waving in the air.

The radiant face of Jesus fanning back and forth in the hands of women whose underarms flapped like chicken necks to the rhythm.

Folks rocking, soothing themselves like babies. Someone shouted, "Yes, Jesus!" because the *Spirit's* not ready to let them go. The Deacons unlocked the stained glass windows with long poles from up high to let in some fresh air—all they could do to keep someone from passing out.

It wasn't quick enough, though, for the heavy woman with the purple shiny hat. She fainted to the red carpet floor, while her scrawny husband valiantly tried to hold her up by her mountainous girth to revive her.

Of course, when she woke up she hit him with her matching purse because he wrinkled her dress.

I cheated! And I've been cheating since my very first step into that church. I'd been dragging myself there in body, but not in spirit. Not in my soul. But today was different.

I didn't have to coax my heart into bearing the hours of mouthing hymns and fainting women.

I wanted to be there.

I wanted to thank God for my family, my relatives, my friends, and my life. And thank Him for Mr. Jake not hating me anymore. And that maybe, I was wrong about him hating me at all. And, oh yeah…that white lie I told Tommy and Terry.

———

Then it came to what I call the meat of the service—the sermon. Reverend Reynolds had a voice that rumbled through the church with the strength to tip the benches to the floor. But today, when he slowed down to come to the end of the service, he added a prayer.

"And for those who missed the funeral service for our beloved Joseph Samuel and his daughter Emma Samuel, we ask that you pray in silence for their journey to our Lord. Amen."

I shut my eyes tight, feeling the tears fighting to escape. I opened them just long enough to check on Miss Violet. Much to my surprise, her eyes were open, directed at the stained-glass window of Jesus on the cross high above the head of the Reverend. At that very moment, I'd swear the golden light of Jesus beamed through his face and onto hers.

A knowing smile creased her cheeks, while my tears made their getaway.

———

The passing of the offering plate always seemed to sneak up on me. Just when I started to relax my bones and flesh, a slow thump of music would begin. The thumping was the Deans and Deaconesses taking each step in unison like zombies. Coming to take your money. All dressed in white nurse-like uniforms with long white gloves to hold the gold plate.

Thump-thump, thump-thump.

You could feel them coming closer, see the plates being passed down the aisle from one person to the other. Some digging for bills and envelopes stuffed with money; some like me, a couple of embarrassing coins and a dollar bill. I dug through my patent-leather purse like I was digging for China. As the plate reached Aunt Alice, amidst the rustle of paper and the jingle of change resonating about the church, it struck me.

Maybe the penny is in here!

It had to be done.

But how was I going to do this?

When the plate finally came to me, I tossed my dollar bill into the plate, and leaned over Uncle Frank's arms to check the pennies. My eyes searched wildly while I flipped the coins on their back. God forgive me, but Uncle Frank started to realize what I was doing.

"Are you tryin' to check the plate for pennies, girl?" He chuckled at me.

"Yes," I said, a little louder than I wanted to over the shouting spirits in front of us.

"Then why don't you volunteer to count the offering today in the basement?" He smiled at me as I held his enormous shoulders in gratitude.

When the plates were collected and the prayers were said, down went the offering to the church basement to be counted. In the meantime, my Uncle Frank gathered me up and took me downstairs with the volunteers, who already had their latex gloves on to count today's offerings, and explained that I collected pennies. I was introduced to Deacon Jones, who admitted that he would be grateful for the helping hands. Deacon Jones sat me down at the edge of a table with a bucket of coins and some empty buckets. Once I had my gloves on I was off like a racehorse out of the block. I gorged my hand with coins, flipping the denominations into separate buckets, while spying only the brown ones.

I continued like this until I heard Deacon Jones say to me, "Whoa there, gal!" as he was wiping down the plates.

"Yes, sir?"

"You sure count those pennies mighty fast there. I know you young people are smart and all but…well, you go ahead then if you know what's best." He smiled and gave me an easy nod to continue if I pleased.

But he was right, I hadn't counted one coin. What I had not noticed was the coin counter on the table beside me. So I dumped all the pennies back into the original bucket to be counted. I sheepishly turned my neck to see Deacon Jones, still wiping the plates, but with a telling grin on his face.

It was the longest Sunday ever, but I will never forget it.

Still no penny.

———

Two hours of sweating and praying and counting coins, the doors finally broke open to the world outside. The buoyant laughter floated above us all, and when it burst like confetti, it sprinkled throughout the sky, lightly sweetening our faces like newfound joy. If this feeling could last forever, if it could find its way everywhere on Earth, there would never be a war again.

But then along came Miss Melanie Neely, McMeanie herself, to step on it. I hadn't noticed before, but McMeanie had unruly eyebrows. They curled up like armadillo worms, twisted white curls of hair across her brow. The ends turned up like a handlebar mustache. Obviously, she'd never heard of tweezers before. Her red taffeta hat rested too low on her forehead against her bushy eyebrows, making her resemble a Russian soldier lost in the Carolinas.

"Miss Alice, Franklin, girls. You all look nice this Sunday morning. Is there an occasion?" she smirked. Lena made a face at her, making me yank her hand to stop immediately. Not too hard, though, since I wanted to do the same.

"No occasion, Miss Melanie. We just try our best...as I'm sure you do... but we make do with what we have." My auntie looked her up and down, addressed her like she was wearing a potato sack. McMeanie's bottom lip buckled right up to her nose in anger. She walked away in a huff, nearly knocking folks over in her path in search of some other poor souls to harass.

The sun was beaming hot, and after the ice cream cones that Uncle Frank had promised, Lena and I wanted to dive head-first into a that running pool of cool water.

"Oh come on, Uncle Frank, it's so hot outside and these dresses got us itching something terrible!" Lena whined.

"You just had a gallon of ice cream, how you gonna float with all that cream in your bellies?"

We tickled him in the belly for that.

"Okay, okay girls. You win. You can go to the river, *if* you have at least one of your cousins with you. Deal?" He stuck his thick fair-skinned mitt at us to strike the deal solid.

"Done!" I cried.

"One more thing, Uncle Frank. Can Margaret come with us?" Lena looked to me for permission, as did Uncle Frank.

"I surely don't mind, Uncle Frank; it'll keep her out of my hair."

"Done!" shouted Lena.

Both Terry and Tommy came around that afternoon to swim with us down by the river. I heard them *beep-beep* in front of the house. Ready to go, I made it to Tommy's car before Lena was even dressed.

"Lena!" I shouted as she finally ran out the door. "What are you doing with one of my best outfits on?" Here she came with my red halter top and matching plaid shorts over her bikini. "What did I tell you about wearing my new outfits?" I hollered.

She had enough sense to crawl over Terry, and squeeze herself between him and Tommy in order for me not to commit my own murder!

"You wore this one already…what difference does it make if I wear it now? It's not like it's ever gonna' be new again." She smirked at me then turned back around facing the road ahead.

"You're gonna' be sorry for that, Miss Lena." I said as I yanked one of her braids.

The river was as cool as a watermelon lifted straight from a bucket of melting ice. Aunt Alice had bundled up a basket of goodies to hold us until dinnertime. My stomach was feeling somewhat heavy, so I let up on the fried chicken wings to take a swim with Lena. I'd been swimming on a recreation team for the past six months, having the skill to breaststroke very well.

A sip of the clear water sucked to the back of my mouth upon every other stroke. My toes, nipped by the hungry baby trout, flit upon strings of grass along the way. When I was just about my height deep into the river, I decided to float on my back so I could soak in the sun. The warmth on my face mingled deliciously with the cool splashing about my body. After a few minutes or so, I finally felt secure enough to shut my eyes…slowly…while the sun still blazed through my eyelids. Taking in the fresh warm air to the last threaded extent of my lungs, then blowing it out slowly through my nose, keeping me steady on my back.

I smiled just enough to keep my balance.

"HELP! HELP ME!" someone cried.

It was Lena. But I had heard her holler that phrase a thousand times before, especially when Tommy splashed water in her face. So I ignored her, to concentrate on my sunny bliss.

"HELLLL..!" The shout ended abruptly with gurgles. That didn't sound like fun anymore.

I flipped over so quickly that I nearly swallowed the entire river up in one gulp. As I got my footing on the mushy river bed, I rubbed my eyes to clear the water. Another scream made my head snap towards the bank.

"LIZBETH!" Now Margaret was screaming my name, jumping and pointing frantically from the riverbank.

Lena's very small hands splashed the water about wildly. When she gasped for air, I could see the fear on her face. Her terrified eyes straining to find help; her hands clawed for anything to grab on to. Then down she went again with the tip of her nose last to sink. My mind crazily thought of what I would tell Mom and Dad if she died.

It was my fault.

I'm sorry God please forgive me for freezing.

You can punish me every day, and I'll cry too! Because I want to.

Because I wouldn't deserve to be happy ever again.

"SWIM LENA! SWIM!" I screamed. She knew how to swim. What was wrong?

"Tommy, somebody, help!" cried Margaret.

I knew that they were too far down the river to get to her before I could, so I had to try...alone.

Like Lena, I started flapping my arms through the water in an attempt to reach her. Kind of a cross between a walking zombie and a fish out of water.

"I CAN'T! I'M STUCK! HELP ME!" she gurgled.

Just as I was about to reach her, under she went again!

"LENA!" I screamed at the water.

I was still standing on my tippy-toes when I reached her, so why couldn't she swim? I sucked a breath and dove down toward where I last saw her.

The water, though clear on top, was not so down at the bottom. I could see a thick blob, which was Lena, but something was holding her back. I shot up like a rocket from fear of what I could not see and fear of letting myself drown. Almost hyperventilating, I dove back into the murky water again. This time with my mind set on getting her out.

Her body was still putting up a fight, yet weak and heavy, like sopping wet rags. My eyes burned from dirt and God knows what else, besides tears in the ready. But I dug deeper beyond my natural fear to set her free.

When I reached her I felt a bump, hard and big against my leg. I nearly choked from shock.

What could this be?

Then I saw the branches and vines entangling Lena's leg. It was a tree that had fallen some time or another into the river. It's upper branches had split, evolving into treacherous daggers beneath the calm plane.

I pulled her leg as best I could, but got a handful of nothing except slippery leaves and the steady seep of blood swirling with the water.

I had to come up for air again. "*Gasp!*"

I knew Lena would not make it if she didn't have the

strength to steal a breath, so I shoved her up upon my shoulder, just high enough for her face to break through the water.

"Hughhh," was all she could get out before descending again. Now she was becoming too weary to try.

I dove down again and saw that her ankle was caught between two wrist-thick limbs. One of which had a two-inch stump dug deep into Lena's leg. The only way to get her out was to rip her out. What else could I do?

I had little air left in me, but I knew there was no time to spare for Lena's life. I had to do it! I had to! So I pulled.

I pulled Lena's leg so hard that I yelled out, choking on the river with her. Blood weaved its way like a saucy swirl of strawberry, thick into the mushy darkness of moss. I thought I saw her neck jerk back in pain. At least I hoped that's what I saw. I took hold of her leg and pulled again, this time anchoring my foot against the fallen tree. More blood, more ripping of the flesh…I imagined the sound to be horrible. The tissue floating away lifelessly from my sister's body.

But I had to keep pulling until…

Suddenly a muffled *pop* and her leg was free. I was able to hold her limp body in my arms, keeping her bobbing head from dipping too low beneath the surface. By the time I'd dragged us two steps toward the shore, Tommy was splashing to our aid. He caused a heave of water to sweep up around her like a tunnel, which seemed to lift her up from the water and drag her into the shore. Upon letting go of her I immediately felt the lead in my legs. I tried to keep up behind Tommy but I couldn't.

When I finally dragged myself to the beach, Terry had already begun to pump her chest. Tommy started to blow life into her small mouth. I stood there, waiting for the pink beads knotted to her bikini top to move from her breath. It dawned on me that the bathing suit she was wearing under-neath *my* new outfit was also mine. Normally I would have fussed at Lena for going into my clothes, but this time it just didn't matter. I only wanted her to live and come back to me, like my Lena.

It was so very hot that within seconds my skin was almost dry, but I was shaking violently. My teeth chattered as if I wore a frozen overcoat. The pain begged me to move about, but I didn't have the energy to move.

I could hear Terry swearing something as he pumped Lena's chest, but I couldn't understand what he was saying.

Maybe the water was still sloshing between my ears.

Maybe all the blood in my body had clotted like jelly in the drums.

Maybe I didn't want to hear that Lena was dead. God forgive me, but I wanted to open her hand. I wanted to see if that penny was clutched in it, ready to take her away from me.

Just as I was about to pounce on her hand to see, Tommy gave her a blow that caused a spurt of water to gush free from her mouth. More followed, with coughing, near choking.

"Lena!" I dropped to my knees. As I held her face in my hands, I could feel the crinkle of a smile in her cheeks. I squeezed her tight into my chest, probably too tight as she began to cough again.

"Liz," she said weakly. She started to whimper as I held her.

"It's okay now, Lena. Just rest." I shook her a bit too hard, unintentionally, trying to hush her fears. Tommy was busy wrapping her leg, so it was my job to keep her distracted from seeing the tower of bloody swim towels beside us.

At that moment Aunt Alice and Uncle Frank arrived, thinking that they would surprise us with a cookout. What a surprise. They descended upon her, and with all of their whooping and shouting, Lena didn't have a chance to see a thing—but I did.

I crept around the back of their hovering bodies to get a good look at her leg.

It couldn't be but so bad…could it? I prayed in my head.

My fingers picked at the sloppy bloody towel wrapped around her leg to get a good look. The sight of the wound almost made me vomit. A long jagged gouge, from the top of her ankle for another eight inches, oozed blood and torn flesh meshed like a crazy painting I'd seen once at the museum. Thick like oil paint, but with the smell of a creature's flesh in the air. I toddled back on my butt to catch myself before fainting.

Clear from Lena's view, I backed my way to the shore to wash her blood from me. My chest cinched up like lead when I found it difficult to clean my red-stained hands. What was I thinking? Blood is thicker than water. I wanted to scream, but I couldn't—rather I knew that I shouldn't. If Lena heard me hollering like a fool it would scare her even more, so I clenched my teeth and swallowed it down hard, let it sit there in my throat to melt away.

I steadied myself to hold her hand, to comfort her, as Uncle Frank placed her in the backseat of the Dart. Trying to find a home with a phone to call an ambulance would take too long and put Lena in greater danger.

"It's going to be okay now, Lena," I said as Auntie began to slide into the backseat beside her.

"What? I'm her big sister. I'm going to ride with her too!" No one said a word. Not Auntie, not Uncle Frank, not Tommy or Terry.

"I'm sorry. I promise she will be alright when we get her to the hospital." Auntie's smile curled up into a frown, fretting me even more.

"I have the right to be with her! Me! I'm her sister!" I demanded. Angry tears, frightened tears whipping about my face as my voice got louder. I'd lost control, that scream began to bubble up from my throat below. Next thing I knew, Terry and Tommy were holding me back and shoving me into their car. I kicked and screamed like a banshee for them to let me go and be with Lena.

"Oh, Dear God," I said over and over to myself.

Tommy and Terry held me up on either side. Normally I would have sat in the backseat, but this time they sandwiched me into the middle in the front with them. Tommy holding my hand tightly as he carefully turned the steering wheel, across the lumpy grass to follow them. I clenched my fingers with Terry's entwined, in praying position without even knowing it.

"She's going to be fine, right?"

No one said a word.

Twenty-four

At the Ahoskie General Hospital, there was this black man sitting next to me with a fish hook clean through the flesh of his left thumb. I knew this because he'd check it every once in a while, removing a bloody bandage that was as thick as a woman's pad from it.

"Mr. Jenkins, Mr. Jenkins, you're next!" A Negro nurse from behind the counter shouted, never looking up to see his condition. She made him stand there for more than a minute before acknowledging that he was even there. I didn't like that. Not one bit. He reminded me of the boy who loved fishing every day. The one who saw Mr. Joseph's car go over the bridge. Funny how this made my blood boil. We're supposed to at least respect each other, even if the white man doesn't!

He was just an ordinary working man, mind you, but still someone enjoying the simple pleasure of the *plop* when the weighted bait hit the water. He didn't deserve that.

Caught up in the hook gouged in the man's finger, I didn't notice the doctor approaching to talk to my aunt and uncle until they startled me by rumbling the bench as they jumped up from their seat. They crowded around him, as if they would understand his words better if they were closer to his nose.

Deaf but able to read his lips. On the other hand, Mom was a nurse and I did understand a little more mumbo-jumbo than most of the kids and even adults in my neighborhood. So I leaned in to make out what the doctor was saying.

"What does that mean?" my Uncle Frank gruffed at the doctor.

"It means that she's okay, but she may have a slight limp for the rest of her life," I stated matter-of-factly, finding myself standing in the midst of the grown-up powwow.

They peered at me as if to say, *Mind your own business or did we ask you?* But then those words washed away from their faces as they realized: it *is* her business and Lena *is* her sister, thus she does need to be included.

As we started to walk down the hall to Lena's room, the woman who was rude to the fish-hooked man stopped us.

"'Cuse me, but I don't think she's old enough to visit the patient?" She peeped at us from above her black framed glasses.

Aunt Al and Uncle Frank stopped stock-still and faced the nurse behind her desk. Auntie nodded at the woman and all three of us continued on our way down the hall.

When we reached Lena's room, we peeped through the small rectangular chicken-wired glass window before knocking on the door. Though the sun shined brightly outside, the room was gloomy. The lights were dimmed low beside her bed. Lena was still asleep, as the doctor had warned us. We entered and stood beside her bed close together, like sardines in a can. Huddled together in hope that the intensity of our presence would pry her eyes open.

We waited. We sat down beside her and waited some more.

And I waited, as long as I could. Then:

"Lena," I hushed to her. "Lena." This time my voice grew with impatience as I nudged her arm.

"Lizbeth!" my auntie said in a quiet shout.

Still groggy, Lena moaned and turned to our shadowed faces.

"Lena," I whispered. This time she blinked her eyes.

"Hey, baby sister. How are you feelin'?" I gently scooted beside her on the bed, cautious not to move her leg. She flinched in anticipation anyway.

"It doesn't feel too bad. I just feel really, really, sleepy. I'm sorry."

I held her hand gently in mine. "Why?" I half expected that she'd say she was sorry for wearing my bathing suit instead of hers. But that was fine by me, unbeknown to her.

"I fell into the river. But then someone…someone wouldn't let me up! I started swinging my elbows…"

I tried to hold her tight like Mr. Benjamin had held Miss Violet, until she became calm. I could already feel the bruises rising on my arms from her sharp elbows.

"Shhhhh, it's alright, Lena. It was an old fallen tree, that's all. Now shhhhh." I continued to rock her in my arms until she collapsed. Then gently laid her back to the pillow.

Evening came along with a call from Mom and Dad. Although Mom had spoken to the doctor not five minutes after putting Lena to sleep, she still wanted the late evening edition of what was happening from my aunt. After fifteen minutes, the phone was handed to me.

"Lizbeth!" She sounded happy to hear from me.

"Mom?" Shoot.

"Hi Peanut, how are you?"

"I'm good, Mom. Are you going to talk to Lena tonight?" Please, please get off the phone! "Mom, I'm sorry about what happened to Lena! I didn't mean for her to get hurt. I was just swimming for a second when…." I started to whimper into the phone.

"Honey, I just wanted to know if you were okay. I'm so sorry that happened to you."

"To me?" What was she talking about? I didn't get hurt.

"Yes, sweetie, you had to see that and be the mom in my place. I'm so sorry. I love you. Is there anything you need?"

"No, Mom. This is just fine, talking to you."

We talked another ten minutes or so until she had me laughing with tales of Aunt Al and her sisters. Though even as I put the receiver down, I could feel the same numbness come over me.

As the days grew on, so did Lena's bravery. Released from the hospital, she passed her time between bunking with Wise potato chip crumbs and trying to walk. She was given a set of crutches, which made her underarms too sore to bother walking sometimes. So she fell into the habit of using just one crutch with a giant sponge Uncle Frank taped on the top. It was kind of fun watching her hop like mad trying to get away from me and Uncle Frank, the "new tickle monsters." She'd tire easily enough, though. Drop to the floor, even if a seat was arm's length away, just like a puppet that'd had its strings cut.

I always sat beside her wherever she landed.

"Let's see what's on the 'Wide World of Sports'!" I suggested a few days after she came home.

Lena and I were sports nuts, especially when it came to the Olympics. You couldn't tear us away from our blankets on the floor, dead center in front of the TV, cheering for the USA track and field team, no matter male or female, black or white. Sports seemed to make us forget about that stuff, and made us all Americans.

"Wait, wait, Lizbeth, get some chips and lemonade while you're at it." She rubbed her hands together with glee.

"Good idea, I don't want to get up in the middle of the show and miss anything."

I beelined it to the only cabinet that kept the chips. "Yesss, Barbeque." I grabbed the bag and nearly ran by the refrigerator in my excitement, forgetting the fresh pitcher of lemonade.

"Hurry Lizbeth! What's takin' you so long?"

"You've got some nerve, Hop-a-long Cassidy." I poured two blue plastic cups just short of the rim. I took a sip off the top of one so it wouldn't spill on the way back. With my hands full and the chip bag clenched between my teeth, I could have carried a book on top of my head and not spilled a drop.

Made it.

Lena and I hooped and hollered for nearly an hour before they finally got to the track and field games of the Olympics, and then the announcer said they were going to show an introduction. We eased back against the front of the sofa, hoping that we weren't going to be bored to tears with this "brief program."

"Here we are folks at the beautiful Olympic Games in Mexico, October 16, 1968..." stated the announcer.

We leaned away from the sofa, engrossed with the replay of the two hundred-meter race, featuring two of our finest athletes. Once again we cheered for America's first and third place winners. Though this was four years ago, I felt my heart begin to sink in fear, same as it did that first time, watching them take their place upon the podium. The first and third place winners were shoeless, with black socks. As our nation's anthem continued, they raised their arms high above them, their fists covered with black gloves. I was so proud, but I knew in my heart, they would pay dearly for their solidarity.

"If I win, I am an American, not a black man. But if I did something, bad, then they would say I am a Negro. We are black and we are proud of being black. Black America will understand what we did tonight."

Tommie Smith, American Olympian

A Coca-Cola commercial interrupted, allowing us to regain our breath.

I felt something tickling my open palm. Little fingers had found their way into my hand. I grasped them to smother them in mine. Lena started to well up, trembling hard to hold it back. I knew what she was trying to say.

"I know… it's hard sometimes, but I will always be there for you…you big bean-head!" I gave her a smile of promise. We stared at each other, holding hands, until the commercial ended.

Twenty-five

I didn't know so many folks gave a darn about Lena or even knew who she was. Visitors came cutting through our carpet daily for at least a week or so, bringing all kinds of gifts. Of course, there were the typical flowers and boxes of assorted chocolate candy, or the homemade yellow cake with white frosting and coconut flakes. Some went so far as to bring the whole meal for that evening.

I was a little picky about my eating and where it came from, and rightfully so. Take for instance, Mrs. Lacey. People swore that her cooking was so good, you wanted to kiss her momma for bringing her into this world. But I was deterred from making such a commotion over her cooking on account of her love for cats. She loved cats so much that she had about ten of them that she could count. Some may have lived outdoors all their nine lives, living wild, tearing mice apart. The rest lounged around her house leisurely, squatting where ever their slinky hairy bodies wanted.

This particular day I had to pick up a recipe for my aunt to try out on the numerous visitors. Mrs. Lacey's home was nothing to comment about. Weeds sprouting between the brick walkway, spots of the lawn with grass about as high as a hen. And the smell—a couple of cats were prowling along the porch, meowing like they were warning me not to take a step closer for fear I'd die from the ammonia.

I decided that they knew best.

"Mrs. Lacey! Mrs. Lacey! It's Lizbeth. I've come to pick up the recipe for my Aunt Alice?"

The screen door screeched and a white-haired woman waddled out to get a better look at me.

"Well, Howdy! Whatcha doin' out there, sweet pea? Come on up here, them cats ain't gonna bother you. Half of them gots no teeth to bite with!" She laughed at herself. I didn't think she was so funny.

"No thanks, Ma'am, I'll wait here if you don't mind."

"Why? You scared of cats? They won't scratch you or nothin'."

I know...they don't have any teeth!

"I know that Mrs. Lacey, I'm just a little allergic to them, the hair and all."

"It ain't the hair that does it to you, it's the dander, sweetie. Their skin. Your eyes water, your throat gets tight and itchy. Lord, that must be maddening!"

I don't care what it is because I'm not allergic to cats. I'm just allergic to coming inside your house with that stinky smell!

She walked back into her house feeling sorry for me. A few moments later she returned to the screen door with something in her hand. I couldn't make out what it was. Did she hear me right? I expected a pink card or a lined piece of paper with measurements on it. But this looked fuzzy. Good gracious, is she handing me a mouse?

Bundles of unruly cats and kittens, and whatever sizes there were in between came running out of the house behind her. Flying out of the door, jumping cross and over each other like robbers in a jailbreak! For every step she took toward me, I took a bigger one back.

"Well, what you doing there, sweetness? All these cats here are mine, you know. They won't hurt you none!"

"Okay. But what's that in your hand, Mrs. Lacey? I think they want it." I pointed to her.

"Oh girl, this here is the recipe your Aunt Alice wanted! They don't want none of this!" she cackled. Then she licked her other thumb, and started to stroke the thing in her fist. As the fuzz started to peel off, the thumb became coated like it was one of the kittens nipping at the hem of her dress. Ughhh!

She finished.

"This is the card, sweetie, don't you want it?" Sure enough, when I was able to control my intestine, I saw that it was a white card. "Why don't you come in for some cake and lemonade?"

Like I said, I never ate anything that Mrs. Lacey made… or her cats! So I politely declined.

———

When I got home, there was another visitor in our driveway. The green car looked familiar.

Oh, jeez o' peas, I thought. As if Mrs. Lacey and her hairy recipe card in my basket wasn't enough. McMeanie was here!

In my short life of experiences, I'd found that sneaking up on the grown folks when they're talking is best. You can't just bust in on them, otherwise they're bound to choke on whatever's in their mouths, gagging for air and coughing out every piece of whatever they were chewing on clear across the room.

So I rode my bike around to the back of the house on the soft grass. A little harder to peddle through, mind you, but not a soul can hear you coming. I would have usually dropped my bike where I stood, but the jangle would stir up an ear, so I placed it on the grass like a blanket. I crept up to the kitchen window and stood on a pipe that came up from the earth and into the wall of the house to listen. The balls of my toes wobbled trying not to fall down, making it hard for me to peep.

Not a sound from the kitchen. I peeked over the ledge of the window to make sure no one was there standing quiet in the refrigerator door. All clear.

I jumped down from the pipe to the ground, making a small squeak from my sneakers.

I opened the screen door so quickly, I almost fell back from the jerk of the knob. Across the linoleum floor I tipped-toed, through the swinging door, then into the dining room.

Two sets of feet came pounding down the steps behind my back. Scared me to pieces.

"I'm sure she'll be fine one day." I could tell McMeanie's irritating voice from anywhere.

"She's fine *now*, just needs to rest and let that wound heal." I could tell that Aunt Al was taking a seat in her favorite chair in the living room. McMeanie would have sat in it first, knowing that it was my aunt's favorite, but she was left to sit on the couch closest to the door.

"Yes, but that's a nasty, nasty wound, Alice. If infection gets in there, why, she could lose part of her leg. Maybe all of it!" Nasty shrugged her shoulders. If she could have a say in it, the worst would happen.

I saw Auntie's face drop. Her bottom lip buckled into her top preparing to speak. I could see the darkness sweep over the pure blue sky. Auntie's shoulders curled up and started to shake. A rumble shook the earth, rattling the dishes still drying on the plastic stand.

Goodness! Did she just do that?

A curtain pulled back from the sky, releasing sheets of rain to pour over all of Ahoskie. Streams of reddish clay veined their way, bubbling through the grass. Foams of water rushed in streams while picking up stranded branches, causing a surfer's dream to roll down the street.

"Auntie?"

Before I knew it, I had stepped into the middle of the living room. They looked at me like I was buck-naked.

"Help me get some of these windows shut, Lizbeth!" Not skipping a beat.

This was the first, and would be the last time I would ever feel sorry for McMeanie. She watched us scurry about the room like chickens with our heads cut off. She didn't lift a finger, other than to help herself to the tray of pecan turtles on the coffee table.

Lightning crackled and split the thick purple-gray sky in two. Though the rain was starting to drift, the boom of the lightning continued to strike with full force. Thunder shattered.

I was scared beyond the frightful weather. I feared that my aunt conjured it up from her anger.

"I think I better go now, before the roads get so bad that I can't get home to my man. We're having a special dinner tonight at a Japanese restaurant—probably something sizzling like duck. Oh, I almost forgot. It seems we have something in common, Miss Lizbeth. I collect pennies. So do you. Isn't that what you told me?"

I didn't know what to think. Did she know about *the* penny? Would McMeanie be willing to give it to me for one of my legs?

"Yes Mc...ma'am." I stuttered.

"What do you think of these?" She dug into her brown pocketbook to show me a small matching change purse. She shook it to tantalize me with the jingle, causing me to salivate like one of Pavlov's dogs. She pulled out my hand, and poured the purse's contents into my palm. I couldn't have imagined this, so I knew it was real. Every penny that I could see was a wheat penny! At least ten were posing on the beach of my palm. Showing off their bronzed tans and ignoring Lincoln like he was a nobody. I shuffled a few here and there to check the year and markings.

Hurry, I thought. *No, not this one. Just one more…*

My face must have said it all. Suddenly she snatched the pennies from my hand, causing one to fall, Lincoln's face up, smack dab on Aunt Alice's carpet.

I stopped breathing in preparation to dive for the one on the floor. But the demon was quick; she kicked it across the floor to Auntie's feet. Slowly Auntie bent over to retrieve the battered penny. How she kept her eyes on McMeanie while lifting the coin from the floor, I don't know. McMeanie knew that she dared not try that stunt on Auntie, or consider losing *her* leg. Auntie stood up slowly, extending her hand toward me.

This might be the penny!

But Auntie sidestepped me and handed the coin to McMeanie.

"You can't bargain with the Devil without losing more than you could ever afford." Auntie placed the lone penny in the cup of McMeanie's hand. McMeanie popped it into the change purse to hide amongst the others. Then she snapped it shut.

"I just wanted to show you something that's rare and fine. You have to understand, not everyone is meant to have these things." She grinned as she stood up and prepared herself to go out into the turbulence. "Now look what you've done, you've kept me too long! Good evening and good luck to little Lena."

As she walked out the door she glanced over to the heavy

stone vase that held the umbrellas. Naturally, she helped herself to the most beautiful one, the one that my mom brought back from St. Thomas as a gift to her sister.

Plucked it like she was picking the best flower out of the garden.

"I'll get it back to you, Alice, as soon as I can."

I knew she had no intention of doing any such thing.

"Sure Mel, sure you will." Aunt Alice stood at the screen door, too calm for me, as McMeanie popped the umbrella open on the porch. Never looking back to give a glance of thank you, she trotted out from underneath the shelter of the house toward her car. I sank into the opposite frame of the door from Auntie, watching the Devil take and never give in return as usual.

"It's not right, Auntie, she's so, so mean…." At an instant, a clap of lightning thundered so loud that I lost my train of thought.

BOOM!

Then it hit. Right before our eyes.

Lightning had struck McMeanie!

The silver bolt hit the point of the umbrella and rammed its way straight through her. She collapsed onto the soggy ground like the dead tree in the river. We stood there for too many moments shocked in our shoes.

I must have shifted like I was about to run out after her.

"Don't you dare go out there Elizabeth!" Auntie grabbed me by the arm, trying to pull me away from the door, but I was too quick for her to keep hold of me.

Auntie must have though that was going to risk my life to help McMeanie.

I broke free from her grasp, running frantically, nearly falling facedown into the slick grass before getting ten steps from the porch step.

"Elizabeth Parrot Landers!" My aunt screamed as another bolt of lightning crashed in the sky, too close for comfort. "Get away from her!"

Not before I did one thing.

I tripped on the grass and slid right up to McMeanie's nose. Her purse gaped open wide beside her. I flapped about wildly in the wet grass to get around her, grabbing for the object of my desire.

"I got it!" I cried, tightening my fingers around the handle of the umbrella.

I didn't open it, though I couldn't imagine that God would strike me dead right then and there, after retrieving my aunt's umbrella from a woman struck by lightning. Wasn't hers to keep anyway.

The closer I got to Auntie's face I could tell that she wanted to slap me upside my head into next week, for pulling such a stunt. She pulled me close to her instead.

Before the ambulance and Sheriff Bigly arrived, my aunt and I did manage to get a blanket for McMeanie. We propped it up like a tent on top of two wood sticks over her body. Just in case.

Good thing, because she wasn't dead!

Nope, McMeanie made it to the hospital in time for them to revive her heart, but not all of her brain. Yes, her once lifeless brain was now not as lifeless. Probably a little better, we hoped.

She had no family to visit her. No real friends who cared enough about her to ask the doctors "what more could be done for her." Nobody to push her around the hospital garden to smell the fresh lilacs from her wheelchair.

Nobody.

Nobody but my Aunt Alice, who God bless her, did just that.

I must admit one thing. While Auntie called the ambulance, and before they arrived, and after the storm had ended, I slipped my fingers into that brown change purse of McMeanie.

Not one penny matched Mr. Samuel's.

Twenty-six

August rolled around, hot and humid. I'd been working at the grocery for almost three weeks. By me being an extra pair of eyes and hands for Mr. Jake, he could take care of the customers at the butcher block, and I was able to handle the register. This way, I was at my leisure to check out all the pennies in the register. It seemed to work out pretty well, especially this particular day.

The bell sang out as usual, to announce that Miss Johnston had arrived, along with the twins she was carrying in her big belly right down to her huge bubbling bottom. She had to turn nearly sideways to get through the front door. She was so big that it took me a thought to believe my eyes had seen another shadow following right along side of her through the threshold. I stretched myself over the counter to follow her with my eyes. Nothing.

Anyway, it was about noon time. That's when it got really busy with the lunch crowd, particularly for Mr. Jake, making all the sandwiches.

"Mr. Jake, how much is this roast beef with horseradish sandwich you made for Mr. Reynolds?" I asked. That's when I saw him. That smelly, dirty, thieving Crawford boy. I'd caught him red-handed stealing a loaf of bread under his arm, and a jar of peanut butter tucked in the front of his grungy pants, just like the chicken he'd stole before.

My back stiffened as that boy's eyes locked into mine. He quick-stepped around Miss Johnston's belly full of twins, like he was dancing on out the door.

"Mr. Jake, Mr. Jake!" I shouted pointing to the thief.

Mr. Jake didn't say a word. Smooth as silk, he came around the block heading toward me. I was pointing frantically across the room, so I didn't quite understand why he was heading my way and not toward the filthy thief. He had to of seen him!

"That'll be a dollar for Mr. Reynolds, Lizbeth!" he answered.

Next thing I knew, he was standing beside me, calm like, counting up the groceries for the Sunday school teacher.

"But Mr. Jake..." I shut my mouth when he raised his hand to me to quiet down.

He thanked the Sunday school teacher, then turned his back to the register and started to count the boxes of Milk Duds on the shelf. My mouth hit the floor hard, as I watched the dirty demon scamper out the door, free as a jailbird, with a loaf of bread and a large jar of peanut butter. And not the cheap kind, either!

"Fifteen," he said. Then scribbling something down on a piece of paper, he handed it to me, and headed back to the butcher block just as calm as before.

It's okay. I'll explain later.

I crammed the piece of paper in my pocket for evidence, just in case Mr. Jake had lost his mind and couldn't remember.

It about tore me apart for the next two hours waiting for him to make time.

Finally he locked the door, turning the *Be right back!* sign to face the street. He took a seat in the green cushioned chair beside me where I stood. He rubbed his hands down his thighs together, as was his habit when he committed to his thoughts.

I waited patiently. There was no sense trying to nudge Mr. Jake along into discussion any sooner than he intended. Not that he'd ever been.

"Elizabeth. Don't you know by now, that things aren't always what they seem to be? There's no such thing as a fair account for every man and his troubles. You work hard and you plant the seeds for the future—yours as well as others you touch. You can only pray that it works out right. Most times it doesn't."

My throat began to thicken, as he'd never spoken to me before like this. Never had four sentences meant so much to me in my short-lived life.

"Listen Lizbeth, let me tell you a story." He thought again for a minute before he spoke again. "My wife had left me some years ago. I wanted children, but as she was more prone to drinking and staying out late at night with…Our arguments became the usual, rather than the unusual. I thought I was a good man, reliable, worked hard, didn't drink much, and never chased women. But, to her, I was not a good husband. I came home one day late from the grocery expecting to find her in bed, sleeping off the night before. What I found was a nicely made bed, with fresh sheets and flowers on the nightstand. I knew she was gone before I even noticed the letter beside the vase."

Tears streamed down my face. He reached out to catch one drop from my chin with a finger.

"That boy that took that bread and peanut butter today? His parents keep a house no better than a pigsty. They spend what little money they have on drinking and God knows what. They've been known to sleep in the motel up the road, because they were too drunk to get home to care for their children. That boy is doing the best he can to feed his siblings. I know that, and he knows that stealing isn't the way. So there's no point in taking his pride away by forcing him to beg. He'll need what little pride he's got left to be a man, a good man. And maybe a good husband to his wife." He paused. "Everyone has a story, it just takes time to tell it."

As he got up from the chair, something came over me that I couldn't fight. I hugged him. Hugged him long and hard.

"Shush now, Elizabeth," he said as he held me. "There's something special inside you. You know it too. Don't let just everybody have a piece of it, you hear?" As he pressed my shoulders back, he rubbed away the last dying tear on my cheek away with his thumb.

"How about an orange pop for the road?" he said.

I managed a crumpled smile for him.

Twenty-seven

Sometimes, when the air would blow down low to the earth, then twirl about the door like a bouquet of butterflies, and the *ring-a-ling* of the bell was warm with sweetness, Miss Violet would appear in the store. I was sure I hadn't imagined this, since it seemed like Mr. Jake sensed the same thing. Though we never talked about her in words, I knew it from the moment I caught his eyes gleam bright when she first stepped through his door.

Grown folks.

They nodded at each other, with their usual "Good Morning" politeness, as Miss Violet continued her stroll down the far left aisle. She couldn't help herself; the draw of the warm sticky sweetness could not be denied. She loved herself some cinnamon buns. Gooey cinnamon buns that Mr. Jake would get up extra early on Saturday mornings for; then drive an hour round-trip to a home bakery in Kokomo. A few times I caught him racing in, nearly sweating to death to make sure he wouldn't miss her.

"Morning, Miss Violet!" I said with an extra something in my voice.

"Good morning to you, Elizabeth. Are you working here full time now?"

"As much as I can, and I'll tell you, those cinnamon buns you love so much, they're piping hot. Know why? Mr. Jake drives to Kokomo and back each morning so that *you* can have them fresh from Mrs. Jenny's oven." I pronounced every word so she would understand that I meant every bit of it, and loud enough that Mr. Jake would hear me. His face turned beat red; I think that meant he heard me.

"Well, not...not just so that I can have them, I'm sure, Lizbeth." She dropped her eyes in hopes that it was true. I was young, but I wasn't stupid.

"As sure as I'm standing here, he would have no talk of not taking the trip, because he knows how much you love him...I mean them!" Ooops.

"That's very nice of you." She turned shyly to catch a look at him.

"Mr. Jake, Miss Violet would like to speak to you about these cinnamon buns for a minute, if you would." Of course he would. How could he ignore the request of a widow? A parent without a child? Black or not? And merely the most beautiful woman that ever set foot in the whole of North Carolina? He couldn't!

Nervously he put the knife down, and cleaned his hands before coming around the butcher block. Thanks goodness he stopped to hang that yucky apron of his up first. No woman wants a man smelling and looking of fresh pork chops and pig feet.

"Miss Violet," he nodded. "Let me get some of those for you first before someone runs off with them." Mr. Jake moved faster than I'd ever seen to get a waxed paper bag. He began to scoop up the big runny frosted rolls with his bare hand.

She tried to help him scoop them up with her hands too.

215

"Oh!" She yelped like a puppy, stung by the hot sticky bun. She involuntarily put the tip of her finger to her mouth.

"I'm sorry about that Miss Violet! Here, set down right over here. Elizabeth!" he shouted. "Go get a cool towel for her hand from the back!"

Gently he guided her to the green cushioned seat.

This man, the one I had thought was the worst creature in the world. A white man who seemed detached from anything that mattered, ached at the sight of seeing this black woman with a painful finger.

I caught myself staring at them from the back door.

I'd never witnessed such compassion between two seemingly strangers.

Strangers? More than that—a white man from the South and a Negro woman from nowhere near except from the same town.

Miles apart yet entwined in all ways that mattered as people.

How could the soul know which one mattered to which?

Mr. Jake caught me peeping through the crack.

He smiled.

I ran to get that cold towel.

Twenty-eight

My Aunt Alice is an amazing woman. After all the nasty, mean, devilish behavior McMeanie had bestowed upon the entire town of Ahoskie, she insisted on dropping by every day to see her since she'd been home from the hospital.

Each day McMeanie seemed to be doing better—at least that's what Auntie thought. I asked her, how could she tell? She said that McMeanie was becoming increasingly ornery each day that passed. Her lips were twisted to the left side of her face, and when she tried to gossip, she seemed to quack like a duck.

Auntie asked me to go with her to McMeanie's to drop off some groceries. I hated the thought of looking at that monster. But I knew if I made too much of a fuss about visiting McMeanie, Auntie would continue to make me go with her.

Before I could beg to stay home, we were knocking on McMeanie's front door.

Concentrate, I told myself.

The slender little hand that reached out for mine belonged to McMeanie's nurse. "Hi there, Miss Alice, and this must be your niece Elizabeth I've heard so much about. Nice to meet you, young lady."

"How are you today, Melanie?" Auntie asked as she stepped into the dining room, which was now the makeshift bedroom. I made myself small behind her, trying to hide from McMeanie's grotesque face. A black silk scarf was wrapped around her head like a turban. Supposedly, the lightning bolt had a burned away a patch of hair about the size of an extra large grapefruit. Her robe was also black, with large white flowers scattered about. She looked like a tiny black bug stuck in a mound of white cotton sheets and pillows. Her nightstand was covered with medicine, nail polish, makeup, and cups with drained tea bags crumpled on a saucer beside them. The mixture of smells nearly made me nauseous.

"I'm just fine," she quacked. I nearly jumped out of my skin at the sound of her voice. An oval mirror was perched like a giant lollipop on her belly, as she tried to trace her lips with bright red lipstick. I had to turn away when she smacked her lips to even out her paint job.

The duck twisted to the mirror to look at her brown bill. *Smack-smack.*

I'd liked to have run out that house like my hair was on fire, but for Auntie being my ride home. Then I saw a knife on the nightstand beside her. It glistened with tiny jewels embedded in the handle made of gold. The knife was too thin and pointy for spreading butter, and had not one notch, making it incapable of cutting a well-cooked string bean.

"Like that don't cha', Miss Lizbeth? I got all kinds of nice things besides a penny or two. It's an Egyptian letter opener. I got it from a mail order catalog. Got real crystals from Egypt in it." She tapped it with her bony fingertips like it was something special.

Ringgggg. Went her phone.

"Excuse me, I have to answer this," she said. She gingerly placed the phone to the side of her face where her lips were least twisted. "A deal is a deal," she quacked. "Wait a minute..." She put her hand over the receiver so that the person on the other end couldn't hear what was being said. "I'm a little tired, ladies, and have some important business to take care of right now. Maybe you could visit me some other time. Hmmmmm?" She nodded to relieve us from our duties. I beat Aunt Alice to the door before she could wave good-bye. I for one had no intention of visiting that woman ever again.

As it was my day off, I followed Aunt Al around the house like a cat begging for attention. If I could have looped a figure eight between her legs, I would have tripped her right to the floor. At the last stop of the day, the hub of the universe, the endless yummy world—the kitchen—I plunked myself down in one of the laminate coral kitchen chairs with a *huff*.

Auntie ignored me and continued to flour and season the pork chops over the sink.

"Maybe you could take care of those beans for me?" she said with her back to me, gazing out the window.

A half bushel of lima beans sat on the center of the kitchen table waiting for me. I pushed my chair away from the table just enough to set the basket between my legs to shuck the beans. Auntie hummed a hymn that we'd sung last Sunday in church while she slapped the chops around. The sun lingered on her ebony face with its glistening hand, while I sat quietly for once.

"It's a beautiful day out there, Miss Lizbeth, so why are you in here following me around?" White clouds of fluff laid still in the blue.

"Hmh." I shrugged A lima bean *clinked* its way down and around the bowl.

Sizzle…sizzles, pop! cried the grease as Auntie laid another chop into the pan.

"Miss Violet and Mr. Jake…I understand why they like each other, but then I don't!" I blurted out.

"What is it that you don't understand Lizbeth?"

"He's white."

"Seems so."

"She's black."

"Got that right." I could feel Auntie's eyes on me now.

"We're not supposed to mix like that…are we?" I kept my eyes on the bowl so she couldn't see me swallow my jealousy.

"Who says so?" She stopped mid slap of a pork chop.

"They say so!" That was the best that I could do on command.

"And who is *they*?"

"Everybody…I guess." I reached down into the basket waiting for a better answer.

"Do you think blacks and whites should mix?"

"Sure." I twisted a little in the chair sticking to my skin.

"Why?"

"People should like…who they like. I don't think it can be helped," I said softly.

"Do you think, if it could be helped, would it be wrong to love someone who is different from you?"

"No."

"Lizbeth, I think you and Mr. Jake had a slow start. You searching for that penny, him still hurting bad in his heart." She stopped for a moment and looked up to the sky, thinking. "Didn't he give you a penny bubble gum for free one day, before he and Miss Violet became friends?"

I hadn't thought about it since then. "Yeah."

"Maybe you're the one that opened his heart in the first place. Maybe without you, he'd never been able to open his to Miss Violet. Maybe you became friends with him first."

"Really, Auntie?" I wanted it to be true.

"The first joy he's had in a long time." She gently placed the last chop into the angry grease.

Hard as I tried, I couldn't contain the smile that spread across my face and the pride growing in my chest.

I popped those beans to Auntie's hymn until the bucket was empty in no time. Jumped out of my chair, took the steps upstairs two at a time, busted into my bedroom, and did a flying leap onto my bed.

Twenty-nine

The only time I went to the bank was with Uncle Frank. We made it a date: every Friday afternoon with the smell of Tate's hot dog special lingering on our clothes. He had a lot of deposits to make today, so I took a seat at the customer service desk inspecting every suspicious face that could have Mr. Samuel's penny in their pocket. It was a silly thought, but it was a fun way to pass the time.

By now it was well into August, and I knew everybody in town. If I didn't know them by name, I knew their face and therefore their family. The same folks came by the bank on this day, at this time, every Friday as always. But today, I heard this woman talking, a voice that wasn't familiar, which made it seem to pierce the air of the spacious bank. I looked up, and she was standing there at the gate of the second teller from the left.

"Oh honey, don't you worry about it. He won't care one bit if you give me a few dollars." She oozed across the counter with persuasion.

The teller wasn't as convinced as she.

"I'm sorry Mrs. Moore.... Oh, excuse me—Miss Lucy. I'm so very sorry!" She pushed her gold wire-framed glasses up her sharp nose, which slid right back down her perspiring slope.

"Don't be sorry, Mizzz..." she searched the teller's chest for her name, "Tatum! I can forgive and I can forget, but I still need that money, sweetie." She giggled too loud for a bank.

She looked familiar to me, but I couldn't see why. Pretty white woman with long dark wavy hair. Big blue eyes! My thoughts went wild, like blind bees buzzing through my brain searching for honey, but they couldn't find any! Until something made me jump out of my comfortable seat and run to my uncle.

"Uncle Frank! Uncle Frank!" I tugged frantically at the frayed sleeve of his greasy shop jumper.

"What girl?" His stumpy cigar waggled while he spoke.

"Who's that woman over there?" I didn't point my finger, but instead used my head to direct him.

He leaned forward a bit, while squinting his eyes as if to make sure he got it right.

"Why glory be, I believe that's Miss Lucy."

"Miss Lucy?" I cupped my mouth to swallow the bark I'd made. "Who's that?" I tried to keep it down to a loud whisper.

"Oh, I'm sorry, Lizbeth. She was long gone before you arrived. I'd say maybe, *hmmmmm*, two, two and a half years ago. Pretty little thing, always was, but..."

"Uncle!"

"Sorry about that. Miss Lucy, as in Mr. Jake's former wife! You know, divorce and all. No kids, just the store. Poor Mr. Jake. We all thought that he'd shrivel up and die after she left him. He wouldn't let anyone near him for the longest. The loss tore him up so bad inside, he didn't eat or sleep for weeks. A puff of air out of a frog's ass could have knocked him over, he was so weak. Even then she wouldn't leave him alone. She'd call and come by for money for her and her new beau when they'd run out. Worthless son of a...awful shame it was."

"Come on, Uncle Frank. We gotta go!" I tugged on his big hand with both of mine, trying to drag him across the floor to the door. I could have tugged at him all day and all night and never budged him an inch unless he wanted me to.

"Where we goin' in such a rush? I was thinking we'd go down to the DQ and get an ice cream or maybe a Blizzard!"

"We don't have time, Uncle Frank!"

"And just where are we going, Lizbeth, that we don't have time for DQ?"

———

I told him where we were going, but not the why. It was just a lot easier and quicker to save the explaining to Uncle Frank for later. Right now I needed to get to Mr. Jake fast. When he reached the steps of the store, he'd barely put his foot on the brakes to park when I bolted out of the car.

"Lizbeth!" he shouted, trying to get his mitts around the seat belt.

"I'll call you, Uncle Frank, if I need a ride home, okay?" I was already running up the steps, near the door before he could answer.

"Call me!" he shouted back.

"Mr. Jake!" I shouted. Then I saw it, the little sign on the door that read *Be right back!*

I banged on the door a good ten minutes before I heard his footsteps inside the store.

"Mr. Jake, Mr. Jake!"

"What in the heck has gotten into you, Lizbeth? And I thought I gave you the day off today?" He dropped a box of Del Monte canned carrots on the counter, then stood before me with his hands on his hips and eyes a blazin'.

"I had to see you!"

"What?"

"I had to warn you!"

"Elizabeth, calm down."

Ring-a-ling, ring-a-ling! So sweet, so fine it sang.

"But Mr. Jake…!"

"Not now, Elizabeth. Hello, can I help you today?" He rubbed his hands together to warm them up from the cold storage room as he headed toward the bell. I watched him. I watched him from beside the tower of peas until his body became a black shadow in the dancing sun light.

A scent of lavender and spice drifted across the room. Had Miss Violet changed her perfume for Mr. Jake? But why? The one of magnolias and wet grass drying in the heat of the day suited her better.

I heard one faint step into the store, then a second.

"Hi, Jake."

He froze in an instant. I ran up beside him, thinking that I would have to catch him before he hit the floor!

"Lucy," he answered quietly.

No, no, no, I shouted in my head. *She doesn't love you, remember? She left you, left you for dead and didn't care. Miss Violet cares. I care!*

"It's been…we know how long it's been. I'd tell you I missed you, if I thought it really mattered. Does it really matter to you Jake?" She took a smooth step toward him, her hand reaching out for his.

I snatched Mr. Jake's hand like I had a right to it!

To my surprise he didn't shake me lose. He just looked at me, and then her. The pressure of his moist hand held mine even tighter.

I knew then, he could not let go. He would never let me go.

"Well, well Jake, who's this little one?" A peculiar smile, twice a mouse's tail, whipped upon her lips. "Oh, I see…maybe the high and mighty Jake Moore had himself some *Negra* one hot winter's night long ago to keep him warm. Funny, I don't see you in her face. Are you sure she's…?"

"Stop it! Why are you here, Lucy? I gave you all you needed, all you wanted and then some." His voice was coarse from scrapping up the long-buried disgust for her in his belly.

"All I wanted? You've never given me all I *really* wanted Jake. If you had, I would never have left you! Would I?"

"You're right, Luce."

"No!" I nearly yanked his arm free from the joint in anger.

"Shhh. Elizabeth." He shook my hand to settle me down. "If I had given you all that you wanted, there would be nothing left of me. Nothing at all. But a form of a man. No flesh, no skin, just dry bones. You'da sucked me dry until there was nothing there. I know that now. I tried, but you got tired of me too fast."

I saw that look in her eye.

"Why you…!" In a flash her hand stretched out to Mr. Jake's face.

I don't know what came over me, and God willing, it won't happen but maybe once more in my life, if the need be, but I caught her wrist just as her fingertips came within inches of his face. He never flinched.

"Mr. Jake is a good man! Better than most! Better than you deserve!" Something was rumbling deep down within me to be able to say that. She jerked her wrist from my hand and prepared herself to lunge for me. But for Mr. Jake grabbing her arms, then shoving her back with enough force for her to land on her ass, she would have torn my face in two. Lucky for her, she was able to claw the countertop to break the fall.

"How dare you…over a…!"

She stopped, then coiled, ready to attack again, checking the range as if she were to spit into his eyes.

"I went to the bank today," she said snidely, with a wicked smile, "and I took your money! I took five hundred dollars of your money and that stupid teller let me have it! I could have taken it all, but I didn't! And maybe, just maybe, I'll come back one day and take all of it. You'll have nothing. Nothing Jacob Eli Moore. And do you know why I didn't leave you dry? Do you?"

He pursed his lips in pain…for her. "Yes, I do. Because you know no matter how much you take from me, it wouldn't make one bit of difference in how I feel about you. I loved you once, but now there's nothing there. You're a bottomless pit, Lucy. Nothing would ever make you happy, except *nothing*. So take it all and be done with me. Please."

He really didn't care anymore. His care was somewhere else.

"Good-bye, Lucy." He dug into his pocket for his beaten brown leather wallet. He handed her a wad of twenty dollar bills.

She snatched the leafy papers from his hands.

She wasn't happy, she wasn't sad, she was just what Mr. Jake had described—pitiful, and she knew it.

Then she walked out the door. She wouldn't be coming back again. I thought

Ring-a-ling, ring-a-ling! went the bells, sounding happy to be free of her.

"Elizabeth, don't you ever do that again!" He shook my arm with such a stir.

"I don't think I'll ever need to, Mr. Jake, so I promise."

A smile wound its way up to the corners of his lips, deliberate like a rusty crank.

"I think you're right," he said.

I smiled back.

"Hey, how about I do some work while I'm here?"

"Nah!" He said. "How about we eat some ice cream?"

We slapped hands and headed for the freezer.

Thirty

I was sweeping up the sawdust from behind the counter, and every other corner when the doorbell rang. White Willy scooted in, seemingly undetected. But before he could slip into one of the aisles, something turned his neck so hard he nearly broke it.

A big brown bag with the name CRAWFORD written on it in black magic marker. He scurried like a squirrel, bumping into folks, scurrying about the floor. For a brief second he turned and faced me.

Our eyes met, then he turned and ran back outside.

I was shaking, but I knew what to do. I picked up the bag and walked it to the door. I stood there, praying that he would come in and get it. I didn't know if he could come back.

He ran down to the bottom steps and turned back again. This time I set the bag on the ledge of the window. He could still see his name, CRAWFORD, clear as day through it.

He turned and ran on away.

"What'd you do to that boy now, Lizbeth?" Mr. Jake snuck up behind me, which made me shudder for a moment in my shoes. He'd only seen Willy come in and then run down the road empty-handed, leaving me standing there like the villain.

"I…I…." I couldn't get it out of my mouth fast enough.

"I thought you understood?" He walked back to the register with disappointment on his face. He hadn't noticed that there was a bag of groceries for the Crawfords on the counter.

I knew that once I explained to him what I had done, he wouldn't be so angry. But then again, maybe he would? Maybe I insulted him by doing this, some kind of white folk mentality that I didn't understand. It didn't matter for now. Mr. Jake was far too busy for me to take his time explaining things.

This went on for a half hour or so before I saw *him* standing at the foot of the steps of the grocery.

Him…was Willy Crawford.

I slowly put down the cleaning rag and headed toward the window. He stood there with his hands in his pockets, face looking down at his holey shoes. I glanced back to see what Mr. Jake was doing. Good, he was busy cuttin' up some pork chops for a customer.

What did I have to do to get Willy to take that bag of groceries?

I'd never spoken to him before. He probably wouldn't believe that the groceries were for him without a trap.

I couldn't go out the door. Mr. Jake wasn't deaf—he'd hear the door bell yappin' and clanging after me, look up, and see what I was up to. He'd see Willy standing outside, melting into his hand-me-down shoes, then holler at me for scaring him to pieces.

What was I going to do?

Defeated, I leaned against the window with my hand.

Knock-knock.

I jerked back to find a round white face with yellow hair looking at me from the porch. It was Willy! I didn't know what to do at first. We just stood there with a glass wall between us. My senses fell through to my hands. I waved to him to come on in.

Ring-a-ling. Ring-a-ling!

I stepped back behind the counter waiting nervously. Those few steps to the counter's end must have been hard, but he did it. I lifted the brown bag.

"Crawford," I said as I handed it to him.

Cautiously, he grasped the rolled-up top of the brown bag with his family name on it. He nodded his head and stepped backwards out the door. All eyes were on him.

Down the steps he went, crabbing backwards, one step at a time. When he made it to the dirt, he stood there for a second. I couldn't believe that he'd made it down without breaking a bone in his body. I walked to the window and waved good-bye.

I guess that was all he needed to know—that it was okay to take the bag of groceries, 'cause then he took off like lightning down the road.

———

At first Mr. Jake didn't seem too pleased with what I'd done. But that wasn't it at all. He just didn't like the fact that I'd spent the little bit of money I'd made to accomplish it.

"You should have told me your plans first." He puffed up his chest like he meant business. "You can give him whatever you want for free from now on, you hear?" Then he walked to the back of the store. I giggled at him, which made him stop dead in his tracks and look over his shoulder at me.

Oops.

He smiled and kept on walking.

Within an hour's time Willy came back, stood on the steps and did something he'd never done before…he waved good-bye to me. I waved back, kind of jittery, hoping he didn't notice the jittery part. He surprised me; he smiled, which made me smile.

For the little bag of groceries we gave him that day, Willy didn't know that he'd paid us in full with the kindness he left in our hearts with that powerful gesture.

It was just about two in the afternoon when Mr. Jake ran into the grocery store. He greeted me, happily as usual, after helping Miss Violet with her groceries and the little chores around her house. I was jovial as usual on the outside, as far as he could tell, but inside, my gut churned. Churned and churned and churned, nearly eating my stomach inside out. There was something I had to know.

"That Miss Violet, she sure is a smart woman. Why, I was telling her about…" Mr. Jake went on and on about her, but I didn't hear a word.

My head hung low as he kept on talking. He knew something was wrong.

"I'm sorry Elizabeth, I've been spending some time with Miss Violet out in the sun lately. Talking to her, trying to get to know her…each other. Her baby dying and all that goes with it. And then there's Lucy…I should keep all this nonsense to myself, not burden you."

"Mr. Jake, can I ask you something? When I first came to town, I heard that you'd been in trouble with the law a few years back, and that you'd had an argument with Mr. Samuel just before he died."

I shut up after that. The silence was killing me, but I kept my mouth shut so I could hear every word he had to say. His chest raised then he took me by the hand.

"I'm glad you asked me, Lizbeth...proud of you too." He took my hand in both of his. "My ex-wife and her beau, at that time, stole a bunch of money from the register one day. To make a long story short, I caught them, but in order to keep Lucy from going to jail, I had to drop the charges...against both of them. Seems like some folks figured I had made the story up just to get back at her. Blackmail her to come back."

"But what about the fight with Mr. Samuel?" I insisted, for I couldn't wait any longer.

"It had come to the point that I could no longer continue to supply goods to Samuel's lumber yard without payment. I didn't mind giving them credit every once in a while, but it started to become a habit. A habit that wasn't good for business. Unfortunately Joseph and I got into an argument in the street that sounded as though I was upset with him, but I wasn't. We apologized later, and that was that."

"I was short with a lot of people back then," he continued. "But not anymore. There is nothing I have that can ever repay you for what you've given me, Lizbeth."

No tears, but my eyes did water.

I wanted to say all kinds of silly things....

I hugged him (as usual) instead.

Thirty-one

I could have skipped all the way home but for the fact that I'd ridden my bike to the grocery that day and Lord knows I couldn't leave it there! Besides, I felt so good. Good in so many ways. I felt like a new bird, blindly soaring high above the heads of trees, one after the other, dead on into the setting sun. Then a light fresh breeze, gliding me low to the aroma of freshly cut grass. The twinkling sound of children laughing below me. Life was great.

I decided to take a shortcut to my aunt and uncle's home that day. No big deal. I had done it once before. Two blocks of homes that resembled shacks no better than Mr. Cockney's barn; and his barn was a whole lot cleaner than those places. Men rocking in chairs on their porch with shotguns by their sides. Kids half dressed in filthy clothes with combs sticking out of their heads.

But still, I was too happy to let that bother me. I was well loved.

I glided past the first block. Kids waving at it me like I was Aretha Franklin, Queen of Soul. I waved back and continued to pump the peddles of my bike. The shortcut really was a good idea until then—dogs, doggone it! A pack of dogs, descendants of the werewolf, running behind me with their tongues hanging out. Barking loud to brake me, scare me to death so maybe I would fall and make it easy for them. Let me know that I'd pay for trespassing on their territory.

Clackity-clack, clickity-clack

I could hear their long nails scrapping across the black-topped street, racing in the hunt for a taste of meat. My meat!

I knew if I kept biking straight-away, they'd be jumping on me soon, knocking my bike down and then…well…

So I took a hard turn onto Blake Street. My legs pumping like a madman. I felt the pain of exhaustion burning up my thighs.

With a right turn at Corn Street, I started to pump even harder. The barking began to fade. The dogs had slowed down. Then, like magic, they stopped dead in their tracks at the cross-roads. I guessed, like the dogs back in New York, there were boundaries—limits to where you can go and bite someone's butt and not disappear the next day in a strange truck.

I leaned into a dead-end called Thomas Way. My heart gradually pounded down toward normal. Relieving the rush of blood to my ears so I could hear the world again. This block looked nice enough. Nice like my uncle's home, but maybe even better. I looked back to check on the dogs. They hadn't followed me. I could slow down now. Rest a bit.

All the lawns on this block were meticulously manicured. As if the neighbors had a meeting and decided that every lawn was to be measured at two and quarter inches high, no more and no less, then watered every Sunday afternoon unless it rained for over an hour that very day. Most had brick-framed porches, with gliding chairs for two, of every color.

A black truck with red and white letters snatched my attention. Something about it was very familiar. I rolled in close enough to make out the sign on the truck, "Samuel Lumber Yard." That's it! I shouted inside my head. This had to be Mr. Benjamin's truck!

In an instant I worried no more. I was as safe as could be.

I rolled up the freshly tarred driveway right up to the porch. I gingerly knocked on the door, hoping that I wasn't disturbing him. The large picture window took a peek at me, or so it seemed from the flick of the cream curtain. I heard steps moving quickly toward the front door. I checked my feet to make sure that I wouldn't stomp tar all over his floor if he'd let me in.

"Hello, Miss Lizbeth!" The same handsome face I remembered.

"Hi, Mr. Benjamin. I hope I'm not interrupting you or anything." I felt my cheeks already aching from smiling so hard.

"Not at all," he said as he looked through the screen door. "Where's your Aunt Alice?"

"I guess she's at home by now. I got kinda lost when some dogs started chasing me up the road." I pointed out the way.

"Yeah, I know about those dogs. I guess no one wants to do anything about it until some child gets bit or worse. Come on in; you all right?"

"I'm fine. I recognized your truck out there and figured that you might let me use your phone to call my aunt."

"Sure you can! Have a seat. I was just getting myself a drink. Would you like something yourself?"

"I am a little thirsty after riding so hard from those dogs. May I?"

"Of course, girl. I'm so sorry about those dogs. We've been complaining about them for months now. This will be just enough for the city to catch 'em and do away with them finally!"

I'm sorry, what would you like?" He was already standing at the archway to his kitchen.

"Orange pop, if you have it?"

"Coming right up."

I sat down on the massive brown leather sectional, with an oval coffee table between me and the two opposing chairs, neither of which were covered with plastic like at my aunt's or my mom's in New York. The television was on, but the sound was off. The photographs on the walls had some faces that were familiar to me: Sheriff Bigly, members of the Samuel clan. Mounted on the opposite wall were some rifles, with a deer's head mounted on either side of them. I didn't care for that kind of thing, but it didn't bother me either. Down at the far end of the coffee table, I spotted a dusty picture frame that had been turned facedown. I skooched my bottom down the sectional and turned the frame over.... And there they were, all of them: Miss Violet, Emma, and Mr. Joseph Samuel. I quickly turned the picture over, sure he could not bear to see their smiling faces anymore than necessary.

"Here you go," he said as he handed me a fancy glass filled with orange pop. He had a light blue short-sleeved shirt on with the collar open wide. Wide enough for dusty brown curls of hair to say *Hi Elizabeth.* "So you must have been bored to tears this summer. Ahoskie is small-fry compared to New York, huh?"

"Not so much, just more concrete than grass. I kinda like running around outside with my shoes off. Can't do that in New York!"

He chuckled at me. "No you can't, can you? I've always wanted to go to the Big Apple. Live there maybe. But that would take some real money. Some ole' lumber yard boy like me could never afford a dream like that." He washed a sip of his drink back hard.

"Why not? Seems like the yard is always busy to me."

"Oh, don't get me wrong. The lumber yard makes some good money. Yes sir! You bet that greedy woman Neely knew it, too. Always callin', threatenin' to take the lumber yard from me! But there's a lot of mouths to feed. And now I'm the one in charge. Everybody's depending on *me* to take care of things, you know." He sat up, and started to wrench his hands. "But that's changed now. Yep."

"Oh. I'm sorry Mr. Benjamin." I realized that I'd stuck my foot in my big mouth once again. I couldn't stop to think first before stirring the man's feelings up about the loss of his brother. How stupid could I be?

"No, girl, it's fine. Everything is fine. I got the money to do things now. Keep things steady. Like that truck out there. Joseph would never have approved of buying something like that." He took another swig from the bottle, bending his neck back, washing his thirst down with the cold liquid. "No, he'd want to save money, put what's left back into the business by getting a used truck. Probably wanted to save it for Violet and…" He put down his glass, then buried his face in his hands.

I turned my eyes away. Once again, I had intruded into his life. My gaze wandered aimlessly across the pile of folded newspapers, unopened mail, and a splatter of change. I blinked, then reached out to a single coin without thinking.

The penny was small in my hand.

A 1909 wheat penny, with a flaw that made Lincoln's ear look like it was caught in a crease.

Not the penny I had fought Bob Jr. over.

Not the pennies in the church offerings.

Not a penny from Mr. Jake's till.

Or from Aunt Ode's jar.

Or McMeanie's purse.

The one that Mr. Benjamin's brother had clenched in his hand when he drowned.

The one that had been taken from the sheriff's office.

Like a thud, I felt a sickness come over me. A sudden shudder of fear rocked me to my heels. I didn't know what to think. I tried to shove that thought out of my mind. An evil thought that Mr. Benjamin...no, he could never do that! Not him! I trusted him! I cared about him!

His own blood.

And if he did this to his own blood.

I swallowed as hard as I could, but it didn't shove the fear back one bit.

Slowly, as he shifted his head, I could see his face. He was staring at what I held in my hand.

I could see his eyes devouring me with confusion.

Then panic.

Then hate.

Though I sat frozen in my sneakers, my mind raced like a tornado, whirling, gathering up scraps of images, pieces of hellos and good-byes, empty spaces coming together. I could feel the blood pulsing through my head, burning my ears, my eyes moistening, and the deafening sound of the beginning of being lost here forever. He stood up slowly, lifelessly. Still I couldn't move.

"I'm ssssorry Mr. Benja..." I hadn't the air to get the rest out. And suddenly I wanted to go. I wanted to break through the door, the wall, anything that would guarantee that I could get away.

Standing upright, he appeared far taller than ever before. A giant, as I was a mere lamb. Tears welled in my eyes. I felt my body sway ever so slightly like a bowling pin. One touch and I would tumble down.

What had I done?

What could I do?

Like Miss McMeanie, I'd met my fate.

Then he spoke: "I swear I didn't know she was in the car."

He turned suddenly and stood before a dark wood desk like a ghost. He turned the key that was already in its hole.

Click.

I should have run right then and there. I should have screamed. But I couldn't.

He opened the drawer and planted his hand in it for a moment. I held my breath as he placed a gun on the desk. Then he just stood there, while I waited with tears running down my chin.

"The next day, I saw it in the sheriff's office. The penny. Knew what it meant. I should a' just left it there, but I was scared somebody'd recognize it and know it was mine. My lucky penny. Made some good decisions with it…and some bad, like that time I used money meant for Mr. Jake to buy that truck. I flipped it into the air one day this past June, right in front of Joe. I guess it was one too many times to count, in front of the workers and all. My father included. So he slapped me in the face. Slapped so hard it went numb. Made me look like fool in front of them. Like I tried to do to him all these years.

"'It's a bad penny, and you made it bad,' Joseph said, scolding me like a child.

"He took the penny from me…he took the lumber yard from me…and he took Violet from me too."

Within an instant the sad tears turned into a dark anger.

"I knew he would be coming over the bridge that evening, the same time as every other evening. He'd done it for over five years. So I waited.

"I hid my car in the bushes, far enough away, in case somebody drove by. There I stood, waiting with my gun in my hand, shaking like a leaf. When I recognized Joe's car coming 'cross the bridge, I eased out from the bushes and walked halfway to the center of the bridge. I saw his face and he saw mine.

"I planted my feet until I was steady.

"Then I squeezed the trigger. I missed.

"Then he swerved right down into the river...

"...right down into the river...so he wouldn't run *me* down!"

We both were broken with tears as to what Mr. Samuel had done.

"It was then that I saw little Emma's face in the backseat. Dear God, what have I done! I never would have done it if I'd a known she was there! I wanted to dive in after her...but even if I could have saved her, how could I ever explain what I'd done...that I was a coward?"

After what seemed forever, I watched his fingers squeeze the barrel of the gun tight as he took deep silent breaths. He lifted the gun up and faced me.

In a flash of my mind's eye, my mother, father, aunts and uncles. Every friend that I had—Tommy, Timmy, Chin-Chin, Miss Violet and Mr. Jake—all those lives shot before me as though I knew this would be the end.

"Please Mr., *sniff*..."

"Shut UP!"

"Please," I whimpered. "I need to call my auntie, please!"

He just stood there. Getting ready in his mind what he had to do. Muttering at last, "I got no other choice. I got no other choice, yah hear!"

I was convulsing, praying so hard for God to intervene.

Let me shrink into a hole in my chest until I disappeared.

I looked at his face, contorted as it was in pain, pouring with mingled sweat and blood. right down to his frayed blue collar. It struck me hard in the chest. I'd never seen a grown man cry before, but as the sweat melted in streams down his face there could be no other explanation.

He stepped closer to me and gripped me by both my arms, shaking me hard. Screaming. Spit flying in my face!

"I TOLD YOU TO LEAVE IT ALONE!" His hot breath smelled strong of smoke and beer as he cried out in my face. I felt my knees weaken as he shook me. If he hadn't held me up by my shoulders, I'd have been kissing the floor. I could taste the bile piercing my throat, ready to pour from my dry mouth.

He pushed me back down onto the sofa and sat down in front of me, with the gun now resting in his lap.

"Close your eyes," he cried laboriously.

I started to cry harder. Louder. The fear had consumed me and I had no control. I couldn't breathe, but I could beg.

"Please!" My teeth were chattering so hard I must have chipped a tooth.

"Stop it!" he shouted.

"Please, Mr. B—"

"Shut UP!"

"I'm sorry…I don't want to die!"

"Shut up, I said!"

"Please!"

BANG!

Thirty-two

My senses awoke to the freshness of air, smelling bright, feeling warm, wrapped in the light of the sun.

My eyelashes were thick with sleepy crust. Then it hit me. A dream.

No, a nightmare. A true nightmare.

In a wooden box or on a metal table at the morgue? At the pulpit or heading into a furnace?

Heaven or hell?

I waited for a sound, a clue really, something...

"Elizabeth?" A soft voice was tossed from the corner landing into my ears. Familiar as it was, I couldn't make out who it belonged to. God may very well be a woman.

I turned my neck unnoticeably, trying to peep through my eyelashes.

"Lizbeth, are you okay?" I couldn't be dead...she asked me if I was okay. God wouldn't ask if I were okay.

I pried my eyes as wide as I could to find the face of my sister Lena above me. I felt the warmth of her little hand on mine. A shower of relief washed over me, squelching any question of death.

Yes, I was still alive!

"Lena?" My throat was dry and horse.

Normally, not one too eager to express any concern or care for me, she let her body fall shamelessly over mine.

"I thought you were gonna' die. Please don't die, Elizabeth, I couldn't take it!" She never looked up at me, though she continued to hold on to me like driftwood on the ocean.

"I'm not dead and I'm not gonna die just yet, Lena, don't you worry." I said as I stroked one of her long thick braids.

———

Once I convinced her that I would survive, there was no shutting her mouth. Apparently I'd been lying in bed for all of an hour in shock. She didn't quite understand what that was, but she knew that I hadn't been bleeding, and that I didn't have any broken bones. The rest of what she said was a little foggy, but I got the gist of it.

A shot had been heard coming from inside Mr. Benjamin's house. The neighbors called Sheriff Bigly, who found me passed out in a chair. As for Mr. Benjamin, he was found with half his head missing and the better part of his brain splattered on the ceiling and the deer antlers.

Mr. Ben had shot himself through, from the bottom of his jaw.

And when the sheriff examined his body, lying on top of his own red slippery blood, he still held the gun in his left hand, and *the penny* in the other.

———

I told Sheriff Bigly everything Mr. Benjamin had said to me. Had to write a report and sign it for the medical examiner. Word started hushing about town as to how he was jealous of his brother Joseph. They said what made Benjamin's blood burn black as ash was not Joseph's marriage to Violet, but their blessing named Emma, who should have been his.

He figured it had come time to do something about it.

Something deadly wrong.

I had imagined that Joseph had thought himself to be without courage, not able to take Emma's life before she drowned. But in the end, it was his brother Benjamin who was the coward. The one who could not live after taking the lives of those most precious to him, in order to cling to his own greed. A coward, a thief who trapped himself into a corner—until there was nothing left to do. He never thought of the veil of agony that he had ever so gently placed over himself when he decided to take his brother's life. In the end, there was no taking it off, no ripping it off, as greed had tricked him into believing. So it had to be done. He had no choice.

Thirty-three

Aunt Alice wasn't much for coddling somebody, especially when nothing was broke, whether physical or spiritual. I hovered around the house for two days, then went back to work at the grocery store.

Ring-a-ling, ring-a-ling! Ring-a-ling-ling-ling!

For the first time ever, I was pleased to hear that darn bell. Mr. Jake hugged me so hard I couldn't speak, but I liked it. I'd never been held like that by a white man before. It didn't seem any different than the hugs of one of my uncles who hadn't seen me in a while. Then he did it. He stroked my coarse hair that Miss Violet had just taught me how to do for myself. I can't explain it, but this little thing freed me. Freed me from feeling less than other white girls in school, with their long straight hair. Freed me from believing that white people could barely stand to brush-up us, skin to skin, on a crowded bus.

Freed me from fearing that blacks and whites could never be friends.

After he let me go, we didn't talk for a long while. It was too much. Besides…I hoped that we would have a lifetime of summer days ahead to figure things out.

The store buzzed with excitement all day long. Word must

have gotten around town that I was working. Mr. Jake tried his best to sift out the nosy onlookers who came in the store to bide my attention or just get a look at me. See if I had any bloodstains on me that I didn't catch in the tub. It got so bad, that by noon he had to put a sign outside on the door that if they wanted to see me, they had to buy something. That would keep them out for sure, he thought.

He made a lot of money that day.

Come time when the store was winding down, I was sweeping the floor kind of lazy in my thoughts.

"Mr. Jake?"

"Yes, Elizabeth?"

"You can tell me that it's none of my business, but I was curious..." I shrugged my shoulders like it was nothing. A terrible question really, to ask a man who won't tell you what's in his sandwich. But I figured he would allow me a reprieve today, since I did survive Mr. Benjamin blowing his head off and then sweeping a few days later.

"What?" He tossed the change into the bank bag.

"That day that you ran after Miss Violet with her grocery bag...."

"Yep?"

"I think I saw you put something in it that wasn't on her list." I stopped sweeping to set myself still for his answer.

"You don't miss a thing, do you Elizabeth?" He smirked, then shook his head in admission. "Yes. Yes I did. It was a bar of bittersweet chocolate."

"Why did you give her that?" I asked. Why not white peaches or flowers? A few sticks of sugary hard candy?

He leaned back against the shelves as he dropped the bank bag on the counter, thought for a moment, then he spoke.

"Sometimes you're in so much pain that you forget to taste what's sweet in life. Go too long, you won't remember.

"That which is bittersweet, is not soon forgotten."

He looked at me with a small smile on his face, then casually went back to counting the change as I scratched my head and moved the broom along.

Thirty-four

It's true: time does fly when you're having fun. How I loved those last few weeks in Ahoskie. I consumed the time like fire burning a crimson Chinese lantern into ashes, playing joyously while being consumed by the heat.

For if I moved too slow, without splendid abandon in everything I did,

Every star that glinted across the dark blue-black sky,

Every aroma that lingered in my Aunt Alice's kitchen,

Every cloud of dust my bike made as I turned the last corner down the hill,

Every sprinkle of rain that I danced to, barefoot with my mouth open wide to catch the drops,

Every blade of grass that cut between my toes, left to bleed into the soil,

Would be missed.

Not one day should ever be forgotten.

I decided to leave my purple bike in Uncle Frank's garage for next summer, no truer sign that I was determined to come back to the Only One. He covered it with a tarp that wasn't half as greasy as the others in his shop. Then hoisted it high in the air with rope, so no one could reach it or nest in it while it waited for my return.

I told Mr. Jake that I would work for him for a dime more per hour starting mid-June next year. He said fine, but I had to work at least one Saturday per month so he could spend more time getting to know Miss Violet. I readily agreed and suggested that I should spend one Sunday a month at the store also, since that would keep me out of going to church so early in the morning to pray. But Mr. Jake said he would have none of that in his grocery. For sure something awful would happen, and it would be my entire fault that the Devil was following me around with his hands clasped behind his back, kicking up dusty trouble in the front.

The day before our flight back to New York, my relatives gave Lena and me the greatest barbeque ever in the history of Ahoskie. The leftover Fourth of July matching paper plates and cups, along with the everyday white paper towels, were used to their very end. Large white lights strung over the tables brimming with delights, lined up in the driveway from end to end. It was good planning, since we'd be there late into the night laughing, playing, and dancing to the music over the radio propped against the screen in the window. I pitied whoever would sleep in that room tonight. The mosquitoes would surely slip through the crack the cord made running into the outlet.

Everyone showed up. Great Aunt Ode wore her best flip-flops that matched her yellow flowered and white apron dress. Although she didn't have her brown liquid bottle weighing her down in her pocket to keep her from taking flight, she did manage to find some white lightning back in the woods behind the outhouse. At least that's what I was told by Terry. He didn't want me to know that I'd seen him out there too in the rickety shed, sittin' around the steaming copper invention, sipping the sweetness off the top. How could I not notice him dripping wet like he'd been locked in a sauna by accident?

Even the one-armed wonder boy, Daniel came by. Funny, the more I saw of him, the more I liked him. We spent some time together eating fried chicken and potato salad and played a little basketball with Terry, Timmy, Chin-Chin, and Red in the thick of the evening.

Just enough time to cause my mouth to water at the thought of kissing him as the evening went on.

Too bad about the family relations.

―――

The best of all was Uncle Frank's surprise. He went all the way to Charlotte to get Lena and me some of the finest, loudest fireworks ever. I couldn't wait for him to light them up.

Aunt Al let us eat all the hot dogs, corn on the cob, and fried shrimp we could shove down. I saved just enough room (I could tell when my belly button hurt when I touched it) for a huge slice of Seven-Up cake. Can't get that in New York, since most folks had never heard of it. And my Aunt Alice made the best.

With all the fun I was having, I took a look around the yard. It bubbled over in laughter and life. Each face, every voice, the colors people wore. The more I watched, the more my heart swelled in delight.

But just when I thought this night couldn't get any better, the dirt kicked up on the road a bit as the top of a red truck slowly pass by the others, then park farther down the packed road. More visitors, I suspected…more of the *sad to see you go,* but not really, just hungry for a taste of free ribs.

If a "quiet" could be described at such a party, this would have been it. The crowd rumbled against the music and tried to stop noticing, distracted by the people coming up the road to the driveway of my grandmother's house.

Had the mayor been invited?

I jumped up on top of the picnic bench so I could see above the array of heads, curious to see who could make such a ruckus at a kids' barbeque.

The closer they came, the more I could feel the energy from the crowd.

A hand, the color of his hair, the scent of warm rain. My eyes had not played tricks on me. It was truly a sight of amazement: Mr. Jake and Miss Violet were there together, weaving through the crowd of brown faces.

I don't know if I could have done it. I would probably have been afraid. What they did—out in the cool evening air— together. What a wonder they were. They seemed to walk softly, but strong. They smiled gentle smiles to the mumbling crowd about them, enticing them to say "Hello, glad you could make it."

"Mr. Jake!" Aunt Al shouted boldly. "Miss Violet!" Her arms were wide open enough to take in the two perfect bodies within them. She held on for a second longer to make sure that everyone knew she cared for them and any hate would have to go through her first—and then Aunt Ode!

I wanted to fly into the air from the bench, but my wobbly legs wouldn't let me. I was so happy to see them that I was stunned speechless. I finally gathered myself enough to leap down from the bench and across the lawn toward them. I could see Mr. Jake grab Miss Violet by her shoulder, pulling her in close to his chest.

I wondered how that would feel.

"Mr. Jake, Miss Violet!" There was nothing more to say. In one scoop they had me in their arms. They hugged me hard and long, showering me with kisses. When we let go, we held hands, and the crowd roared. At that very second, the firecrackers burst into the black sky catching our unsuspecting faces like the flash of a camera.

There we stood, Lena, me, Miss Violet, and Mr. Jake, holding hands like a string of precious beads.

God, I will never forget that moment as long as I live.

———

Later that evening, I went to check up on Aunt Ode in her bedroom. It wasn't unusual for her to sleep right through a party, so finding her in bed sound asleep was just the moment I needed to tell her how much I loved her. Just one more time alone, before taking off to New York to be with her favorite married-into-the-family-nephew, my dad, and my loving mommy.

"Auntie, Aunt Ode." I nudged her as gently as I could in order to wake her without getting my hand bit off.

"Auntie." I felt my pulse begin to rise. I turned her over on her back and shook her, waiting for that milky eye to look back at me. Tears began to roll down my hot face. I must have cried out for her so loud that Tommy came in to see what was wrong.

Thirty-five

I sat up in my Queens bed, to find that promise sitting on my desk. As my bare feet took to the well-worn path across the carpet, my face began to break free with a stiff smile.

I dumped the jars on my bed and spread them to every corner of my bed without one falling off. Then I dove into the cool ripples to make an angel out of them. The more I fanned my arms, the happier I became. I thought of Aunt Ode and the long walks she would take, only to return home to her rocking chair on the porch.

I rolled to my side to wipe away the last of my tears.

My eyes were still wet, when a penny seemed to wink at me in my peaceful moment. I picked it up to give it the attention it and all the others deserved, and would receive.

For a moment, I thought I was dreaming, drunk from the swarm of coins surrounding me. But I wasn't.

He had found me, Mr. Lincoln. With all the markings of a wheat penny that made him grand. I held him to my chest.

"Thanks, Aunt Ode. I love you."

To receive a free catalog of Poisoned Pen Press titles, please contact us in one of the following ways:

Phone: 1-800-421-3976
Facsimile: 1-480-949-1707
Email: info@poisonedpenpress.com
Website: www.poisonedpenpress.com

Poisoned Pen Press
6962 E. First Ave. Ste 103
Scottsdale, AZ 85251

CPSIA information can be obtained at www.ICGtesting.com
Printed in the USA
BVOW04s1251171014

371211BV00003B/3/P